A Crafty Christmas

Center Point
Large Print

**This Large Print Book carries the
Seal of Approval of N.A.V.H.**

A Crafty Christmas

Mollie Cox Bryan

CENTER POINT LARGE PRINT
THORNDIKE, MAINE

This Center Point Large Print edition
is published in the year 2014 by arrangement with
Kensington Publishing Corp.

The text of this Large Print edition is unabridged.
In other aspects, this book may vary
from the original edition.
Printed in the United States of America
on permanent paper.
Set in 16-point Times New Roman type.

ISBN: 978-1-62899-350-9

Library of Congress Cataloging-in-Publication Data

Bryan, Mollie Cox, 1963–
A Crafty Christmas / Mollie Cox Bryan.
pages cm
Summary: "Sheila wins a free scrapbooking cruise, but her dream
vacation turns disastrous when she trips over a dead body on deck"—
Provided by publisher.
ISBN 978-1-62899-350-9 (library binding : alk. paper)
1. Scrapbooking—Fiction. 2. Cruise ships—Fiction.
3. Murder—Fiction. 4. Christmas stories. 5. Mystery fiction.
6. Large type books. I. Title.
PS3602.R943C73 2014
813'.6—dc23
                                                        2014032385

Dedicated to Kevin Reid Shirley.
Here's to long train rides and good friends.

Also dedicated to Paula D'Allesandris, who always has an open heart and space for me. Here's to making dreams come true in the big city and old friends who never forget.

Acknowledgments

When I attended the Malice Domestic session where panelists were discussing murder on the high seas, I already had written the first few chapters of this book. I'm so glad I sat in. Those panelists were Trish Carrico, Maria Hudgins, Liz Lipperman, Marcia Talley, and Elaine Viets. I enjoyed that panel so much and found it so informative—and it also reiterated what a fascinating, ripe topic cruises and yachts could be. I had an inkling. Also, special thanks to Joanna Campbell Slan, who filled me in on what it's like to be on a scrapbooking cruise. Cathy Wiley, my 2012 Bouchercon roomie, sat with me during that panel and then shared some notes. Turns out she's writing about a cruise, too. Much love and thanks to Cathy. Thanks to Amber Benson for answering my questions about cruises. Special thanks to Luci Zahray, aka the Poison Lady, for answering my questions.

My beta readers deserve a huge shout-out this time for putting up with my poking and prodding. Thanks so much to Missy Starliper, Leeyanne Moore, Mary Sproles Martin, and Jennifer Feller.

A huge amount of gratitude goes to my editor, Martin Biro, for helping to keep me on track while juggling an intense schedule and for his continual and steadfast support. Much love and gratitude goes to the whole Kensington team.

I'd love to mention some of my new mystery writing friends here, but I'm so afraid I'll forget a name or two. Suffice it to say that the mystery writing community has been a godsend. I am honored to be a part of it.

Speaking of godsends, I want to mention my agent, Sharon Bowers, without whom none of this would be possible for me. Hugs and kisses to you.

And to my readers: I offer you heartfelt gratitude. More to come.

Much Love,
Mollie

Chapter 1

Was that a person lying half in the shadows of the ship's deck?

When Sheila had tripped, her eyeglasses flew off her face. She'd stumbled and landed on her knees, groping around for them. On this, her second day of running on the deck of the cruise ship, images of disaster ticked at her brain. What if she couldn't find her glasses? What if they were broken? She didn't have a spare. Finally, she found them and slipped them on.

Now, what was it she tripped over? What was she touching as she groped around?

She tried to get a better view as she struggled to her feet. But the sun hadn't cracked the Caribbean sky yet this morning, and the ship's lights were dim. The glasses weren't helping, either. It looked like there was a sack shaped like a body lying on the deck, with an arm strewn over the path. *That can't be right.* She pulled the glasses off her face. *These are not my glasses.*

A huge floodlight flicked on, and Sheila now saw the object she was looking at was indeed a person, lying there in a most uncomfortable position. *Drunk, of course.* She thought she saw her own glasses just beyond the person's arm, and as she reached for them, a member of the ship's crew came walking over.

"Is everything okay here?"

"My glasses. I tripped," she said, stumbling backward over the person's arm again.

"What's this?"

"It looks like someone had quite a night," Sheila said, smiling. She was no prude and enjoyed a drink or two, but she'd never seen so much drinking in her life as what she had witnessed on this cruise.

The crew member's expression grew pained as he leaned in closer, shaking the person gently.

"Dead," the man said.

"What?" Sheila said with a sharp tone, dropping her glasses. Was he joking with her? What a sick joke.

"Stay right there," he said, and pulled out his cell phone. "I'll call security."

"I'm in the middle of my run," she said, dazed.

"Ma'am," he said. All business. Very stern. "I need you to stay here."

"Well, all right," she said, picking up her glasses and slipping them on. Her heart was thumping against her rib cage.

As she stood next to the crumpled body on the deck, she crouched over to take a better look. She blinked. The side of the face was clear: mouth open and skin sickly blue. Sheila stood fast. Yes, that was a dead person on the deck. And she had been groping around the body. Touching the body as she searched for her glasses. As soon as it sank in, she proceeded to do what any normal, red-blooded woman would do. She watched everything melt around her . . . and she swooned.

When she came to, she heard a familiar voice. "She runs every day," the voice said. "Nothing unusual about that."

Sheila blinked her eyes. Where was she? She looked around. There was a CPR poster, a table with medical supplies, and she was lying on a cot, underneath a soft blanket. She figured she was in the infirmary—and, man, her head throbbed. She reached her hand to her forehead and felt the swollen area. It hurt to touch it. When she'd passed out, she must have fallen forward. Of course. She was such a klutz. Why couldn't she have swooned with grace, like they did in the movies?

As she lay on the cot, her mind patching together what had happened, she began to feel sick. She'd tripped over a dead person, and what was more, she'd been pawing around the body to find her glasses. Where were they, anyway?

She started to sit up, but dizziness overtook her. She wanted to cry.

Here she was on a scrapbooking cruise, as the guest of honor—a once-in-a-lifetime opportunity— and she couldn't even sit up.

"Mrs. Rogers? Please don't sit up yet," said a male voice coming from the side of the room. She couldn't see without twisting her aching head. "You took quite a fall and have a nasty head injury. We don't think it's a concussion, but we need to keep an eye on you."

"Sheila!" a familiar voice said, and Vera's face came into view. "How do you feel?"

"Like hell," she managed to say. "What happened?"

Vera's presence calmed her. She was Sheila's best friend. They'd known each other their whole lives. It was hard to imagine life without Vera.

Vera's mouth twisted. "I was hoping you could tell us. We were paged. They said you had an accident. We came rushing down here. And this security guy starts questioning me like I'm a common criminal. Then he starts questioning us about you."

"Vera, you're babbling," Paige said as she came up behind Vera.

Paige was here, too. That was good. Another friend whom she'd known for a long time. And for some reason, Sheila felt like she needed as many as she could get.

"I tripped and fell during my run," Sheila said, nearing tears.

"That's not like you," Vera said. "You've been running your whole life. I don't think I've ever known you to fall."

"She said she tripped," Paige said. "Anybody can trip."

"Yes, I fell over a . . . body," Sheila said. "I've got this horrible headache. Anybody know where my glasses are?"

"Here." Paige handed them to her.

"No, these aren't mine."

"You fell over a body?" Vera asked, ignoring the part about the eyeglasses.

Sheila nodded.

"These are the only glasses I see here," Paige told her, and then turned. "Any idea where her glasses are?"

"Those aren't hers?" the male voice said.

Sheila sighed in frustration. "No, they are not mine. I'm sure I had them when I passed out. I think. Maybe they fell off again. These glasses must belong to the . . . the deceased."

"Which means that the dead woman has your glasses on," Vera said, smirking, then giggling.

"What's so funny?" Paige asked.

Vera shrugged and laughed. "It just seems funny. I don't think she has any need for eye-glasses if she's dead, is all."

These two had been sniping at one another since they'd gotten on board. Paige was mad because Vera had brought Eric along on what was supposed to be a girls-only trip. Vera became upset when she realized Paige was mad, yet Paige's son had joined them on board to surprise his mother. Yet another man.

"Hi, Sheila." The male voice suddenly merged

with a face as he gently moved the two women away. "I'm Doctor Sweeney. How do you feel? Head hurt?"

She nodded. A nurse brought her an ice pack.

"Let's keep the ice on that bump for a while. I'll get you some pain medicine. Are you allergic to anything?"

"Nothing," she said. "I'd really like my glasses. Everything is a blur."

"We have someone working on that," he said. The nurse brought water and some pills. "This should help with the pain. I hope your vision is a blur because you don't have your glasses. You really smacked your head."

"Well, here they are," said another man, who walked into the room. He was tall, well built, and wearing a linen suit. His long black dreadlocks were pulled back into a ponytail.

He handed Sheila her glasses, and she slid them on her face. The world around her took on a familiar clarity.

"Mrs. Rogers, I'm Matthew Kirtley, from Ahoy Security. I have a few questions for you," he said. His voice was softer than what his body and his professional attitude would have led one to believe.

"Can it wait?" the doctor said. "We're not sure how she's doing."

"Certainly," Matthew said, and smiled. "Whenever you're up to it. My vic is not going anywhere.

Well, nobody is. That's one of the interesting things about security on a ship. Nobody's going anywhere. Not even the murderer."

"Murder?" Sheila said. Her hand went to her chest. Paige and Vera rushed to her side; both paled at the word that stuck in the air and hovered around them.

Finally, Matthew Kirtley cleared his throat in the quiet room, which made Sheila's heart nearly leap out of her chest. They were on a cruise ship with a dead body and a murderer.

Nobody's going anywhere. Not even the murderer.

Chapter 2

Sheila sank further into the pillow. Her head ached, the room spun every time she opened her eyes, and this was her big dream vacation. She had won the free scrapbooking cruise with two free guest tickets from entering a scrapbooking design contest. Who would have thought a murder would take place among a group of two thousand scrapbookers?

She decided to not think about it. Instead she tried to focus on the good things about the cruise. Who would have thought such a devastating and cruel act could take place when they had stepped on board two days ago? Sheila could never have imagined such finery as what she saw when she'd first set foot in the atrium.

"They said it was going to be luxurious," Paige had whispered as they all stopped in the bustling crowd to take it all in.

The somewhat worn but very excited group from Cumberland Creek had stood on the white and brown marble floors and surveyed the huge, elegant room. A crystal chandelier sparkled from five floors above them. A white baby grand piano sat in the corner. A gentleman in a tuxedo played "White Christmas" with a pleasant smile on his handsome face.

Christmas trees and poinsettias filled the hall. Tall, thin trees were lined up against the gold columns that reached from floor to the ceiling. Wreaths with glittering gold ribbons hung from the balconies of the open restaurants and bars. In the center of the room was the largest Christmas tree any of them had ever seen.

"Welcome aboard," said a man dressed in a uniform as he came toward them. "Are you Mrs. Rogers?"

"Yes," Sheila said.

"Our guest of honor," he said. "I am Captain Marsten."

Sheila beamed. "These are my friends." She introduced Vera and Paige, who were taking advantage of the free trip. Then she introduced Eric, Vera's boyfriend, and Randy, Paige's son.

"What do you folks think of her?" the captain asked, opening his arms wide to indicate his ship.

"She is breathtaking," Randy said. "Much bigger than I ever expected."

"Ah, but turn around," the captain replied.

And when they did so, Vera gasped out loud. Two huge spiral staircases led up to the top floor and strands of lights draped down the center of them—giving the area a glistening sheen. Vera, the dancer in the crowd, loved her sparkles.

"I love the idea of hanging lights from the ceiling like that," she said. "Amazing."

"The ceiling is pretty amazing, too," Eric pointed out, looking skyward. Circular patterns etched in gold and light filled the ceiling.

"What do I smell?" Sheila asked.

"I think that's the gingerbread," the captain said. "We have every kind of restaurant and food shop you can think of on this ship. Right over here is one of my favorite places, our pastry shop. They are giving out gingerbread cookies right now, to welcome our guests. Please help yourselves. I really must take my leave, but I am at your service."

Due to Sheila's award-winning status, they'd been the first passengers allowed to board the ship, and so they were also the first to enter the pastry shop, which was exactly the opposite of the atrium in terms of atmosphere. It was cozy and quaint with dark-colored woodsy walls, ceiling, tables, and bars. Servers were dressed in red velvet shorts with suspenders over white crisp blouses, and each of them wore a Santa hat. They held up trays of spicy-scented cookies.

Sheila reached for one. "Oh my gosh, I'm going to gain ten pounds on this cruise," she said. The cookie was still warm.

"I'm glad they took our bags," Paige whispered, as she fussed around with her cookies.

"Why are you whispering?" Vera asked.

"I don't know," she said, her voice getting a little stronger. An awestruck look came over her. "I guess if this is a dream, I don't want to wake myself up."

The group took their cookies and walked through the shop to the other side, where there was a smaller atrium with a fountain in the center. It glowed red and then green as the water spurted in streams.

"I really need to sit down," Sheila said as she spied some tables and chairs in the corner. The group followed, sitting and eating their cookies.

"Not bad," Randy said. "Could have used a bit more ginger." Randy was a pastry chef in New York City. He'd joined his mother on the cruise because he was going through a rough breakup with his boyfriend of many years. He needed some time away from the city. And some time with his mother—they had been estranged for a while.

"Hmph," Paige said. "I was thinking they need more sugar."

"I think the cookies are perfect," Sheila said.

And for two days the cruise had been perfect. Scrapbooking with people from all over the world was just the beginning of the perfection. Some of the world's most well-known professional scrapbookers were here. And, because Sheila had won the contest, they were all introduced to her.

Everything had been perfect—until this morning.

She lay in the infirmary trying to gather her strength, keep her wits about her. *Don't panic,* she kept telling herself. *Think of all the good things about the cruise, of all the good things that have happened and that will happen.*

But it was so hard to think between the pounding jabs in her head.

Chapter 3

Annie was sitting in front of the computer, working on her new book about the Mary Schultz murder, when she heard a strange beeping noise. It was a new computer—she'd taken part of her advance to purchase it. She didn't have time to read the manual, so she had just plunged in to using it. The beep came again. What the heck was it? Was her computer freaking out? Then she saw the Skype icon light up. Ah-ha.

The screen popped up with Vera's and Paige's faces on it.

"Hello, hello, one-two-three, testing," Vera said as if yelling through a megaphone.

"Okay, yes, I see and hear you," Annie said, smiling, then waving. Amazing! Her friends were out at sea and yet she saw them on her screen. "How's the cruise?"

Their white faces didn't look like they had gotten any sun yet. She was expecting them to be sunburned by now.

"Sheila took a fall and has a mild concussion," Vera said. "I'm very worried about her. She had to miss her first appointment this morning."

"Fell?"

"Yeah," Paige piped up. "She tripped over a dead body."

"What?" Annie's heart skipped a beat. They'd all had too much death in their lives the past few years. It had finally calmed down in Cumberland Creek and now Sheila trips over a body on a cruise? "How?"

They filled her in.

"Who is this person?" Annie asked. A mixture of morbid curiosity, reporter's instincts, and concern for her friends coursed through her.

"We don't know. They are not telling us a thing," Vera said, eyes wide. "It's like a big secret or something."

"They probably don't know who it is yet," Paige

said. "I told you that." She said it with an edge to her voice. Paige was annoyed. "You've got close to two thousand people on board. There was no identification on the body."

"I'm sure it will all come out eventually. They probably need to contact the family first. What makes them think it's murder?" Annie asked, trying not to sound panicked.

"We have no idea," Vera said, shrugging.

"Other than all this, how is the cruise?" Annie said. She tried to ignore the fear she felt creeping along her spine. *Her friends were on a ship with a killer.*

"It's gorgeous," said Paige. "The water. Saint Thomas was wonderful. Just so beautiful."

"Yesterday was a lot of fun," Vera said. "We went to a session on altered books. It's amazing what you can do. Eric even liked it. I'll tell you more about altered books later."

"Eric's there?" Annie said, surprised. She noticed Paige crossed her arms. *Ah-ha. That's what the problem is.* Annie almost laughed.

Vera nodded. "He surprised me and came along."

"Speaking of surprises . . ." Paige looked off camera and then her son, Randy, was on camera, grinning. "Hiya, Annie," he said. "Do you mind if I steal them away for lunch?"

"Good to see you, Randy," Annie said. She was thrilled that Paige and Randy would be spending time together without Earl, who still hadn't fully accepted his son was gay. He was working on it, but he sure was stubborn.

"Well, ladies, we have to go or we'll miss lunch," Randy said.

They said their good-byes and Annie went back to work on her story. It was the most fascinating story of her career, one she'd never have known about if she hadn't been living in Cumberland Creek. Funny how one story could lead to another. While writing about the murder of two young women, she had visited the local prison to talk with Mary about the local Mennonites. She had eventually trusted Annie enough to talk with her and agreed to allow her to write a book about her own story.

Hard to believe she'd been here five years. They'd first moved here thinking she'd retire from reporting to stay at home with her boys. But she got sucked back in because there had been several murders in Cumberland Creek and she was contacted by an editor to write about them. They had really needed the money. It wasn't easy living on one income, even in Cumberland Creek.

The Mary Schultz book might be a big break for Annie. Mary was a young Mennonite woman who'd killed her father, after years of abuse and asking for help everywhere she could—even her church. The petite, soft-spoken Mary had finally taken matters into her own hands. With an ax.

Hard to imagine how a small young woman could have the strength. It must have been the element of surprise and the adrenaline rush of finally fighting back.

Murder. It had been on Annie's mind a lot the past few years and even more while working on this book. She swallowed hard. Several of her friends were on a ship with a murderer. She didn't want to scare them—she was certain they were already frightened—but cruise ships remained murky when it came to the law and security. They'd been in the headlines recently because of it. Annie wondered if the crew was so secretive because of the PR problems cruise lines were having.

She sat back in her chair and, once again, wished she could have gone on the trip. But her deadline prevented it. That and the fact that tomorrow was the first day of Hanukkah. She wanted to be with her boys for the holiday.

Mike walked into their bedroom. Her husband of fifteen years wrapped his arms around her.

"How's it going?" he said, then kissed her cheek.

"I just Skyped with Paige and Vera," she said. "How about that?"

"Aren't you a techie these days?" Mike teased.

"Poor Sheila fell," she said, and then told him the story. "I feel so bad. This whole cruise is such a great opportunity. She's finally coming into her own. I'm so proud of her. I hope she rallies."

"I hope they find out who the killer is soon.

Wouldn't want to be on that ship," Mike said, and shivered. "I'm glad you didn't go, babe. How's the book coming along?"

"Okay. I think I need to write a few more chapters, but then the first draft is done."

He bent down and nipped at her cheek. "Care to take a break?"

She glanced at the clock. Mike had a dentist appointment in an hour.

"I might be persuaded," she said.

Chapter 4

Beatrice would never admit it, but she was proud of Sheila. She wondered if Sheila's mother, Gerty, was doing happy flips in her grave. She had scrimped and saved her whole life for Sheila to study design in college, and then she'd run off and gotten married right out of college, which nearly broke her mother's heart. You just never knew about your kids.

Still, there Sheila was, middle-aged and starting anew. It took guts. And talent. Sheila had always had plenty of both—she simply needed to get her bearings.

"Thinking about Sheila again?" Jon said as he walked into the kitchen.

"How did you know that?" she said, looking up from her tea and cookies.

"You always get a sort of happy, bemused look on your face when you think of her these days," he said, leaning over, then kissing her cheek. "Good morning."

"Good morning to you," she said. "But it's almost supper time, ya know."

He'd just wakened from one of his long afternoon naps. He was French, and he claimed it was bred in him to nap. The fact that he was in his seventies had nothing to do with it, of course.

"Have you heard from Vera?" he asked.

"Not yet. I expect to hear from her today," Beatrice said. "Lizzie will be home from day care soon."

"What kind of cookie is that?"

"It's a sugar cookie. Have one. There are a few on a plate there on the counter. I made a batch and froze them. Lizzie and I will decorate them later. I might make pumpkin bread tomorrow."

"Pumpkin? Mmm." Jon had fallen in love with pumpkin since he moved to the States. He'd never had anything pumpkin in France. He bit into the cookie. "Delicious," he said, sitting down at the table.

"I have a gingerbread cake in the oven."

"Ah, that's what I smell," he said, clapping his hands together.

The house phone rang, and Beatrice answered.

"Hi, Mama," Vera said. "How's it going?"

"Fine here. Just baking up a storm, getting ready for Christmas. How's the cruise?"

Vera didn't respond right away. Beatrice's psychic antennae went up.

"What's wrong?"

"It's nothing, really. Please don't worry too much," Vera said, and then told her about Sheila falling and the mild concussion.

"Oh dear," Beatrice said. "She's still able to make some of those engagements, right?"

"We hope. She's missed a couple already. She had an appointment with an editor of a design magazine. Had to cancel."

"Well, now, that sucks," Bea said. "How did she fall?"

"What do you mean?" Vera asked, her tone a bit forced.

There was more to the story. Bea was sure of it. Did someone push her?

"I mean, I've known her as long as I've known you, and she's been a runner for a long time. How did she fall?"

"She tripped. That's all."

"What did she trip on?"

"Oh, Mama, damn you. She tripped over a dead body. Someone was killed on this ship. We're on a cruise ship with a bunch of designers, drunks, and at least one murderer. Did you really need to know all that?" Vera said without taking a breath.

"Hmph."

"Okay, so I know you're sitting there thinking you told me so, that cruises are nothing but trouble. But I'll tell you what. I'm determined to have a good time. No matter what."

Bea laughed. She hated cruises, and Vera knew it. No point in arguing with her. There never was.

Bill, Vera's ex-husband, walked into the house with their daughter, Lizzie, who was staying with Beatrice and Jon.

"Grammy!" Lizzie ran up to her and wrapped her arms around Bea's legs.

"Is that Lizzie?" Vera's voice softened. "Please put her on."

"Okay, but you be careful. You hear me?"

"I'm always careful, Mama."

"Yeah, right," Bea said. *That's why I've had to bail you out of jail, take you to see a shrink, and pull you out of the cold Cumberland Creek as you dumped your wedding photos in it, standing in your bare feet. You're so careful.*

As if she didn't have enough on her mind, now she was worried about Vera and the others being out in the middle of God knows where with a killer. Beatrice bit her lip. She had a bad feeling about this.

But at the same time she had to admit a certain satisfaction. She'd told all of them not to go. You heard nothing but bad things about cruises these days. Accidents. Disappearances. Rapes. Now a

27

murder. She was certain it was not the first time a murder was committed on a cruise. But her only daughter was on this one.

"The people on this cruise are some of the finest scrapbookers and designers in the business, Mother. It's not like it's just any cruise," Vera had said.

Not just any cruise, indeed.

Chapter 5

Croppin' with Cathy was about to start. Sheila had talked the doctor into letting her try to attend. After all, Eric was there and could watch over her, if need be, as Vera's new man was a doctor. The ship's physician had entrusted him to watch over her while she cropped. Eric was a pain in the ass, always hanging around with them, so much so that Sheila found herself biting her tongue a lot. She was happy if Vera was happy. But damn, he was smothering their friendship.

She still felt a bit woozy, but the pain medicine helped. "Jingle Bells" sounded over the intercom and the room was lavishly decorated with holiday greenery and lighting. As beautiful as it was, Christmas was the last thing Sheila wanted to think about. All she really wanted was home and her own warm bed, preferably with her husband in it so she could cry on his shoulder.

She knew that wasn't the "modern woman's" way of thinking. She should be grateful for this opportunity—and she was. But tripping and groping around a dead body, and then bumping her head hard when she passed out, had her feeling glum about the cruise. A few days ago, it was like a dream come true: two thousand scrapbookers all in one place. So many of the big names were gathered here.

Surely she'd get over her malaise. But, right now, she missed her sleepy little town of Cumberland Creek and she missed her family.

She took a deep breath and motioned for the beautiful young man who was dishing out glasses of wine. Surely one glass of wine wouldn't hurt. They were lucky the cropping events on board all offered free drinks, which included alcohol. And the Cumberland Creek contingent took advantage of it, since outside the scrapbooking events the drinks were extremely expensive.

Cathy was one of the big names on board. Sheila had a dinner scheduled with her this evening, so she was happy to be able to participate in this event today.

Sheila dug around in her scrapbooking cart and pulled out the photos she wanted to use for this crop, from her son's violin recital. She was working on a music-themed scrapbook for him. Of all things she would have chosen for her son

Jonathon to be good at, violin was not one. But he loved it and excelled at it.

"What are you thinking about?" Vera said. "You thinking about that dead body?"

Sheila nodded. "Sort of."

"What did it feel like?" Vera asked, eyes wide.

"Vera, honestly," said Paige.

"Seriously," Eric said. "Leave it alone for now." He wrapped his arm around Vera and pulled her close to him.

How was the woman going to get any cropping done with him hanging out with her?

"Thank you," Sheila said to the server as she reached for the wine.

"You know, I don't think I've ever seen so much booze in my life," Paige said. "It's everywhere. All the time."

"Thank God," said Sheila as she drank from her glass. It was sweet, good, and she wanted more. But she put the glass down. Out of the corner of her eye, she saw a man looking at her. He turned the minute her eyes met his. Strange. Was he really looking at her? Did he know what she knew? Or worse, was he the murderer?

"Mrs. Rogers?" someone said from behind her, causing her to gasp and jump.

"Oh, I'm so sorry. I didn't mean to startle you," the young woman said. "I'm Sherry. I'm a big fan of your designs. I was wondering if I could get you to sign my program?"

Sheila's eyes widened and she felt a blush creeping on to her face. She smiled. "Of course," she said. "Thanks so much."

Sherry held the program book up to her; it was open to the section that featured her work. It was then Sheila remembered Allie Monroe had borrowed her winning scrapbook two nights ago and was supposed to return it this morning at breakfast. Oh bother, that's exactly when she had been in the infirmary.

She signed the book and handed it back to Sherry. "My first autograph," Sheila said. "And probably my last."

"Oh no." Sherry became serious. "My money is on you to become very famous. What are you going to do? Develop your own line? Work in digital?"

"Well, um, er . . ." she said, trying to find her words.

"She's entertaining offers," Vera spoke up. And thank goodness for that.

Sheila's head was swimming; she wasn't used to complete strangers wanting her signature and she was a bit flummoxed.

"Why, thank you so much," said the young woman, and then she walked away.

"Oh my, my, my, my," Paige said, and whistled. "I didn't know we were in the company of a star."

"Stop it." Sheila waved her off.

"You better get used to it, dear," Vera said,

cutting some paper with her paper cutter before she stacked it in a neat pile next to her page.

"What do you have on that page?" Paige asked.

"It's a doily. They handed them out at yesterday's altered book workshop. Didn't you get any?"

"I didn't see them," Paige responded.

"Here, have a few." Vera reached into her bag. "I never would have thought to use a doily in my scrapbooking. I'm getting so many ideas and this is only the third day. You can use them plain, paste a photo on them, or whatever. Or you can paint them. One woman at the workshop put together a page with painted doilies. It was gorgeous. Another woman—I think it was Allie Monroe—used doilies as a kind of template. She painted over them and when she took the doilies off it left behind this intricate design."

"That reminds me; I need to find Allie," Sheila said. "She has my scrapbook. Have you seen her?"

"No, thank God. What a snob," Paige said.

"She's got a lot to be snobby about, I suppose," said Vera.

Allie Monroe was one of the most successful scrapbooking designers in the world. She and Sheila had hit it off immediately and had sat together at dinner a few nights ago.

"Very talented woman," Sheila said. "She was supposed to meet me this morning. I'm afraid she might think I stood her up. She borrowed my scrapbook before I even got the chance to take it out of the plastic."

"Why?" Paige asked.

"She wanted to look it over one more time," Sheila said, noticing the man looking at her again. She ignored him. It was that or hit him over the head with her scrapbook. She could not abide rudeness.

Soon, young fresh-faced servers placed themselves at the end of their aisles, handing out bags of scrapbooking swag.

"Good afternoon," Cathy said into her microphone. "Welcome. I hope you enjoy a sample of my new line of scrapbooking paper, called Cherry Blossom. I was in China last year and was so inspired by the blossoms."

"I love this paper," Vera said, eyes wide.

"Nice freebie," Paige said, as she opened her bag of scrapbooking paper, stickers, and embellishments.

"Must be costing her a fortune to give all this away," Vera said.

"It's good marketing," Sheila said. "We're her market. If we like it, we'll buy more. Besides, she's not hurting for money."

She loved the black and white paper with the silver cherry blossoms. She changed her cropping plans and decided to use the photo of her son and his violin on this paper. But first she needed to get a message to Allie. She wanted that scrapbook back.

"I'll be right back," she said. "I'm going to the message center to try to contact Allie."

"Maybe you'll find her along the way. This place is packed," Vera said.

"I'll come with you," Paige said. "I need to stretch my legs before I settle in here for the afternoon."

The message board set up by the conference organizers was jammed with messages. It was a confusing mess.

"Shoot," Sheila said. "You know what? I'll just go up to her room and slide this under the door. I think she said her room number was one hundred thirteen. Yes, that's right. I remember it because of the thirteen and bad luck and all that. We joked about it."

"I'll walk with you," Paige said. "How are you feeling? You still look a little dazed. Well, a little more dazed than usual."

Sheila chuckled. "I'm fine. That wine took the edge off a bit. Now, let's see here." They walked over to the elevator, went inside, and pushed the button to the first level of suites.

They exited the elevator and walked along the deck. The sky was a beautiful robin's egg blue, with no clouds in sight. The water and the sky sometimes looked like they were one. This was a different ocean than either one of these born and bred Virginians had ever seen. Theirs had a hard sand and rocky beach and was barely blue. This water was smooth as glass or silk. It was hard to take their eyes from it at times.

They walked around the corner, looking at the numbers on the doors.

"There it is," Paige said.

But something was very wrong. Part of the hallway was blocked off with people and there was a flurry of activity both inside and right outside Allie's room.

Matthew Kirtley walked out of the room. "Mrs. Rogers, can I help you?"

"I'm not sure," Sheila said. "I came to see Allie. But is she here? Is she okay?" Her stomach flip-flopped as she realized something must be wrong if the security team was here.

"I'm sorry, Mrs. Rogers. She's not here. Can I help you?"

That was the second time he'd asked her the same question, yet he was being no help at all.

"I stood her up this morning. We were supposed to have breakfast. She borrowed my scrapbook. I came to get it back from her. May I?" She motioned to the door.

"I'm sorry, no," he said. "Look, you're going to find this out at dinner tonight. That's when the announcement will be made."

"Announcement?" Sheila said.

"Everything in Allie's room is evidence right

now. I'm surprised to hear that you knew her. . . . You didn't recognize her this morning?"

"What? This morning?" Sheila's hand went to her cheek. *Oh, this is very confusing. What is he getting at?*

"She was the victim on deck this morning," he said.

Sheila blinked and thought she might pass out again. She took several deep breaths as Paige's arms slipped around her.

She shook her head no. "It didn't look anything like her. I mean, I didn't get that close of a look. . . ."

"No," he said, his voice lowered. "Her face was contorted. She must have been in great pain. The poison . . ."

"Poison?" Paige said.

"Yes, normally we have to send out to labs to confirm. But this time it was pretty clear. Cause of death: poison. Details to come. Excuse me, ladies."

"But wait—my scrapbook . . ."

But Matthew kept moving, and shut the door behind him.

Chapter 6

Annie's new dishwasher barely made a sound. Was it possible to love an appliance?

She straightened the kitchen table, where the boys had just been doing their homework. A pile for Ben. A pile for Sam. It was a half day of school today, which meant they'd gotten home around eleven o'clock. Mike was overseeing the baths—the boys had decided on early baths, since they didn't get them last night.

She sat down at the table and started to sift through the stack of mail. The mail carrier didn't seem to have a set schedule, which drove Annie crazy. In Washington, she could set her watch by the efficiency and timeliness of the mail carriers. Nothing exciting here: bills, junk mail, and— Oh, wait. A pretty blue envelope addressed to her.

She opened it and saw it was a lovely handmade Hanukkah card. Who could this be from? Her family had never even sent cards. Most of them didn't practice at all anymore, let alone celebrate Hanukkah. But she did; now that she was a mother living in the Bible Belt she wanted her boys to know about their family traditions.

She opened the card and was surprised to see it was from Hannah, a young woman she'd met during the New Mountain Order murder cases from a few years ago.

"Honey, do we have any clean washcloths?" Mike yelled in from the bathroom.

"In the closet, Mike," she yelled back.

"I don't think so, honey," he said, in a sing-song tone. He was trying not to lose patience with her. She was probably the world's worst housekeeper.

She set the card on the table and went in to help Mike. Okay, so the washcloths weren't where she said. But they were folded in a nice stack on the dryer.

"There ya go," she said, handing the cloth to him. "Sorry. I guess I forgot to put them away." *But at the same time, he could have put them away himself.* She stacked them neatly inside the bathroom closet before going back to the kitchen table and card.

> Dear Annie, I want to wish you and your family a Happy Hanukkah. I miss seeing you at the farmers' market and hope to see you in the spring again. I will be working all week at the bakery. Maybe you can stop by and see me? Love, Hannah.

That might be a good idea. Maybe she could pick up some baked goods for Hanukkah tomorrow.

Her mind sorted through memories of Hannah,

how she'd befriended her during the investigation and had kept in touch. Hannah and her family were Old Order Mennonites, which meant they dressed in plain clothes, didn't have cars, and didn't use modern conveniences, like electricity. Hannah had been a good friend of the two women who had been murdered two years ago, one of whom was also a Mennonite.

A naked boy zoomed past her through the kitchen, giggling, as Mike followed with a towel.

"Ben, please," Mike said.

"Why can't we just all be naked?" Ben wondered, his curly hair wet and dripping.

"Silly boy," Mike said, and grabbed him, toweled him off, then set him free. "Now go and get your pajamas on."

Mike sat down on the chair next to Annie. "That boy," he said, and grinned.

"Where's his brother?" Annie asked.

"In bed, reading. You know, I miss reading to him, but I guess it's a good thing that he wants to read himself."

"I know. I miss it, too."

"What's that?" he said, pointing to her card.

"A Hanukkah card from Hannah. Remember her?"

"Oh boy, do I. How is she?"

Hannah had been next on the killer's list; he had actually managed to kidnap and drug her before Detective Adam Bryant and his team found her. It took many months for the young woman to get over that.

"I think she's fine," Annie said. "She invited me to come to the bakery. Think I'll go and pick up something for the first night of Hanukkah."

"I have their whistles wrapped," he told her.

"Oh good. The boys will love them, but I'm certain we'll be sorry we bought them," she said with a laugh.

Chapter 7

Beatrice stood at her turquoise Formica counter and poured the brownie batter into her pan. Herb Alpert's Christmas music was blaring in the background. She loved baking with the music on. She sat the pan aside and opened the oven door. The nut cups smelled done. She took in the scent of them and pulled them from the oven, sat them aside on the counter, and placed the brownie batter in the oven.

She planned to let the nut cups cool and then take them out of the pan. She checked the time: 11:35 A.M.

In the meantime, the phone rang. She saw from the caller ID it was Elsie, one of the women from the Christmas bazaar she was helping with. This year the historical society was helping raise money for the Cumberland Creek Area Food Bank and Beatrice was in charge, much to the chagrin of Elsie Mayhue.

"Hello, Bea, this is Elsie," the voice said.

"Yes?"

"I just wanted to let you know that we've gotten another three vendors and I'm wondering if you think there's space for one more."

"Of course there's room," Bea said, thinking this woman really needed to learn to do things for herself.

"Okay, I'll let them in and also let Leola know so that she can place their names in the program," she said.

"Okay, sounds good," Bea said, and hung up the phone just as the doorbell rang. She took a deep whiff of the rich scent of brownies as she walked into the foyer. Through the peephole she glimpsed two men she'd never seen before in her life. Standing on her porch, both were dressed in suits and one had a briefcase.

She opened the door. "Can I help you?"

"Beatrice Matthews?" the taller man asked. He was blond, baby faced, and wore Clark Kent glasses.

"Yes," she said, wiping her hand on her apron.

"Investigator Len Springer, and this is my associate Ben Waters." He showed her his badge. "May we come in?"

"I don't know," Bea said. "What do you want?"

"We need to talk with you about a group of

women you know who are on the *Jezebel*," he replied.

"What's that?"

Suddenly Jon was by her side.

"That's the name of the ship that is holding a scrapbooking cruise," the other agent said. "May we come in?" he asked again.

"I guess," Beatrice said, and opened her door. "Have a seat." She gestured to the living room area, which held two couches and several chairs. "Can I get you something? Tea? Coffee?"

"No, ma'am, but thank you," the blond one said. "We'd like to talk to you."

"Sure," Bea said. "What's going on?"

The other suited man sat down on her favorite chair, so she sat on the chair next to it, while the blond sat on the couch with Jon.

"We've been sent by our office, who was contacted by the cruise line."

"I presumed," Beatrice said.

"There was an untimely death on board the ship—"

"I know. I just spoke with my daughter. I don't know what I can tell you about any of that," Beatrice said.

"Is your daughter Vera Matthews?"

"Yes. Is she okay?"

"We think so. We're not here about her. We're here about Sheila Rogers," the other man said. "She listed you as next of kin."

"What? What about her husband? And is she okay?"

"We stopped by their house and he wasn't at home. So we wondered if there was any information you could give us."

"I've known her a long time," Beatrice said. "Since she was born, as a matter of fact." *Did he say "next of kin"? Isn't that what they say when someone dies?* She grabbed her chest and repeated, "Is she okay?"

"This is so hard," the younger, dark man said. "But no, she's not okay. We regret to inform you that Sheila was killed this morning. We think it was food poisoning. We're so sorry."

Bea gasped. "No! There must be some mistake. I just spoke with Vera. She'd certainly have told me this."

"It just happened," one man said. "This morning."

The other man reached into his bag and fumbled around with his paperwork. He fished out an official-looking paper and showed it to Beatrice and Jon. There was a passport photo of Sheila and a death notice from the cruise line. Attached to that was a report that the cause of death looked like poisoning. "The subject had gone to the infirmary complaining of stomach cramps approximately two hours earlier."

Beatrice's head spun. This didn't make any sense. Certainly Vera would have told her if Sheila had been ill. Who were these men?

"Gentlemen, I'd like you to leave my home," Beatrice said. "I'm sure that Sheila Rogers is still alive. I don't know what kind of game you're playing or what kind of idiot you take me for—"

"Beatrice," Jon interrupted, and reached for her hand. "Please calm down."

She pulled away from him and stood up. "Out! Out! Before I get my gun after you! How dare you come into my home and spread such vicious lies."

The men stood.

"Are you threatening federal officers?" the blond said.

"Hmph, if that's even who you are," she said. "And I'm giving you until the count of ten."

"Mrs. Matthews—"

"Ten," she said with a sternness that scared even herself. Damn, she still had it.

"Fine, we're leaving. But we'll be back," the young man said.

"Nine," she said.

The blond turned around to look at her. "We are sorry for your loss."

"Eight," she said.

After the men left and the door was shut, she deadbolted it.

"What was that all about?" Jon said.

"I don't know," Beatrice said, her voice now quivering. "I'm going to call Vera."

When Vera picked up the phone she seemed breathless. "Yes, Mama? Everything okay?"

"Everything is fine here, except that two FBI officers were here and claimed that Sheila is dead."

"What?"

"Where is Sheila? She there with you?" Beatrice asked.

"No, Eric and I left the crop when she didn't come back."

"She didn't come back?"

"She went looking for someone with Paige and they didn't come back. We figured they found something else to do."

"So you left the crop," Beatrice said, trying not to raise her voice, but she heard the edge in it and hoped Vera did, too.

"Well, yes. Eric and I . . . were a bit tired and decided to nap," Vera said.

"Nap, heh?" Beatrice said, and paused. She suspected there was no sleeping going on during their "nap." "So you're certain Sheila is okay?"

Vera didn't answer right away and Bea heard shuffling going on in the background. "I don't know anything for sure," Vera said. "But we saw her an hour ago and she was fine."

Beatrice didn't know what to say to that. There was some kind of weird misunderstanding going on.

"Don't you think that someone would have told

us if something happened to Sheila?" Vera said after a minute.

"I don't know, Vera. But you better go and find out, don't you think?"

Chapter 8

"Is there a problem here, Sheila?" A warm voice came from behind her. It was Grace Irons, the woman in charge of the whole scrapbooking cruise.

"Well, I . . . I . . ." Sheila started to say. "Allie borrowed my scrapbook and you know what's happened, right?"

"Yes, it's a shame. I feel so bad," she said, her face red with emotion. "This has never happened during one of my events, I assure you."

"I don't mean to seem insensitive, but my scrapbook is in her room and I want it back," Sheila said, crossing her arms.

"Just a minute," Grace said, and walked by her.

"Well," Paige said. "This cruise is getting more interesting by the minute. Allie was killed? This will be big news."

Sheila turned to face her. "Who would want to kill her?"

"I know she was nice to you," Paige said. "But she was a bitch, from what I heard. She didn't treat her employees very nicely. The cops might start questioning the people who worked for her."

"But there are no policemen here on this cruise," Sheila said, under her breath. "Only this security outfit."

"Aren't they police?" Paige asked.

"No, I don't think so. They're hired by the cruise company."

"Surely they have police training or something," Paige said, bewildered.

"I have no idea," Sheila said, and flung her arms out. "Just what exactly is taking them so long to get my scrapbook back to me? Seems like it should be easy enough to retrieve it."

"Sheila! There you are." Vera's voice rang through the corridor. She ran down the stretch of the hallway, with Eric trailing behind her.

Sheila stood, discombobulated by Vera's hysteria. "What on earth?"

"Mama called and was worried about you," she said, a bit breathless. "I told her there was nothing to worry about."

"Why was she worried about me? I don't understand. The old bat," Sheila scowled.

"No, seriously," Eric said. "Evidently she thought you were dead. Poisoned."

She gasped.

Paige's hands went to her mouth. "So odd," she said.

"Someone is dead all right," Sheila said. "But

it's Allie. I have no idea why anybody would think it's me."

By that time, Grace had walked back out to her, followed by Matt.

"Matt, Mrs. Rogers is one of our guests of honor. She's one of the reasons we're all here on this cruise," Grace said.

Sheila beamed.

"Why did someone visit Ms. Beatrice Matthews in Cumberland Creek, Virginia, and report that Sheila was dead?" Eric asked, point blank. "What's going on here?"

"I have no idea who would do that, let alone why. Someone must have mixed up the reports," Matt said. "I am so sorry."

"That's terrible!" Grace said. "Is Ms. Matthews okay?"

"Of course she is. She's my mother, by the way. She didn't believe a word of it. But it frightened her. She wanted to know what the hell is going on here. As do I," Vera said. "What kind of a cruise is this where someone gets killed and it's reported that someone else was killed? What a bunch of hooey."

Sheila stood in shock. Hooey, indeed. But in the meantime, she still didn't have that scrapbook.

"I do apologize," Grace said. "It's so embarrassing."

"Where's Sheila's scrapbook?" Paige said, after a few moments of awkward silence.

"We've been asked to leave the room as is until the FBI can do a sweep," Matt said. "Standard procedure. They will meet us at the next port of call. When an American citizen is murdered on a cruise, the FBI takes over the investigation."

"FBI?" Sheila said. "I'll never get my scrapbook back!"

"We'll make sure you do," Grace said. "Please don't worry."

"The next port of call is in two days in Mexico," Vera said. "Do you mean that we'll be on the ship with a murderer for the next two days?"

"Our security staff will ensure the safety of our passengers, but please keep all this to yourselves. We don't want mass hysteria on board," Grace said, with a tight smile, her cheeks stiff with stress. She wore bright red lipstick, perfectly applied, yet her face glowed with a sheen of sweat. "Why don't you all go to the crop? Sit back and relax. Have fun. We'll take care of everything."

"I wish I could believe that," Paige said as she turned to go.

"Please let me know when you have my scrapbook," Sheila said, turning and following Paige. Eric and Vera trailed behind them.

The captain of the ship smiled at them as he walked by on his way to Allie's room. "Mrs. Rogers, good day to you."

They had had dinner together the first night she was on board. Sheila found him an absolute bore.

She smiled and nodded politely, but kept moving.

They found their way back to the crop, where Randy was saving their seats.

"Where have you all been?" he said, flinging his arms out.

"You would not believe it," Paige said, sitting next to him. She motioned to the young server who was passing out champagne.

"I'll take one, but do you have anything stronger?" Paige asked.

"What would you like?"

"Bourbon, straight up, please."

"Make mine a double," Vera said.

"What's going on?" Randy said, looking over his almost done page. He'd watched his mother and her friends scrapbook for years and sometimes joined the crop when he was a kid, but he hadn't scrapbooked in a long time. "It just needs a little something. Maybe glitter?"

"Stay away from glitter," Paige said. "There's a reason I outlawed it in our house. Lethal stuff."

"Hmm," he said, and placed his page back on the table.

Paige then told him what had happened.

"Murder?" he whispered. "This sounds crazy. Nuts!"

"Mama," Vera said into her cell phone, "Sheila is fine and right here."

But Sheila wasn't certain she was fine. This morning she'd fallen over the dead body of Allie

Monroe. Her head still ached from her concussion, and her scrapbook was still in a room where a murder investigation was taking place. She took a sip of her champagne and shrugged. At least she wasn't dead. She glanced around at the people surrounding her—that man was still there. She took another sip and pushed her glasses back up on her nose. She glared back at him and he turned his head quickly.

"Now, croppers, I have a treat for you," a voice said over the microphone. "I know it's Christmas, but I love Halloween. So I'm unveiling my new Bloody Bash Halloween papers, inspired by the song 'Monster Mash.'"

Much laughter from the crowd as "Monster Mash" blared through the intercom.

"Ladies and gentlemen, it's Halloween in December time! Woo-hoo!"

Servers came out dressed in costumes: vampires, mummies, and Frankenstein's monsters. They handed out packs of paper tied with a blood red ribbon.

"Well, now," said Vera, reaching for her bourbon. "Isn't this just in keeping with the day?"

"Cheers!" Sheila said, holding up her glass of champagne. As she did, the ship rocked and swerved a bit, causing the champagne to spill all over her pretty new paper.

Chapter 9

"We made these apple and cherry turnovers without any lard," Hannah said, pulling out a tray for Annie to look over. The golden brown semicircle desserts looked nearly perfect. "They are kosher."

That's one definition of kosher, Annie thought.

"I'll take six of each," Annie said. "Thanks for the card."

"Oh," Hannah said. "You got it already?"

Hannah was pale and freckled and blushed easily.

"Yes," Annie said, digging in her purse for cash. "Are you about due a break? We can have a coffee. How's that sound?"

Hannah warmed. "Sounds lovely." She gave Annie back her change and handed her the box of turnovers.

Annie walked over to the corner table, where it was at least semiprivate. Hannah followed her with a coffee tray and some gingerbread muffins.

"I hear Sheila won a design competition," Hannah said. "How exciting to go on a cruise!"

"Yes," Annie said, keeping the murder to herself. She didn't want to freak Hannah out. She'd been in therapy—after much cajoling. The Mennonites preferred to keep to themselves, even with their health issues. But Hannah had been so affected by the murders that she had become uncommunicative. Her family tried to work through the church, but nobody was able to help her. So she went outside the Old Order Mennonite system and found another Mennonite who was a qualified psychotherapist.

"We're all very proud of her," Annie said.

"How are your boys?" Hannah asked. She stirred three packs of sugar into her coffee.

"Good, but very excited about Hanukkah," Annie said, and then took a sip of her black coffee. "So, how are *you,* Hannah? Are things getting better for you?"

She looked away briefly, but nodded positive. "I guess," she said. "Every once in a while, I still dream about the murders."

"I do, too. In fact, I dream about every murder case I've been involved in. I think that's a normal kind of processing," Annie said, taking one of the muffins. "These smell delicious. Gingerbread?"

"Yes. I'm so glad to see you. I'm leaving in a few weeks."

Annie's mouth almost dropped open—it probably would have if the muffin wasn't so good. She chewed hurriedly. "What?"

Hannah laughed. "I'm going on something similar to an Amish Rumspringa. I'll be gone for a year."

Annie had no idea that the Mennonites practiced

something so similar. "Your parents are going to let you do that?" She felt her eyes widen and her pulse race. What were they thinking?

The young woman beamed. "Yes. I'm going with a group of women my age. There will be a chaperone, of a sort," she said, and quieted. "I hope that by going away I'll be able to forget. . . . It's sort of unusual for the women of my family, but my parents thought it would be good for me to get away."

Annie's heart sank. Loss was never easy, but for young people it cut deeper. She didn't think Hannah would ever quite get over the murder of her two best friends. Annie had never gotten over several things in her life—but she'd learned to live with them. Stay busy. Don't look too hard at it. She still hurt when she thought about Cookie Crandall, her friend who had disappeared a few years back.

"Where will you be going?" Annie asked, upbeat. Stay focused on the exciting parts.

"New York City," Hannah said with a wide grin.

Annie gulped her coffee. Talk about throwing lambs to the wolves. She didn't think this was a good idea at all. But it wasn't her business, Annie reminded herself. She was Hannah's friend, not her mother. But she supposed she'd always feel protective over Hannah. After all, they had almost lost Hannah to the same man who killed her friends.

"I've gotten an internship with a Mennonite magazine. I'll be writing mostly for their Web site, but I was promised a couple of articles in print," she said. Her eyes took on a spark that Annie hadn't seen in her in a long time. Maybe this was a good thing.

"I had no idea you wanted to write," Annie said.

"I write mostly poetry. But my teachers all thought I had promise as a journalist. Of course, it won't matter if I'm the best journalist in the world. Soon after my internship, I'm expected home to marry and settle in."

"What if you don't want to?"

"It's a risk we all take when we leave. Some return and some don't. But what does your faith mean if it's never tested?"

"Ah, that's true, I suppose," Annie said. Once again, Annie was struck by the simplicity and the profundity of Hannah's faith. When Annie had been in the hospital, Hannah came in and prayed for her. Normally, Annie would scoff. She was a secular Jew and jaded when it came to spiritual issues. But she could not scoff at Hannah and her faith. It seemed pure.

She suddenly was thinking of her Jewishness and how she'd never thought deeply about it until moving to Cumberland Creek, where hers was the only Jewish family. She had been thinking about making the trek on Saturdays to the

Charlottesville Synagogue to give her boys more of a sense of their heritage.

Annie tapped her fingers on the Formica table and reached for her coffee. "What about this marriage business? Anybody you're interested in?"

"It's already planned. I'll be marrying John Bowman," Hannah said, and looked away.

"How can it already be planned when you are off to New York?"

"My family and his family are certain I'll be back and that I'll make him a good wife."

"Wow. That's different. How do you feel about this?"

She shrugged. "What do my feelings have to do with it? My family knows what's best for me, right? We believe that love comes after marriage."

Love comes after marriage? Annie felt like she had stepped back to the 1600s. Surely not!

"Haven't your feelings for your husband deepened over the years?" Hannah asked.

"Well, yes. But I fell madly in love with Mike when we met and then we made a life together. Of course our feelings deepened," Annie said, thinking that sounded a lot more romantic than it actually was. Sometimes it was easy in marriages. Sometimes not. Sometimes you had to work to keep it together. Adam Bryant's face flashed in her mind's eye. Thank the universe she had not impulsively acted on her attraction to him.

"But look, if this is the way you do things and

are happy with it, who am I to say?" Annie said, and smiled. "I have to get going. If I don't see you before you leave, be careful. Take my number and call me if you need me. I mean, if there's a phone around. . . ."

Hannah laughed again. "Don't worry, Annie. I'll be fine. I'll write to you."

But as Annie walked out of the bakery, she could not shrug the protective feeling that had come over her. Hannah in New York City? Annie was uncertain that Hannah was ready for this. What were her parents thinking?

Chapter 10

"Beatrice, you need to eat your sandwich," Jon said to her.

She stared out the window at the bare landscape, then briefly looked at her sandwich.

"You've gotten yourself too excited. I am sure that this will all get resolved. It was a simple error," he said.

"I know that, Jon. Don't treat me like a child," she snapped. "For heaven's sake."

He clicked his tongue and went back to his cold leftover chicken sandwich.

"What has the world come to when FBI agents give you false bad news?" she said. "I only knew they were wrong because I had just talked to Vera.

If I hadn't, I would have thought Sheila had died on some godforsaken scrapbooking cruise in the middle of nowhere."

"It was an honest mistake, Bea." He shrugged his shoulders. "What can you do?"

"Okay, okay," she said, waving him off. She turned her thoughts to the sandwich, picked it up, and took a bite. If he couldn't understand her anger, then screw him. Time to move on from the subject; it wasn't worth fighting over. She wasn't going to let it spoil her day.

"How are the plans going for the craft fair?" Jon asked. She knew he was also trying to change the subject.

"Okay," she mumbled after swallowing her bite of chicken sandwich. "I have more baking to do. I'm not sure I trust some of these others to get the job done."

"DeeAnn surely—"

"Oh yes, DeeAnn will come through. She donated some of her scones. I'm sure they will sell quickly. But we need more than DeeAnn."

The doorbell rang, prompting Jon to rise from the kitchen table and answer it. "Detective Bryant," Beatrice heard him say. She grimaced.

"Beatrice in?"

"Yes. Please come in. We are just having some lunch. Can I get you anything?" Jon said.

"No, just ate. Thanks, Jon," he said as he strolled into the kitchen.

"What do you want?" Beatrice said, feeling the hair on the back of her neck prick. Whenever he came into her house, she knew it was never a good thing. It usually meant there was a murder or a kidnapping or that her daughter was acting crazy. He was a harbinger of bad news.

"Nice to see you, too, Beatrice," he said, and sat down at the kitchen table.

She kept eating her sandwich.

"I've been sent by the local yahoo FBI officers," he said, and grinned.

She dropped her sandwich. "You know about that then?" she said, her voice raised.

"I'm afraid I do. I've been sent to apologize to you."

She twisted her mouth and tried to keep it shut. Difficult.

"There was a mix-up with the security on the *Jezebel*. Whoever wrote the report confused Sheila's name and the person who was actually killed. I don't know how something like that happens, to tell you the truth. Not like those cruise guys are very busy or anything. But the officers are very sorry to have troubled you."

"Why didn't they come tell me this themselves?" Beatrice said.

Bryant's face colored. "They think you're a bit . . . off. They asked about your mental health and your gun permit."

"I didn't believe they were from the FBI.

Assholes. Shoulda shot them when I had the chance."

Jon crossed his arms.

Bryant ignored her words. "For future reference, when someone says he is from the FBI and shows you his badge, you should believe it," he said. "And act accordingly."

"I don't trust anybody anymore, particularly men who come to my door to report the death of a woman I think of as my second daughter," she said. Her voice cracked. *Old fool . . . She was an old fool.* She blinked back a tear. She refused to cry in front of Bryant. She wasn't sure if it was Sheila she was frightened for, or if the incident had prompted her to recall the horrible memories of losing Gerty, Sheila's mom, to breast cancer way before her time. She'd promised she'd take care of Sheila. And had she?

Lawd, Sheila was a grown woman now, with four kids of her own. Beatrice had been a sort of surrogate grandmother to her kids and tried to be kind to Sheila—but maybe she should try harder. The momentary thought of losing her gave her old heart a spin.

Jon reached out and grabbed her hand. "Dear, dear Beatrice."

Bryant looked embarrassed. "It is an odd thing to have happened. What do you hear from the cruising ladies?"

"They are fine, I guess," Beatrice said. "But

Sheila took a fall—tripped over a dead body and has a concussion."

The detective's jaw set and his mouth twisted. He was trying not to laugh. He looked away from Beatrice and tried to compose himself.

Chapter 11

"Ms. Rogers, so lovely to meet you," Theresa Graves said as she stood up from a private table and extended her hand to Sheila.

"Oh please, call me Sheila."

"Are you okay?" Theresa said, gesturing to Sheila's bandaged head.

"I'll be fine. I fell this morning and have a mild concussion," Sheila said with a light slur. Goodness, she should not have drunk so much at the crop. She sat down and sipped from her water.

"I'm so excited to meet you," Theresa said. She had a Texas twang; "you" had at least three syllables by the time she was finished with it. Sheila made a note to *concentrate* in order to not mimic Theresa. She loved the accent—but anytime she was around people who had an accent of any kind she found herself copying them. *What was that about anyway?*

"Thank you," Sheila managed to say, like a Virginian, not a Texan. "The pleasure is mine. I've admired your products for many years."

"That's good to know," Theresa said. "We love hearing from our customers, of course. Especially from ones with the design skills you have."

The waiter approached them with the menus. It had been one buffet after the other. A menu was a pleasant change.

"Thanks for that," Sheila said. "I love what I do."

After they ordered, Sheila's eyes wandered to the ocean. So shockingly blue and pristine. A feeling of peace and joy came over her, even though her head was starting to pound again. She reached into her bag for another ibuprofen.

"Virginia's ocean doesn't look like that," she said.

"I imagine not. I rarely go to the coast. I'm just so busy with working and keeping up with my four kids."

"Four kids? Me, too," Sheila said.

"It's rare to meet another mother with four children," Theresa said, and smiled. "Maybe we should order a bottle of champagne."

"Sure," Sheila said, mustering a smile. Good God, if she had any more booze today, she might just tipple right over. She'd be sure to eat plenty so she'd not make a complete fool out of herself.

"Our company is considering starting a branch that's just focused on education. We've always been education focused, but we're putting even more of a focus on it. We're starting a Life Arts

Academy," Theresa said after their lunch came, then the bottle.

"Sounds interesting," said Sheila.

"We're looking for teachers," Theresa said. She was a very thin woman and reminded Sheila of a bird. Kind of a droopy, long, skinny bird. She had long jowls and sad, long eyes. "Would you be interested in joining us as a faculty member?"

"Where would this academy be located?"

"Actually, there will be a headquarters at our offices in Houston, but it will all be online. Isn't that exciting?" Theresa's hound dog eyes lit up momentarily with excitement.

Sheila shrugged. "Maybe. I think that in-person classes are so much better. I'd miss the inter-action."

"But you'd interact online. And a few times a year go to conferences to teach," Theresa said, then took a bite of her pasta salad.

"That does sound better." Sheila didn't want to cut off any opportunities, but she was really hoping for a freelance design job from home. Maybe she could do both. "I've designed this scrapbook-journal, which I entered the contest with. Did you see it?"

"Loved it," the woman said, now intent on picking something out of her salad. "I loved the color scheme."

"I was wondering about getting something like

that published or made into my own scrapbook line."

Theresa looked up from her food. "Ambitious. I like that." She held up her champagne glass as the waiter poured first in her glass and then Sheila's.

"To ambition!" Theresa said, and clinked Sheila's glass.

"Here, here!" Sheila said, and sipped from her glass.

"I'd like to take another look at that scrapbook-journal."

"Well, I have photos, but I don't have the book. Someone borrowed it last night and—"

"Okay, I'll take a look at the photos after tonight's crop. How's that sound?"

If she had really remembered the book, why did they need to meet again? Hmmm. Sheila wondered if Theresa was blowing smoke up her ass.

"Well, okay," Sheila said, trying to seem enthusiastic, but she had a bad feeling about this.

Later, she met her friends back at the crop table. Deeply involved in scrapbooking, none of them paid much attention to her entrance. Randy finished a few pages and Paige was agog over them. "Who knew?" she said, and shrugged her shoulders. "My son!"

"It doesn't surprise me," Vera said. "He's a pastry chef. So artistic."

His pages featured several of his desserts and journal entries about them: how he came up with the ideas, what had inspired him, and how many tries it took to get the dessert to the perfection he needed.

"Makes me hungry," Sheila said.

"How was your lunch?" Vera asked.

"Okay. Theresa and I are going to meet later. She wanted to see the book I designed, but I told her I only have pictures. I've no idea when I'm getting that back. It's so frustrating. But I have another meeting tomorrow with David's Designs. I'm hoping to have my scrapbook back by then."

"That's the one you're most excited about, right?" Randy said.

"I love David's Designs. They do all kinds of things. I had a friend who had furniture that was David's Designs—to die for. I love designing and I love their work. But Life Arts offered me a job," she said, and then explained about the offer.

As she did so, the ship listed to the side, sending papers, glue, cutting instruments, glitter, and every kind of embellishment imaginable reeling over the sides of tables. Sheila grabbed on to what she could while trying not to fall over herself. Sounds of screams, gasps, and curse words filled the air.

"Please remain calm," came a voice over the intercom. "This is your captain. We've run into an unexpected turbulence. We're cutting back the engines."

The ship slowly righted itself.

Paige was on the floor, with Randy helping her up. She was covered in glitter and growling about it as she spit it out of her mouth and tried to brush it off her clothes.

Vera and Eric huddled together on the floor before making their way to the table.

"Ladies and gentlemen, this is your captain again. We've cut engines until we get the weather all-clear from the Coast Guard. As you were. Have fun cropping."

Easy for you to say, Sheila thought. What a messed up day—topped off by being on a cruise ship with a killer.

Could this cruise get any worse?

Chapter 12

Pancakes and eggs would be served for supper. The boys loved breakfast for supper, Annie mused. Tomorrow night would be brisket, from a recipe of her grandmother's.

While she was stirring her pancake batter, the phone rang.

"Hey, DeeAnn," she said.

"Hey, what are you doing?"

"I'm about ready to start supper. You?"

"Taking a bit of a break at the shop. I saw an e-mail from Paige. What the hell is going on with that cruise? Someone was killed? We need to get them off that ship!"

"Calm down, DeeAnn," Annie said. She pictured DeeAnn's face red with worry.

"They are on the ship with a killer," DeeAnn said. "And guess what? I just saw a weather report that one of those freaky storms is heading for the Mexican coast. Right where they are supposed to be in two days. Oh Lawd, Beatrice was right. They should have stayed home."

Annie's heart raced a bit. "Did you say a storm is heading for them?" She stirred her batter harder.

"No, it's heading for the coast where they're going," DeeAnn said.

"I'm sure the cruise people know that," Annie said. "I mean, they need to be watching the weather, right? That's part of what they do. Don't worry about that."

DeeAnn sighed. It was a long and heavy sigh. "I just wish . . . if they had to go we could be there. We could at least provide some sanity. Sheila has a concussion. Vera and Eric are all disgustingly love struck, evidently, sneaking off to their room all the time. Are any of them paying attention?"

"C'mon. They know a killer is on board. But they are still trying to have a good time. Especially Sheila. Think of the opportunities," she said.

DeeAnn was silent. "Poor thing."

"I'm sure Vera and Eric will take care of her.

And there is a doctor and medical facilities on the ship. There's nothing we can do for any of them from here."

DeeAnn took a sharp breath. "I suppose you're right. I've got work to do. I guess I better get off the phone. Got in an order for twenty loaves of lemon poppy seed bread. Thank God people don't bake anymore. Keeps me flush, but it's exhausting. I'm starting to hate Christmas."

Annie laughed. "Are we still getting together tomorrow night?"

"Absolutely!" DeeAnn said. "We'll crop till we drop in Cumberland Creek while our friends are on the high seas."

After they hung up, Annie spooned the pancake batter onto her griddle and listened to the hiss, smelled the grease and butter as they came together.

She missed her friends—and that surprised her. They had only been gone four days. They had flown to Miami, hopped aboard the *Jezebel*, and headed for Saint Thomas. Their next stop was Mexico, where Sheila was expected to lead a scrapbooking photography class.

She had thought about joining them, but she and Mike had made a commitment to spending the Jewish holidays at home with their boys. It was something Mike had when he was a boy and wanted to continue with his children. Annie's home life as a child was not as constant. Giving up a cruise with her friends was worth the harmony that she felt at home. There would be plenty of time, later, for travel. Though maybe not a cruise. She was sort of with Beatrice on this one. Cruises were low on her priority list.

She flipped the pancakes over and listened as her boys excitedly discovered that breakfast was for supper.

Later, boys in bed, her phone rang. It was Beatrice.

"How do?" Beatrice said when Annie answered.

Annie heard Christmas music in the background. "I'm fine."

"What do you think about all this nonsense on the cruise?"

"It makes me a little nervous, but there's nothing we can do about it."

Then Beatrice told her about the FBI agents visiting her, which infuriated Annie.

"Honestly! One hand doesn't know what the other is doing. And how could the ship's security make such a huge mistake?" Annie felt the hair on the back of her neck prick. Was it her reporter's intuition? Or a simple fear for her friend's safety?

"I agree. It's egregious. If they were paying for the cruise, I'd demand their money back," Beatrice said. "But it's all free for all of them with Sheila's prize tickets—except the guys, I guess."

"How's it going with your bazaar?"

"Good. I hope you come by. It's next Saturday.

Hopefully, they will all be home by then. Lizzie misses her mama."

"I bet. She can come over here tomorrow afternoon if you want."

"Nah. Her Dad's taking her for the weekend. Thank God he's finally getting it together and is not running around with young women anymore."

"It's finally over with Kelsey?"

"She's back in jail. And I don't think he cares to see her."

"I hope so," she said, remembering what a blow that was to Vera and how disturbed the young woman was.

But then Vera had found love again with Eric, which was driving Sheila a bit bonkers. Say what you will for Vera's first husband, Bill, but he didn't hang around all the time like Eric did. He'd even come to some of their weekly crops—until it had become sacred "women" time. No men allowed.

It didn't bother Annie at all when he came along, but Sheila huffed and puffed and rolled her eyes behind their backs, which was interesting. Sheila and Vera had grown up together and had been friends their whole lives. Annie envied their relationship—most of the time.

"How's the new book coming along?" Beatrice asked.

"It's going well, except for the nightmares."

"Nightmares?"

"It's hard to write about this kind of murder without having bad dreams. She was abused for years. That's hard. And then she took an ax to her abuser, who happened to be her dad. Really difficult to wade through in any meaningful way, trying to get beneath the surface of all of it," Annie said, and then paused a beat. "You want to say 'good for her' on the one hand, but on the other . . . well, wasn't there another way?"

Beatrice was silent. Unusual. Then, "I guess it is hard to relate. But sometimes you are so isolated—or feel that way—that you can't think of another thing to do."

"I don't think she was thinking. I believe some strange thing happened in her brain. She just snapped," Annie said. "And for me, losing control is the most frightening thing of all."

Chapter 13

After her conversation with Annie, Beatrice realized she was hungry. A snack before bedtime, that's just what she needed. She padded her way into her kitchen and fixed herself a plate of molasses cookies and a glass of milk. She took her snack with her to the computer, where Jon was sitting, the blue of the screen reflecting on his face. Something about his posture gave Beatrice a chill.

"What's wrong?" she said, setting her plate down on the desk.

"I've been reading about the woman who was killed on the *Jezebel*," he said. "The story is out. She was involved in a messy divorce. Sounds awful. Children involved. Money." He clicked his tongue.

"So her soon-to-be ex-husband would be a suspect," Beatrice said.

He nodded. "Oui."

"Do they know how she was killed?"

"They say it was poison. They think ricin, from the look of the body. But the medical facilities are limited on the ship, so they can't be certain yet."

"Ricin," Beatrice said. "Where would she get a hold of that?"

He shrugged. "That would seem to be the million-dollar question. Evidently, when a murder happens on the high seas, it is very, very difficult to investigate."

Beatrice bit into her spicy cookie. Damn, it was good. "Mmm-mmm. That's one of the reasons I hate cruises. All kinds of disappearances. Rapes, and stuff. And people get away with these crimes because the law is so tricky. But when something happens to an American citizen, usually the FBI gets involved."

"As we know," Jon said, and smiled. "But by the time they get to the scene, what will have happened to the evidence?"

"Your guess is as good as mine," she said, then smacked her lips together. "Though I guess the ship's security will step in and keep it safe, right?"

Jon let out a huge sigh. "I am sorry, Beatrice, but the more I look at ship security, I wonder why these cruises bother at all. The security people are not concerned with justice. They work for the cruise lines. When something happens, the first people they call are the lawyers—the ship's lawyers—to see, how you say, how liable the company is."

Beatrice swallowed the last bit of her cookie. "Oh my, you have been researching."

"It is troubling. So many people go missing from ships, too. Maybe they fall over? Maybe they are kidnapped?"

"Kidnapped?"

He nodded. "They disappear. At least one person disappears from a cruise every three weeks, worldwide."

A shiver rippled through Beatrice's body. "Land sakes, I've always known about cruises and the risks, but I never knew the extent of it."

Beatrice looked over Jon's shoulder as he read.

"'Allison Elizabeth Monroe, age forty-three, died today on the *Jezebel*, while attending a scrapbooking cruise. Monroe, who was a headliner at the event, was perhaps one of the wealthiest scrapbook designers in the United States. The mother of three daughters, she started her business fifteen years ago in the basement of her home.' "

"That's odd," Beatrice said. "What a coincidence. The same as Sheila. Only she has just been selling the supplies, not designing. Yet."

"Didn't Sheila say this woman took an interest in her or something?" Jon said.

"Yes, they had been e-mailing back and forth and Sheila was hoping to work for her, I think," Beatrice said. "Maybe she was a role model for Sheila. Poor Sheila. To trip over her body like that."

" 'She built her scrapbooking design business into an empire of fifty lines of scrapbooking supplies and recently launched a digital line, with a Web site that has six million unique visitors every month,' " Jon read aloud.

"Good Lord, that's a lot of people," Beatrice said. "No wonder she was rich."

She scanned the article further. But there was no mention of her being murdered. Typical.

"It says that the cause of death is unknown," Jon said, as if reading her mind.

"Hmph," Beatrice said. "They have a couple of thousand people on a ship in the western Caribbean and there's a killer among them. I'm sure they don't want to set off a panic."

"I hope Vera is careful," Jon said after a few minutes. "All of them. I hope they mind their own business and do not try to get involved."

"I would say they probably have had enough involvement, with Sheila tripping over the body," Beatrice said. "They probably don't want to think about the murder too hard. I know I wouldn't."

"But still, remember the last time they got involved with a murder?" Jon asked.

"How could I forget? Though every time they've been involved the murder affected them somehow. Last time, Vera was a suspect," Beatrice said. "She was dragged in whether or not she wanted to be."

Jon clicked on another site. "I love this," he said. "We can track the *Jezebel* as it travels. It's a very classy program they've designed for family members and friends. There's a newsletter and photos of people. Really nice. I love this tracker."

The screen went blue; the islands of the Caribbean appeared, then an icon for the ship, which was standing still.

"Hmm, last time I checked, the little boat was moving," Jon said, and refreshed the page.

"Probably something wrong with the page," Beatrice said, and took a drink of her milk.

He clicked on the boat and a notice appeared on the screen:

Due to a tropical storm front moving in to Mexico, the *Jezebel*'s passage is changing. We are currently awaiting further instructions from the US Coast Guard.

Beatrice nearly choked on her milk. "Hand me the phone, Jon."

But try as she might, she was unable to reach her daughter.

Chapter 14

The announcement came over the intercom about Allie Monroe's untimely death while the croppers were at an evening session on card making. There was no mention of murder.

"They said it was an accident," Vera said. "Didn't they tell us she was poisoned?"

The woman who was behind Vera at the next table over twisted her head and looked at her. She was also getting the evil eye from Sheila.

Eric put his arm around Vera and whispered into her ear. She nodded.

Even though "murder" and "poison" weren't mentioned in the announcement, it still sent a hushed chill over the room as the crafters folded their card stock and sought out stamps and stickers, buttons, and other embellishments. Christmas music played softly in the background. Lights twinkled as the sun began to set.

"I'll be meeting Theresa soon and I really wish I had my scrapbook. I don't understand why they are insisting on keeping it," Sheila said. "My scrapbook didn't kill her."

"Do you have the photos?" Vera asked.

"I do," Sheila said. "But it's not the same thing as having the scrapbook to show."

She placed a paper daisy in the center of her card and held it up to eyeball it. "I really like making cards. I've often thought of starting my own line. I'm not good at the words part though."

"You and Annie should go into business. She writes beautiful poetry sometimes," Paige said.

"Really? I had no idea," said Vera.

"Yep. She says she doesn't write it much anymore. But I saw one of her poems in a literary journal. How many Annie Chamovitzes can there be? So I asked her about it," Paige said.

"How about that?" Sheila said.

The room was filled with low murmurs, laughter, and the sound of cutting boards and scissors.

"I've been thinking," Paige said. "Why don't we see if Allie's room is open? We could go in there and get the scrapbook and nobody would know. She's got to have tons of scrapbooks in her room, right?"

"Now, that's an idea," Sheila said, grinning. Why hadn't she thought of that?

"I don't think it's a good idea," Eric said. "That's a crime scene. You shouldn't be there."

"Eric's right," Vera said. "Just stay here and have fun. Your scrapbook will be fine."

"It couldn't hurt to look," Randy said, after a

few moments. "The door's probably locked anyway."

"Let's go," Paige said. "If the door is locked, there's nothing we can do, right?"

"But if it's unlocked, I'll slip in and get my scrapbook," Sheila said.

"I don't think this is a good idea," Vera repeated.

"Nobody asked your permission," Sheila said with a bit of a bite to her voice.

Vera flung her arms out. "Fine. I'll stay here and finish my card with Eric."

"Whatever suits you," Paige said. "We'll be right back."

The three of them left their crafting behind and stole away into the hallways of the cruise ship.

"Do you know where the room is?" Randy asked.

"Yes, we were there this morning. No worries," Paige said. "We know where we're going."

The three of them walked through the gray, snaking corridors until they arrived at the right room. Sheila reached out for the doorknob.

"Wait!" Randy said. "Use this." He handed her a handkerchief. "Better to be safe." His eyes sparkled with excitement. Sheila was happy for it; he'd been so sad lately.

"Smart," Sheila said, reaching for the linen cloth. "That's my boy," she said. Then she froze and listened. "Hold on. I hear voices."

Randy leaned nonchalantly against the wall and

Paige pretended to be passing by. Sheila just stood there, eyes wide.

The group of people passed through the hallway.

"Maybe this isn't a good idea," Sheila said. Her heart was racing and her palms were sweaty. *What if they got caught?*

"Don't be ridiculous. We're here now," Paige said. Her blue eyes were lit with excitement.

Sheila knew there was no turning back. She hoped the door was open and she hoped her scrapbook was easily found.

She wrapped the doorknob with the cloth and twisted. The door came open.

"Isn't that something?" Paige said. "Anybody could come in here and steal her things." Indignant. As if that's not exactly what they were doing.

Sheila stepped into the pitch black room, surprised that Allie didn't have more luxurious quarters with windows. She took her handkerchief and used it to flip on the lights.

What she saw made her gasp. Paige and Randy clung to each side of her.

"This is freaky," Randy said.

The room was completely empty. The bed was perfectly made. It smelled of disinfectant. It was one clean room. No suitcases, clothes, and certainly no scrapbooks.

"What are you doing here?" a male voice said from behind them.

It was Matthew Kirtley, with his dreadlocks and beautiful white teeth.

"I thought I might come in and find my scrapbook," Sheila said, her voice quivering.

"Look, lady, I told you we'd get the scrapbook to you," he said, his hands on his hips.

"I don't have very much confidence in that," Sheila said. "Sorry. That book means a lot to me."

"I can see that, but you can't go off to find it on your own. You'll need to trust me on this," he said.

"Trust you?" Paige said. "This is Allie's room, right?" She gestured, as if to say, What the heck is going on here?

"Yes," he said after a moment. He cleared his throat. "But by the time we got here the room had been cleaned out completely, unfortunately."

"So when we were here earlier—"

"Yes, I'm sorry, but we really couldn't tell you there was nothing in the room," he said.

"So when you tell me you'll get my scrapbook back to me—"

"It's missing," he said. "But we're on a ship. It's here somewhere. And we will find it along with the rest of her things."

Sheila noted his weariness. Dark circles under his eyes and a raspy voice led her to believe the man had not been sleeping.

"I'm so sorry," Randy said. "We really shouldn't

be here. Ms. Rogers has a meeting tonight and wanted her scrapbook for it."

Matthew glanced at Randy and smiled a weary smile. "I understand. But now that you know, can we keep this to ourselves? And try to stay out of trouble?" He cocked an eyebrow at Randy.

Randy made a sound almost like a laugh. "Well, that's no fun, chief."

There was brief eyeball exchange between the security chief and Randy. Sheila was not certain, but she thought Randy was flirting with the chief of security. A blush crept onto Randy's face.

She shrugged. She wasn't certain about much these days, but she was beginning to come to terms with the fact that she'd probably never see that scrapbook again.

"Are you okay?" Paige's arm went around her.

"I think so," Sheila said. "I think I'm giving up on that scrapbook. Maybe I'll make a new one based on what I remember."

"It's a shame," Paige said, looking at the chief, still eyeing her son.

"Let's go, Randy," she said, reaching for his arm. "Let's finish our cards and get ready for dinner."

Chapter 15

Annie dug underneath her cupboard and pulled out her box that held the menorah and other items she used for Hanukkah. She just wanted to have them on hand for tomorrow.

Mike passed by her and patted her on the rear end. "I'm heading for bed. Are you coming?"

"I'll be there soon," she said. "I have one more load of laundry coming out of the dryer."

"Okay," he said, and headed for bed, knowing better than to suggest she leave it for tomorrow. She was particular about some of the laundry. The boys' shirts needed to be folded immediately after they came out of the dryer or their sons would walk around a wrinkled mess, giving people even more reason to talk about them—the only Jewish boys in town.

It was getting a bit easier for them, thank goodness. Ben was becoming more popular with the boys his age because he excelled at soccer. Annie was glad it was soccer and not football. Sam was starting to play a lot of soccer, too, but he didn't take to it as much as Ben.

The dryer's buzzer went off and Annie pulled out the clothes. Hot. Fresh smelling. She scooped them into a basket and decided to take them into the living room and catch some news while she folded the clothes. A wave of weariness overtook her. *Bed soon,* she told herself. *And in the morning, one more chapter on the book.*

She sat the basket down on the coffee table and clicked on the remote. The TV was turned to the Disney Channel. She flipped around the stations until she reached CNN. Then she pulled some T-shirts out of the basket and listened to the news as she folded. The stock market seemed to be rallying. That was good news. Gas prices still skyrocketing. Grrr. That she knew. She folded clothes and the world turned.

She was trying to ignore this creeping sensation in her belly. She was worried about Hannah going to New York. But she was even more worried about her friends on the cruise ship. She hadn't been worried before they left—but since there had been a murder on the ship, Annie's hackles were raised. And then the really odd thing with the FBI agents visiting Beatrice and trying to tell her Sheila was dead . . . Talk about screwed up.

Maybe it *was* just an honest mistake.

If there was anything she'd learned by dealing with law enforcement that people would find surprising, it was how many mistakes they actually made every day. Of course most of them were good, adequate folks, but mistakes happened, just as they did in every profession.

But maybe it wasn't an honest mistake. That thought ticked at Annie as she folded yet another

T-shirt. Maybe it was something else. But what?

She caught herself. Rolled her eyes at herself. *Get it together, Annie, you are getting paranoid.* Still it couldn't hurt to use her press credentials to get a copy of the report.

She picked up the remote and flipped the television to the Weather Channel. It had become a habit. She loved to watch weather patterns. God, she was becoming her parents, who could talk for hours about the weather.

She folded a pair of jeans and then another. The talking head on the Weather Channel said that Virginia was in for some snow. The boys would be thrilled.

"In other news, we are watching a tropical storm in the western Caribbean as it makes its way to the east coast of Mexico," said the talking head.

"Mexico?" Annie said out loud. "Isn't that where the *Jezebel*'s heading?"

Suddenly, instead of the news being a backdrop in her domestic scene, her attention honed in on the TV. Her friends were headed for a storm. A freaky, huge storm. Surely the ship's crew watched the weather, right? The same crew who had misinformed the FBI about who had died on the ship. Annie's stomach flipped a bit.

The weatherman droned on: "This storm appeared out of nowhere and we are really not certain if it will hit the coast or if it will turn toward the islands. If it hits the Mexican coast at full force, it will be devastating. If it runs in the other direction, the storm may lose momentum as it heads toward the islands. We are keeping a close eye on this system. Several ships in the area have turned around or have adjusted their routes. At this time, we have no further information on individual ships."

Annie folded the last pair of jeans as her heart began to race. She wished she had more confidence in this ship's crew. Of course they knew what they were doing when it came to weather and the sea and so on. Of course they did—or else they wouldn't be sailors.

When a murder happened, fear took over and mistakes sometimes would be made, especially by people who'd never dealt with that type of death before. She could see the errors in dealing with the murder case.

She placed the folded clothes back in the basket. Her hands felt warm from the clothes, but they were a bit sweaty, too. She didn't want to think about Sheila, Paige, Vera, Randy, and Eric on the high seas during this storm. She couldn't think too hard about it. It would make her panic.

Instead, she decided to call Vera. She knew it would be expensive, but she needed to hear her friend's voice.

Of course, she couldn't get through.

Annie called Sheila next. Then Paige.

All of the cell phones gave no message, no signal, nothing.

Annie headed for her computer.

Mike was already asleep. He was snoring softly in the background when she turned her computer on. He wouldn't wake up. He was used to the soft blue light of the screen and the clicking of her keyboard.

She clicked on the Skype icon and the wheel kept spinning. Nobody was available on Skype either.

She searched online to see if there was any news. Nothing recent. Just the news of Allie Monroe's death.

Annie drew in a breath. What was going on?

Chapter 16

By the time Beatrice finished reading *How the Grinch Stole Christmas!* for the fifteenth time, Elizabeth was out. Before she crept out of the child's room, Beatrice turned to look at her lying peacefully in the bed with the quilt pulled up around her and her stuffed elephant in one hand snuggled up to her chin. The child loved elephants. At three years old, she could tell you all about them, their habitats, what they liked to eat, and so on. She showed no inclination toward dance, which her mother loved so much. Beatrice smiled—the child resembled Vera, but she thought she might be more like her with her love of science. She shrugged. It didn't really matter. But it always fascinated Beatrice to see the stew of genetics and what eventually ended up foaming at the top.

Beatrice left the room as quietly and gracefully as her old body could muster. That was a challenge.

Lawd, if anything happened to Vera, what would she and Elizabeth do? She clutched her chest as she made her way into her room, where Jon was tucked into bed with a book, but was almost asleep. The book was tilted down, slipping from his hands. His glasses perched on the end of his nose and his eyelids hung low with weariness. He grunted at her.

She sat on the edge of the bed and reached for her book. She swung her legs over. They were strong, mountain-walking legs. She slipped them under the covers.

"Why don't you turn your light off and go to sleep?" she said.

"Waiting on you," he mumbled. "Worried."

"Me too," she said. Her book was heavy in her hands. She turned the page to read about Agatha Raisin in the Cotswolds of England. Far away.

"I'm worried that you're becoming an Anglophile," Jon said, swatting at her book.

She playfully bopped him on the head with

it. "Oh you! You know I'll always be a Franco-phile."

He grinned.

"Now to sleep with you," she said.

"You too?"

"You know I have to read a few minutes, but I'm sleepy, so it won't be long."

He kissed her, then rolled over to his other side.

Beatrice turned her attention to her book. Soon, Jon was snoring softly and she realized that even though she was turning the pages and her eyes were skimming the words, she wasn't reading at all. She closed her book and set it down on her bedside table, where her battered copy of *Leaves of Grass* had sat untouched for a few weeks. She noted that the lace tablecloth underneath it showed the dirt and dust in this light. She made a mental note to take all the tablecloths off in the morning and wash them.

She was trying very hard not to think about her only daughter on a cruise ship in the western Caribbean where a storm was headed. From the very start of that child's life, she had tested Beatrice. She wasn't interested in the same things as Bea: math and physics. Her daughter wanted to dance. Vera had been through so much the last few years of her life—a new baby, a divorce, a failed love affair, and a new one that appeared to be going well. Then there was the sleepwalking and the time she was a suspect for murder.

Even though Vera had not followed her mother's path, Bea admired her daughter for going her own way and forging ahead with her dance studio and her life. That much Vera had gotten from her, she supposed.

When Beatrice closed her eyes, she saw a ship rocking back and forth and waves slapping onto the deck.

Surely not. Those ships were huge. Surely they would be untouched by rough waves of any sort.

But the scientist in Beatrice knew that the power of the ocean could certainly take down even one of the biggest ocean liners, let alone the *Jezebel*. . . . She turned over to her side.

Of course, the captain and his crew would be well trained and prepared for such things. The fact that they messed up the notification of the murder victim should not have any bearing. That was an unusual circumstance. They were probably flustered and had never dealt with such a thing before. Who gets murdered on a luxury cruise ship, right?

Beatrice turned over to her other side.

Damn, the whole thing rubbed her the wrong way. No use pretending that it didn't. Sometimes you could fool yourself into a calmness. But not this time. Not tonight. She flung the covers off and reached for her robe and slipped it onto her body, bones creaking.

She tiptoed out of the room, leaving Jon to

sleep. Someone would need to be rested tomorrow to think clearly and calmly. It wasn't going to be Beatrice.

She headed down the stairs and toward the kitchen, remembering the coconut pie in the fridge. There was at least half of it left. Maybe that would help her sleep. That and a big glass of warm milk—with a shot or two of bourbon in it. "Good for what ails ya" is what her daddy always said.

Chapter 17

Dinner was a lavish affair. Each night the ship seemed to outdo itself from the previous night. Buffet tables piled high with fresh seafood, gorgeous vegetables and fruit welcomed them each night. Even though Sheila's grand prize allowed her to eat for free at any of the onboard restaurants, she chose to dine with her friends at the buffet. They all came to love the lavish dessert tables. A chocolate fountain surrounding delectables like pound cake, fruit, and pretzels consumed their attention this night. Even Randy was impressed.

"I've often thought about working on a cruise ship," he said. "I'd get to see the world."

"It would be fun," Sheila agreed. "You're young and now would be the time to do it."

"I'd never see him then," Paige said.

"You hardly see each other now," Vera said. "How's it going with Earl?"

"We spoke on the phone yesterday," Randy announced. "He said he was sorry to hear that Fred and I broke up." His voice cracked and he gazed off.

Sheila wondered if he was emotional because of chatting with his father or because of the break-up with his partner.

"Wonders never cease," Vera said. "Your dad is talking with you. That's great."

A huge smile appeared on Paige's face. "Earl is just working through it. He loves Randy. It's going to be okay."

Randy, fair and blond, blushed easily and his face reddened as he sipped his wine. "Maybe it's time for change in my life," he said. "Maybe I'll check into pastry gigs on the ships."

"You know, I don't think I've ever had such good lobster," Vera said. "The food is amazing. I swear I'm going home at least ten pounds heavier. And everything is so clean. Hard to imagine someone has been poisoned."

"But they didn't say food poisoning, did they? I don't think so. It's not just the food, but the booze. I mean everywhere you go, they are shoving drinks under your nose," Sheila said.

"Yeah, for a hefty price," Paige said. "Unless it's in crop rooms. I've been able to sneak some into my flask so I have my own portable bar. Screw them and their twenty dollars for a glass of wine."

"My mom," Randy said, laughing. "Class act."

"How's your head?" Eric asked Sheila.

"It hurts. After dinner, I'm going to meet with Theresa, then go back to my cabin and go to sleep. You all will have to party without me." She grinned.

"Truth is I'm about partied out. This cruise has been exhausting. Maybe tomorrow I'll relax by the pool. I love to scrapbook, but this has been intense," Paige said.

"I'm a bit weary, too," Vera said after a few minutes. "And with the murder and everything . . . I don't know. I'm a bit freaked out. I can't stop thinking about the poison. Is it in the food? In the water? Where is it? Maybe I'll join you at the pool tomorrow, too. Until Sheila's journaling class. We won't miss that."

"Tomorrow night is the award ceremony?" Eric asked.

"No," Sheila said. "It's the next night. It was supposed to be after my class in Mexico, but it doesn't look like we're going to get there. I ran into the captain and he gave me a heads-up on that."

"Doesn't look like we're going anywhere," Eric said.

"They're just being safe," Vera said. "I don't mind if they turn around and go to some other ports. Just as long as we get there safely."

"Seems like a long time," Paige said.

"Well, they said to reroute requires permission from several agencies and islands," Randy said. "It must be taking longer than what they expected."

Sheila finished the last bite of her meal and excused herself to go meet with Theresa again in the Cut and Paste lounge. That name tickled Sheila, even though she knew that the *Jezebel* had adopted it temporarily for the scrapbooking cruise.

She looked around the dark lounge, her eyes adjusting from the brightly lit hallway. She didn't see Theresa. She walked around a bit and then she saw her. She was sitting with a man—maybe it was her husband?

Sheila walked toward them and Theresa stood up to greet her. "Sheila, so glad you could make it. This is Harold Tuft," she said.

Sheila extended her hand. He offered his in a cold and clammy weak handshake. How weird.

"Nice to meet you," he said meekly. His eyes and nose were red and swollen. Was he sick? Drunk?

"I'm sorry, Sheila. Please have a seat. We were just talking about Allie. Her death . . . it's such a tragedy. She was so young and vibrant," said Theresa.

"Yes," Sheila said. "I had just been with her the night before she died."

"Really?" Theresa said. "Why?"

"She loved my work and wanted to borrow my scrapbook to look at it. I've not seen it since—"

"Oh, that's why you don't have it," she said.

Harold patted his eyes with a handkerchief. "I'm sorry, ladies. I really must go back to our—my—cabin. I'm feeling quite under the weather."

He took his leave and Theresa's eyes followed him.

"Poor man," she said. "He and Allie were close. I don't know what the man is going to do."

"You mean—?"

"Yes, they were planning to be married, as soon as her divorce was final."

"Oh," Sheila said. Why weren't they sharing a room together? Maybe they were. Maybe she never really stayed in her own cabin. Oh hell, she'd have to find the security guard and tell him what she knew. It could help with the case—and help find her scrapbook. Her head was pounding. She reached into her bag for an ibuprofen and slipped it into her mouth. How many had she taken today?

"So let's look at your photos. I hope it will jog my memory," Theresa said with a flat note in her voice.

Sheila pulled out her envelope from her bag and showed her photos to Theresa. She wished the woman would say something other than "lovely, just lovely."

Finally she did.

"I remember this book quite vividly," she said, looking at Sheila over her glasses. Those droopy bloodhound eyes were shot. "I think it's average, I'm sorry to say. I was surprise that Allie liked it so much and put her weight behind it. And I was surprised that this book was designed by the same person who designed the exquisite digital pieces. That's where your strength as a designer lies. We would never hire you to design scrapbooks, I'm sorry to say."

Sheila couldn't believe what she was hearing. She choked back a tear. She thought her scrapbook was unique—everybody else had told her that. But maybe they were just being polite. But wait. She'd won a major competition. You didn't win a competition like this unless you were good. This was confusing.

"I don't understand," Sheila said. "I won the contest." Her voice came out weak.

"As I said, Allie really liked it and persuaded some of the other judges. But our company's designers have a much higher standard than hers," Theresa said with a tight smile.

Sheila fought back anger as she realized this was not about her. Theresa and Allie were competitors. And while Allie's body was still in the ship's morgue, Theresa could not muster a kind word for her or for Sheila.

"If that's all," Sheila said, gathering up her

photos. "I've got a raging headache." Her voice was steady. She'd be damned if she'd let this woman know how she'd upset her. "I really need to lie down." She grabbed her things and left.

"Hope you feel better soon," Theresa said with a fake lightness.

I bet you do.

When Sheila turned around to look at her once more, she was grinning off into another direction at nobody in particular. It looked evil and malicious. Maybe murderous.

Oh Sheila, now you really are losing your mind!

She walked over to the elevator, pushed the button, and waited. Oh Lord, she wanted her bed. Tomorrow she'd meet with David's Designs, teach her class, and then lounge by the pool with her friends. Yes, that's what she'd do. That thought warmed her.

She slipped into the elevator and smiled at the woman already there. Sheila's room was on the top floor. She felt a bit pampered in her luxurious quarters; her friends' rooms were on another deck completely and did not have windows. Sheila was treated like a star by everybody. Everybody except Theresa, that is.

When she exited the elevators, she noted sounds of scuffling or something, which was odd because the halls were usually quiet and kept clear. She turned the corner and saw Harold splayed on the floor, with three women crowded around him.

"He's dead," one woman cried.

"What do we do?" another woman said through her sobs.

Sheila spotted an emergency phone and ran toward it. "I'll call security."

This cruise was becoming a nightmare. Only this morning she'd tripped over Allie's body. Tonight she watched as the security team and medics took Harold's body and comforted the three women who'd found him.

"He was heading to his room," one said, and gestured to the room next to Sheila. "He said he wasn't feeling good."

"He looked very sick," another one said.

"Ms. Rogers . . ." Matthew Kirtley came up beside her. "Fancy seeing you again."

Chapter 18

Annie arose at 4 A.M. to get some work done on her manuscript before the start of the day. It was the first day of Hanukkah—okay it really didn't start until sundown, but she allowed herself to feel the joy of the holiday.

She clicked on her computer and the information about Allie Monroe and the ship was still on her screen. It was a tragedy, to be sure, this young woman killed on a cruise ship. She read over Allie's death notice. She was surprised to read that Allie had been in the process of divorcing her husband of twenty-three years. Wow. Three kids, money, and a divorce. That sent alarm bells off in Annie's head.

She typed in "Allison and John Monroe" and bingo, a list of blog articles came up on the computer:

Scrapbooking Superstar Allie Monroe Fights for Custody of Her Three Children

Mega Millionaire Allison Monroe Tells Her Divorcing Husband "Not a Dime"

Allie Monroe Can't Scrapbook This: Husband Accuses Her of Cheating for Years with Fledgling Assistant.

Wow, what a tangled, sordid web.

What if Allie's husband is on the cruise?

Would a jealous soon-to-be ex-husband go to the trouble of killing his cheating wife while she was miles away from home?

Annie's guts twisted. Probably. Especially since there was a lot of money involved. And she'd been cheating on him. That would sting anybody, especially since it was so public. The humiliation would be searing. Some men would have to get revenge.

Annie knew she couldn't get a list of passengers

on the ship, but she racked her brain trying to remember if she knew anybody that could.

She reached for her cell phone—she would text everybody she knew on the ship. At least one of them would be bound to get it.

Looking into murder vic's background.
Bad divorce. Her soon-to-be ex on board?
His name is John.

Send.

She typed in the words "Jezebel Cruise" and saw that the ship was at a standstill on the sea due to the storm and would be rerouted.

Whew, that was a relief.

But still. Her friends were on a ship in the middle of the western Caribbean with a murderer *and* a pending storm.

The coffeepot beeped. Ahhh, coffee. It was just what she needed. A toilet flushed, announcing that one of her boys was up—it was probably Mike.

He sauntered into the kitchen.

"Coffee?" she asked.

He nodded. "Man, I was up and down all night. I shouldn't have had that beer." He kissed her cheek. "Good morning, Annie."

"Morning," she said, pouring him some coffee.

"Get much work done?"

"Not really. I've been distracted by the murder on the cruise ship."

"Ah, yeah," he said, bringing his cup to his mouth. "Find out anything?"

She told him what she knew.

"I'm glad you didn't go," he said, smiling.

She liked the way her man looked in the mornings. All dark and rumpled. Unshaven.

"What?" he said. "Why are you looking at me like that?"

"Because you're cute."

He laughed. "Okay."

She drank more coffee. "I wonder if there's a way for me to hack into the ship's database and get a passenger list."

He grinned. "I bet I know someone who could help you with that."

"Really? I'd feel better knowing if her ex is on the ship."

"Whose ex?"

"Allie Monroe's ex-husband. If he's the one who killed her, he's not much danger to anybody else. But if it was just some random killing . . ."

"Your friends would be in more danger. But, Annie, there's not much you can do from here."

"I can warn them."

"If you can get through to them. With a storm so close by, I imagine communication will be rough."

She grimaced.

"They are a resourceful and smart bunch of women," Mike said.

"True."

"I mean, there's Vera, one of the strongest women I've ever known. She's not going to get herself killed after everything she's been through," he said, and grinned.

It was true that Vera was the cliché of a "steel magnolia." On first meeting Annie thought she was vapid, prissy, and not very bright. Boy was she wrong. Vera was a smart businesswoman who knew what she wanted and never had a problem saying what that was.

"And then there's Paige." Mike rolled his eyes. "I mean, c'mon. I'll never forget when you all went up on Jenkins Mountain after that cult. Paige told you not to do it. And then she helped figure out all that historical stuff for Bea."

"She's definitely the voice of reason. And she has Randy with her," Annie said. "He's a bright young man."

"And Sheila? Well . . ."

Sheila was a mess on the outside—but it was because she had so much going on in the inside that she couldn't be bothered brushing her hair most days. It had taken Annie a while to realize what Sheila was about; she was so creative that she sometimes didn't concern herself much with the little things in real life. Things like matching her clothes and brushing her hair. Annie smiled.

"Sheila is a trip," she said.

"A crazy talented trip," Mike said. "It's a shame

this has all happened to her when she's finally coming into her own. Maybe it won't bother her much."

Annie thought for a moment. "You know, Mike, I think it's going to bother her a lot. It's been a struggle for her to accept her talent. She's put it aside for years. When she's finally acknowledged, this strange murder takes place on the ship. I hope it doesn't hold her back. But in some ways, Sheila is the most fragile of all of us. What I mean is that she's on a precipice of great change in her life. And that makes her vulnerable."

Chapter 19

Beatrice woke up with a headache. Had she overdone it with the bourbon last night?

The scent of frying bacon let her know that Jon was up and fixing breakfast. That man. He was a good one.

She sat up slowly—her bones weren't happy with her this morning. Was a storm going to blow in? She made a mental note to check the local weather, not only the Caribbean weather. From what she could tell last night, the little boat on their Web site was moving again, which meant that it had been rerouted because of the storm. That was a good thing.

She reached for her robe and slipped it on and padded downstairs to the kitchen. She stood a moment to marvel at her man frying bacon and eggs. She glanced at the coffeepot, full and fresh. He was a winner.

"Good morning," she said, coming up behind him, wrapping her arms around him.

"Good morning, mon amie," he said. "There is your aspirin." He pointed to the counter where a glass of water and an aspirin sat ready for her.

"Well, now. How'd you know?" she said.

"You left the bottle out. You always get a headache from it," he said. "No matter what your daddy told you, I do not think it is good for what ails you."

She smiled, then took her aspirin. "The good news is the *Jezebel* is moving again. Of course, it's not heading for the Mexican coast anymore. Thank heaven for that. I was worried because it doesn't seem like the cruise is being run professionally."

Jon sighed and fiddled with the sizzling bacon. "The Mexican coast is getting hit hard. It's devastating to these small coastal communities."

"It's a shame," Beatrice said, and reached into the cupboard to get a cup. Lawd, she needed some coffee. She had too busy a day ahead to let a headache get the best of her.

After pouring herself the coffee, she sat down at

the table and drank it silently. Jon piled plates high with scrambled eggs, bacon, and biscuits, and brought them to the table.

"Thanks for making breakfast this morning. I'll clean up," she said.

"No thanks needed, Bea," he said, and kissed her forehead.

After a mostly silent breakfast, Jon informed her that snow was expected, which didn't surprise Beatrice, given the way her bones ached. They always seem to know, unfortunately.

"It's supposed to start tonight," Jon said.

"Tonight? Maybe I'll try to move the meeting up to this afternoon." She had one more official meeting planned for the Christmas bazaar.

Lizzie came bounding her way down the stairs and climbed up on Beatrice's lap.

"Good morning, sugar. You hungry?" Beatrice said.

Lizzie nodded and Jon set a plate in front of her. She dug her head into Beatrice's chest and sobbed. "I miss Mama."

"Aww, baby," Beatrice said, as she slipped her arms around her. "I miss her, too. She'll be home soon."

"In the meantime, your daddy is going to come and get you today and he's going to take you to see Santa. Isn't that exciting?" Jon said.

She sniffed and nodded.

Beatrice's heart ached. That child loved her

mama, of course. They'd been through a lot together, perhaps making them closer than most. Bill's odd relationship with one of his law students was something both Vera and Elizabeth had suffered through. Some people should never have children. Bill was one of them. Beatrice hated sending her granddaughter off with him this morning, but the man had proven he was a fit parent according to the court's definition. It struck Beatrice, then, as it did from time to time, that half the world's problems would be solved if people were tested before they were allowed to become parents.

Oh, she could hear the crazies calling her fascist and inbred now. But, Lawd, some people should not breed. For years, she thought she might be one of them. After all, if she were to be honest with herself, physics was her first love. But then there was Ed, and when she met him she had grappled with the desire to bear his child. They got one in right under the wire. And she was a doozie.

"I had a dream about Mommy last night," Elizabeth said. "I dreamed she was fighting an octopus!"

"Did she win? Did she kill that ol' octopus?" Beatrice said.

"No, I don't think so," she said. "I woke up before the ending. But his arms were around her and she was crying."

"Dreams are funny things," Beatrice said.

"You've been watching too much Jacques Cousteau," Jon said, setting a plate of biscuits on the table.

"But he's neat," she said. "I like the way he talks. He talks like you, Grandpa."

Beatrice loved to hear her call him Grandpa. So sweet.

Jon's eyes caught hers. He loved it, too.

"He's just another crazy French guy," he said, and smiled.

"Yep," she said, and nodded her head. Then she turned her attention to her food.

After breakfast, Bill showed up for his weekend with Lizzie. Beatrice had to admit that he was good with her. It was the rest of his life he was not so good at—but bad decisions affected parenting, too.

As soon as she was gone, Bea sauntered over to her computer and clicked it on. She checked the ship's Web site to make certain the ship was moving away from the Mexican coast. She needed the certainty of knowing.

It was there that she read the news that another death had occurred on the ship. Harold Tuft, who had been a friend of Allie Monroe. Cause of death: unknown.

Unknown? Did that mean he was killed, too? Hmmm. Beatrice searched for him and Allie online. Sure enough, she found rumors about them dating and so on. Lawd, there were a lot of things online about this woman. Some kind of scrapbooking star. Hmph. Scrapbooking star or not, someone didn't like her or her boyfriend.

Chapter 20

For the first time in several years, Sheila didn't start her morning with a run. She felt like crap. Her head still ached and she was sore everywhere from her fall. She hated to miss a run, but even Eric had mentioned to her the night before that she should not run with a head injury—as mild as it was.

She picked up her cell phone from the bedside table, wanting to call her husband. He might be able to pick up a call from her by now; he was leading a group of Boy Scouts through a part of the Appalachian Trail. She smiled at the thought.

She saw a text message from Annie.

> Looking into murder vic's background. Bad divorce. Her soon-to-be ex on board? His name is John.

Sheila placed her glasses on her face and read the text again. That Annie. She couldn't resist sleuthing, even if she wasn't even on board. But a chill traveled up through Sheila as she remembered the dead man last night. Allie's boyfriend was offed, too. It would seem that Allie's soon-to-be ex would be at the top of everybody's suspect list. It would be good to know if he was on board and exactly who he was so she could make certain to stay the hell away from him. Still, if she could put this together sitting in bed with a cell phone in her hand, surely Matthew Kirtley and Ahoy Security had already done so. It seemed so clear cut.

But later, showered and ready for breakfast, she grabbed her passenger list from the table. Not everybody was privy to this list, but as the Creative Spirit winner, she was. She couldn't read through all two thousand names, but she and her friends could together.

She grabbed her purse and phone and pressed in Steve's number again. She still couldn't get through to him. No signal again. Yet, Annie's message had gotten through sometime in the middle of the night. Off and on again; it was maddening.

She had her meeting with David's Designs and then she was teaching a class. She planned to meet her friends at the pool later. All of this scrapbooking was intense, even for her. She needed a break, especially after last night. Evidently, her designs weren't as good as she thought. She swallowed, willing away tears of embarrassment. Everything she had worked toward had seemed to crash around her at the meeting with Theresa.

When Sheila walked into the dining room, her eyes went immediately to the large decorated Christmas tree, brightly lit and trimmed in red and gold. Christmas music was being piped through the intercom. She was overwhelmed by a longing for home, to be sitting next to Steve and their own tree with all of their kids around them. She felt no Christmas spirit here. After last night, it had gotten worse.

As she glanced around the room for her crew, she observed the man who had been watching her so intently yesterday. She scowled. Then she spotted her group and walked toward them.

"Good morning, sleepyhead," Paige said, looking up at her as she approached the table.

Sheila grunted and sat down, immediately reaching for the coffee.

"Are you feeling okay?" Vera said. She looked up at Sheila from a stack of fruit and crepes.

"I feel about the same as yesterday," Sheila said.

"It's going to take a few days," Eric said, then took a huge bite of sausage. "Try to eat something. The buffet is fantastic."

"Coffee and toast for me this morning," Sheila said. Her stomach was still queasy.

Randy was standing up to get his second or third helping from the buffet. "I'll bring you some toast," he said. "Maybe it will settle your stomach and then you can eat more."

"Thank you, Randy," Sheila said. *What a nice young man. Too bad his relationship hadn't worked out.* "Have you heard about last night?" Sheila turned to her friends, who were all happily mooning over their food.

"What? Your meeting?" Paige said.

"No," Sheila said. She took a drink of coffee. She didn't want to talk about that right now. And she was sure that the meeting with David's Designs would be the same kind of thing. *Who did she think she was? A real designer?* "There was another death."

"What?" Vera exclaimed. A man who was seated at the table behind them turned and glared at her.

"Keep your voice down," Sheila said.

"Really!" Vera said, her face reddening. "You can't lay something like that on me and not expect me to get a little excited."

Sheila took a breath. "Okay. The man was Allie Monroe's boyfriend." She mouthed the word "boyfriend."

"I thought she was married," Paige said.

"She was going through a divorce. A bad one." Sheila said.

"Ahh, so now Annie's text makes sense," Paige said.

"You got that, too? I wondered what that was about," Vera said.

Sheila pulled out her passenger list and divided it among the group at the table.

Randy came up with a plate of food for himself in one hand and a plate of toast for Sheila in the other. He set it down in front of her. She smelled the toast and wasn't sure if she could manage to eat.

"What's this?" Randy said.

"This is the passenger list. We're looking for a John Monroe on the list. Allie Monroe's husband," she said.

"Oh, he's not here," Randy said. "I mean, you can look to double check, but I saw Matthew last night and they had already searched through the passenger list looking for him, probably thinking what you're thinking. The other murder . . ."

"Murder?" Sheila said. "Then he was killed?"

He nodded. "In exactly the same way as Allie Monroe."

"How do you know all of this?" Sheila asked.

"I told you," he said, and sat down next to his mother. "I saw Matthew last night. We met for drinks."

Everybody stopped eating and looked up at him.

"What?" he said. "It was just drinks. It wasn't a real date or anything, and he kept getting pulled away to deal with everything."

"Well, Randy, is there anything else you found out last night that you'd like to tell us?" Paige said.

His mouth full, he shook his head, then finally

said, "Nothing I can think of. But Matthew is very cute, don't you think?"

Paige's neck, then face, reddened. Vera looked away and Sheila took a deep breath and bit into her toast.

"Not to scare anybody," Eric said, "but I doubt the guy would be using his own name. If you were planning to kill someone on a cruise, would you?"

It was no use. Sheila swallowed her bite of the dry toast, but then set it down on her plate with a thud.

Merry effing Christmas.

Chapter 21

Not on the ship. Unless he's using a fake name, said the text message from Sheila.

Annie put her phone down. After taking the brisket out of the freezer to thaw for their Hanukkah dinner tonight, she sat down at her computer to write another chapter on the Mary Schultz book before the boys got out of bed. They were really sleeping in this morning.

She turned her thoughts back to the *Jezebel*.

Well, there was no way she could find out anything about the man if he was using a fake name. So he could be on the ship. But if he was out to get his ex-wife, maybe he posed no threat to Annie's friends. Maybe. But if he was crazy enough to kill someone—anyone—he might do it again.

She clicked on the cruise Web site again, as if it could provide her with some peace of mind. She'd read over this site a dozen times in the last twenty-four hours. What was she looking for? Clues? Comfort?

She clicked on the newsletter, read it over. It gave the upcoming events of the day, as well as highlighted a few things that took place yesterday. In the left hand corner of page three, a death was mentioned. A death? A Harold Tuft of Sarasota, Florida—hmm . . . the same place Allie lived—was reported dead. Annie shivered. Could this guy have known Allie? Surely he did—she was a scrapbooking star from his hometown and they were on a scrapbooking cruise.

She heard the rustling around of her boys heading to the kitchen. She left her computer and followed the sound.

"Morning, boys," she said.

"Morning, Mommy," they said together, and ran to her, hugged her.

"Morning sugar is the best kind," Annie said, and smiled. "Go sit down and I'll make you some eggs. How does that sound?"

They both made their way to the table and Annie headed for the fridge. She took out the eggs and readied her frying pan. She loved mornings with her boys now that they were a little bit older.

Annie beat her eggs and tried not to think of Sam beating up that boy because he said terrible things about the Jewish people. And then there was the time that Ben came home sobbing because a friend said his parent would never let a Jewish boy into their home.

Annie tried not to think about it too much, but being Jewish was on her mind because of Hanukkah. After dinner and family time, she was heading over to Sheila's basement to meet DeeAnn for their weekly crop. She was thinking about a special book. A book about being Jewish. A spiritual scrapbook—sort of like Cookie's scrapbook of shadows. *Cookie.* Finally, she was able to think of her with some fondness, without the horrible, black, bereft feeling. Still, she was unable to make complete peace with the disappearance of her friend.

She poured the eggs in the pan as Mike was entering the kitchen.

"Juice, boys?"

They both said yes. Mike tried to skirt around Annie, brushing up against her, which he couldn't help. Their kitchen was tiny and they were always tripping over one another.

The Chamovitzes were saving for a down payment on a bigger house. As the boys were getting older, space was more and more of an issue—along with the fact that they only had one bathroom.

"How did you do on that math test yesterday?" Mike said as he set the filled juice glasses on the table in front of the boys.

"I think I did okay," Sam said. "I won't know until Monday."

"I got a one hundred on my spelling test," Ben said.

"Good for you," Annie said. She scooped the eggs onto plates for her boys and sat down at the breakfast table.

After breakfast, Mike took the boys out and left Annie to work. When she went back to her computer, the screen with the cruise on it was still up. Before she got settled in to her writing she decided to give Vera a call. She knew it would be expensive, but she needed to talk with at least one of them. She really wanted to talk to Sheila, but she knew that she was in meetings off and on and had events planned. Better to call Vera.

"Hey, Annie," Vera said.

"Hey, Vera. How's it going?"

"Honestly?" she said, and laughed.

"Well, as honest as you can make it," Annie said, smiling.

"The food is great. The scrapbooking is intense. We took a bit of a break from it today. We're all at the pool. Well, everybody but Sheila. She's at a meeting with David's Designs."

"How is she?"

"She still has a headache and not much of an

appetite. I swear she had maybe two bites of toast this morning. Poor thing. We're all worried about her, but we're keeping an eye on her."

"How did her meeting go yesterday?"

"Honestly, I don't know; she didn't mention it at breakfast. We talked about the murder. She had a passenger list and was ready to go over it, but then Randy saw the ship's security chief last night and he said they'd already looked through it."

"Yep, I guess that would be the first thing a security team would do," Annie said, more to herself than to Vera. "But what about this Harold Tuft? How does he fit in?"

Vera explained to Annie everything she knew about Harold.

"It's been awful," she said with her voice lowered. "I keep looking at men and wondering if they are the one. Also, they say they've got the poison situation in hand. That it wasn't food poisoning. But I don't know what to believe. Eric says I'm paranoid. But I can't stop thinking about it. I can't wait until we make land. The FBI is going to meet the ship at the next port. I'll feel so much better then."

Chapter 22

"So where are you headed now?" Beatrice asked Vera.

"We should reach Grand Caymen later tonight or tomorrow. Sheila will be leading a photo expedition. She was supposed to be doing that in Mexico, but with the storm and everything . . ." Vera said. "Oh, Mama, it's just so beautiful looking out over the pool and in the distance is the sea, such a beautiful blue color."

"Try to stick together."

"We're all here now, except for Sheila. She has a meeting this morning, then is teaching a class. We're all going to try to get there," Vera said.

"How is Sheila?"

"Not good, Mama," Vera said in a hushed voice.

"That's too bad. Call Elizabeth. She's with Bill. She misses you," Beatrice said, and hung up.

Poor Sheila. But, Beatrice knew Sheila enough to know that it was hard to keep that woman down.

Her timer went off and she walked into the kitchen, grabbed a pot holder, opened the oven door, and pulled out her poppy seed cake. Ohhh, it looked perfect—and smelled of sugar, cinnamon, and poppy seed. She sat it on the counter and glanced out the window. A fine snow was starting to fall and blanketed the grass.

Beatrice's phone rang. If that was Elsie again, she might scream. This Christmas bazaar should be an easy function to put together. Why was she making mountains out of molehills?

"Hey, Beatrice. I'm on break at the bakery and thought I'd check in with you. How are you?" DeeAnn said.

"I'm fine, other than Elsie driving me crazy and the fact that my daughter is on a cruise with a killer," Beatrice said.

"Did you hear about the second killing?"

"Yep. If her ex-husband is on the ship, there's no trace of him."

"Maybe what we should do is get Annie to check into the background of the other guy. . . . What was his name? Harold?"

"Yes, Harold Tuft. But I don't know what good that would do. He's dead."

"But why?"

"Obviously he was boffing that Allie woman and it upset her husband. Imagine that," Beatrice said with a clipped tone.

"I'm kind of worried about Sheila. I mean, she knows these people and is kind of hanging out with them. What if she gets in the middle of something?"

"You're borrowing trouble. We have to trust that they will be careful and not get themselves into a bad situation," Beatrice said, but inside she was quivering. She'd promised Gerty, Sheila's mother, that she would watch out for her daughter.

After she hung up from DeeAnn, she called Annie, a voice of reason. Most of the time.

"What do you think, Annie?"

"I think it's odd that there's not been much in the news about this. Yesterday there was a bit about Allie, but nothing today. I keep racking my brain trying to remember if I know any journalists in the area who could look into the situation more. But I don't think I do."

"What bothers you about it?"

"For one thing, the person you'd suspect right away would be Allie's soon-to-be ex-husband."

"A no brainer," Beatrice said, stirring cookie dough. "And he's not on the ship—unless he's using a fake name."

"There's no way to figure that out. He could be anybody."

"We could figure it out by process of elimination if we had the list. We could start by eliminating any man who's there with his wife. Guys on a ship in the Caribbean surrounded by scrapbooking women. Poor schmucks. You know they aren't up to murder. And then we go from there."

"I'll text Vera to see if she can e-mail me the list."

"I was also wondering if you still subscribe to your databases."

"I do."

"Why don't you run her ex-husband through some of them," Beatrice suggested. "You never know what might come up."

"I plan to do that later today, after I finish talking to you, make lunch, and put the brisket in the oven. I'm on it."

"Good," Beatrice said, then hung up. She reached over to the radio and turned it up. One of her favorite Christmas songs was playing, "Silver Bells," by Perry Como. She looked out the window. It had stopped snowing, but clumps of snow were clinging to shrubs and grass. She took a deep breath—the cookie dough smelled fresh and sweet. But the nut filling smelled even better. Nut-filled cookies were a must for her season. It was a recipe her mother had used when Beatrice was growing up. It wouldn't be Christmas without those cookies.

The snow. The cookies. The music. It was the holiday season, but she knew she wouldn't fully feel it until Vera and the others were back home safely.

Chapter 23

Just as Sheila walked into the lounge, the ship lurched and she found herself plastered against the wall. Her bag went flying and the items in it splayed all over the tiled floor. After she gathered herself and all of her things, she stood up, brushed herself off, and proceeded to walk.

David of David's Designs was sitting at a table already, but he was speaking into his cell phone. He was dressed casually, in khakis and a white-striped golf shirt. There was a woman seated next to him who rose and greeted her.

"It will be just a moment," she said in a professional voice, but tinged with apology. "Please have a seat."

Sheila sat down. This was awkward. She didn't want to listen to his conversation—or for it to appear that way. So she very obviously looked out the window at the ocean, which appeared to be choppier than it had been this morning.

"He got what he deserved," David said into the phone. "He broke up a happy marriage. What did he think? That there would be no revenge?"

She could not believe what she was hearing. Was he talking about Harold?

A waiter came up and asked Sheila what she wanted to drink.

"Water with lemon, please," she said, thinking she'd kill for a sweet iced tea. But apparently it wasn't on the menu; she'd tried to order it several times. *What did you have to do to get a sweet iced tea outside the South?*

"Theresa is right about that. But listen," David said, looking at Sheila, "I need to go." He placed his phone on the table. "Ms. Rogers," he beamed.

"So good to meet you." He held out his hand and they shook. His handshake was firm and his manner charming. But one minute he was talking about revenge and the next oozed charm.

"This is my associate, Heather Reynolds," he said. "She's in charge of my scrapbooking line. We work very closely together. I give her as much creative free range as possible. But everything gets run by me before it's released."

"If you were to describe our designs in one word, what would that word be?" Heather asked.

Sheila thought a moment. "Classic."

A huge smile cracked across David's face. "Indeed. Now, let's talk about your designs. I'd call them shabby chic, wouldn't you?"

Sheila sat a bit taller. "Absolutely," she said. "But I have designed some classic paper and so on. I also have ideas for a nostalgic line inspired by a carnival."

His eyes widened. "Sounds interesting. You know, you really are very talented. I'm not one to beat around the bush. I don't have time for it. We'd love to have you join us."

"Really? Me?"

"Why do you seem so surprised?" Heather asked.

Sheila shrugged. "I had this meeting with Theresa Graves and she wasn't impressed with my work at all."

David and Heather looked at one another. Heather rolled her eyes.

"Theresa wouldn't know good design if it jumped up and bit her. I don't like talking about colleagues, but that woman's company is a design mess," he said. "You don't want any part of that."

Interesting, Sheila mused. She thought the designs were okay—some lines better than others. But she was astounded by the competition between the scrapbooking companies. With such a family-oriented hobby business, Sheila had assumed that all of the big shots were friends.

The server brought Sheila a glass of water. She squeezed the lemon perched on the edge of the glass and dropped the peel into her water.

"So, tell me," Heather said, after taking a sip of some kind of dark soda. "How would you see yourself fitting into our company?"

Sheila's heart raced. David's Designs was interested in her. She hadn't anticipated this at all because Theresa had said her designs were amateur. She hadn't rehearsed this moment, which is what she would have done if she thought she stood a snowball's chance in hell. Twinges of excitement pulsed through her.

"What I'm looking for is freelance design work," she told them. "I still have children in school in Cumberland Creek. I have a complete home office and studio and see no reason why I couldn't manage to work from there."

"Would you be able to come to New York, say, once a month?" David asked her.

"Certainly," she said.

"I'd like you to consider coming to work for us. I like to put this all up front. When you work for me, you sign a contract. You can't work for anyone else. And I own your designs. It's a standard work-for-hire agreement."

Surely not! This doesn't sound right at all. She felt her eyebrows knitting.

"I'd suggest you think it all over," Heather said. "You'll be getting other offers, I'm sure. Please let us know something within a few weeks. We'd love to have you on board. What I admire about your work is your sense of color. I've not seen such inspiring work in a long time."

"Thank you," Sheila said. "How kind of you."

"I like the way you're comfortable with both digital design and traditional design," David said. His eyes sparked with passion. Design really mattered to him; Sheila saw that. "I loved that scrapbook of yours, the one you entered in the competition. Where is it?"

"That's a good question," Sheila said, and then explained the situation with the scrapbook.

"How utterly maddening," David said. "I'll put in a word for you with security just to reiterate that you are to get that scrapbook back."

"I hope they find it soon," Heather said. "In the meantime, you have pictures, don't you?"

Sheila nodded.

"Oh, thank goodness," she said. "We wanted to

buy the rights from you to create a prototype and actually sell scrapbooks with your design."

Sheila's mouth dropped open.

"Are you okay?"

She nodded. "Yes, it's exactly what I wanted." *Except for the rights issue—and I'll deal with it later.*

"Fabulous. We'll draw up some contracts and treat this project a little differently than the freelance work," David said. "I'll text legal right now."

What a perfect meeting it had been. Sheila slipped away into her room for a breather before she had to teach her class. She took a photo of herself on her iPhone and looked at it. *This is what an artist looks like.*

She mailed it to herself and uploaded it onto her computer, then pulled it into her scrapbooking program and journaled about her day. She chose a pallet of blue and green with waves, clouds, and starbursts.

She typed in the word "artist" large across the top of her picture and read over her journal.

At forty-four, I am finally an artist. I am a mother, friend, wife, businesswoman. I can be all of those things and be happy. I stepped into my own skin today as one of the biggest designers in the country spoke to me—as if I mattered. I always thought of myself as a little bird of some kind, struggling to fly. Hell, sometimes struggling to walk. But I have pretty, colorful feathers. Today I felt like an eagle. Strong and soaring.

She stepped back, considered her face on the screen with all of the color and words around it. *Not bad. Not bad for an old broad from Cumberland Creek.*

Chapter 24

Annie had it narrowed down to twelve men. Twelve single male passengers were aboard the *Jezebel*. One of them had died last night. One of them was Randy. And, of course, there was Eric. So that left nine. She sent the names to Vera, Paige, and Sheila, in hopes that one of them at least would receive her message. In the meantime, she pulled up one of her databases that listed criminal records. She keyed in "John Monroe." Several were listed, as it was a very popular name. She scanned the list. There was one in Sarasota, which was where the Monroes had lived. She clicked on the link. The computer took a moment to catch up to itself.

His arrest record stretched back ten years, most of which was domestic violence charges. There were two DUIs. And the last one? Embezzlement. He had embezzled $325,000 from his wife's scrapbooking company. *Ouch.*

And he was currently in prison. So, unless he hired someone to kill his soon-to-be ex-wife and her boyfriend, he was in the clear. He certainly wasn't on board the ship and Annie doubted he could have hired anybody, given that embezzlement was his crime. He was probably broke and the authorities would be watching all of his accounts.

Could someone else have had it in for Allie Monroe? Maybe her boyfriend, Harold? Did someone else not want to see them together? It seemed an odd thing for someone else to be so engaged with her and her life, so much so that they killed her and her lover. Annie would look into Harold's background next.

"How about lunch?" Mike asked as he entered the room.

"Sure, what do you have?" Annie replied, turning away from the computer.

"I made some egg salad. The boys are already scarfing it down," he said, and wrapped his arms around her as she stood.

She kissed him. It was a rare thing for him to make food. She knew that he was capable—hell, more than capable. He just relied on her to do it. And during the week, she really didn't mind since he was working and she was at home. Still, she had work to do as well, and didn't feel like cooking. She didn't really want to leave her computer—or her train of thought—now, but she felt that she should because he had gone to the trouble of cooking.

The boys were already at the table and Ben's face was already smeared with the egg mixture. Mike had toasted some good rye bread and cut the sandwiches into triangles.

"Nice," Annie said, sitting down.

"So tonight's the first night of Hanukkah, boys. We'll have a good dinner, then light the menorah. And Mom and I have a little something for you," Mike said, before biting into his sandwich.

"The menorah was my grandmother's," Annie said. "My mom never had one. My grandmother had Hanukkah for us at her place every year. When she died, she willed the menorah to me. I think Uncle Josh was a bit upset about that. We both had such fond memories of it."

Ben and Sam ate happily. She didn't know if they realized how much the menorah meant to her. They probably wouldn't realize until it was passed on to one of them. She could almost hear her grandmother singing the prayers. She closed her eyes and swore that she could smell her lilac perfume, mixed with spices.

"Annie?" Mike said. She opened her eyes, surprised to find they had the pricking of tears in them. "Are you okay? Where were you?"

She smiled and waved him off. "Ay, yes. I'm fine. Just remembering my grandmother."

"Tell us about her," Ben said.

And so she did.

She told them about the menorah, how it was one of the few items that made it to the shore of the United States when her grandmother came from Russia as a young girl. The ship had hit a storm and the crew and passengers lost many of their items.

"Our menorah is from Russia?" Ben's eyes lit up.

Annie nodded. "And your great-grandma gave it to your grandmother. Who gave it to me. I wish you could have known her. She was strong and beautiful and kind. Everything a grandmother should be. She wore dresses every day of her life. Loved a good brisket and oh, did she love her chocolate."

The boys and Mike sat and listened to her memories of her grandmother Doris.

Later, after Annie placed the brisket in the oven, having followed Doris's recipe to a tee, she was overcome with a longing, a melancholy for her grandmother's arms, for her voice chattering as they cooked together.

She reached into a cupboard drawer and pulled out a blank journal and a box of photos. She searched for the photo she was thinking of—the one where she was sitting on her grandmother's lap and they were looking at something off in the distance. What was it? Annie wished she could remember.

The boys had left some acrylic paints on the table. She painted a page with a strip of red, then yellow. She tore out another page and wrote in longhand. When was the last time she had done that? She wrote down some memories of her grandmother, her kitchen, her warm bed, and how the thought of her grandmother on a big ship had always troubled her.

By the time she wrote it all down, the paint was dry. She placed the photo off-center on the page, then cut the paper with her writing into four pieces so it resembled a puzzle. She placed each piece in a corner and thought about that ship that brought her family across the sea. What kind of life had they left behind? Her grandmother had never wanted to talk about it.

The thought of the sea brought her back to her friends and the murder. She set her book aside and went to her computer and keyed in Harold's name to the database. Hmmm. He had no arrest record.

But as she reviewed his personal information, she found out that he was married. So both he and Allie had been married, and trying to divorce their respective spouses so that they could be together. Annie's brain sifted through another assortment of possibilities for her friends on the high seas, none of which settled the gnawing in her guts.

Chapter 25

"We're getting ready for Sheila's class," Vera said into the phone.

"How is she doing? Any better?" Beatrice asked. She was sitting at her kitchen table after a lunch of tomato soup and a grilled cheese sandwich. She was a bit tired after a morning of baking and standing on her feet.

"I can't get through to Annie, Mama. I don't know why, but if you're talking with her, can you tell her that I've gotten her list of unattached men on the cruise?"

"Sure. That sounds interesting," Bea said, and chortled.

"She came up with a list of men who aren't here with their wives."

"Oh yes, we talked about that."

"You can tell her that we are going to check these guys out."

"How are you going to do that?"

"We'll find them and talk with them and ask what they are doing here and so on. Who knows? Maybe we'll find our killer."

"And then what?" Beatrice asked.

"We'll tell security. Or the FBI. They are supposed to be meeting the ship at the next port of call."

"Well, you know to be careful. I don't want to get another visit from law enforcement at my house."

Vera quieted. "I love you, too, Mama. And God knows I miss you and Elizabeth."

"She misses you, too," Beatrice said. No point going down that sad road. "Have your learned the latest froufrou scrapbooking techniques?"

"It's intense," Vera said. Beatrice heard Eric mumbling something in the background. "I love scrapbooking, but I'm glad we took a bit of a break from it this morning. These people take their scrapbooking very seriously."

Beatrice harrumphed. How seriously could one take scrapbooking?

"Sheila fits right in. Kind of. We haven't seen her since this morning. She was supposed to meet us at the pool, but she went back to her room to get some rest," Vera said.

"Rest? That doesn't sound like her."

"I know it," Vera said, and then the phone went dead.

Typical.

The tropical storm was still in the area; Beatrice had been tracking it. The *Jezebel* was heading in the opposite direction, but the storm was still affecting communication. And Beatrice was still worried. Yet Vera didn't appear to be worried at all about the storm. She was more concerned about finding Allie's killer, which did not serve to alleviate Beatrice's anxiety either.

Her timer went off. Finally, her last poppy seed cake was done. She opened the oven door and sucked in the scent, felt the heat pouring out of the oven. That was all for today, she told herself. She had a meeting to go to this afternoon. It was the first year Beatrice was chairing the committee and some of the others suffered from power withdrawal—they made every little decision into a cataclysmic one and it drove her bonkers.

"Do we really need to discuss how big the signs should be for twenty whole minutes?" Beatrice had said at the last meeting.

Even with all that nonsense, she looked forward to the bazaar every year. She loved the crafts, the baked goods, and even some of the entertainment. Local kids would be singing Christmas carols and Donna Trevor was going to sit in the corner and play her dulcimer on and off all day.

Beatrice found herself thinking of the last craft fair she'd gone to. It had been in Charlottesville and she had Cookie with her. Beatrice grimaced. Whatever happened to Cookie? She was one of the few people who had liked to go to craft fairs with her. She loved the quilts, but never bought one. And as far as Bea knew, she didn't own one either.

She placed the poppy seed cake on the cooling rack and saw tiny snowflakes forming into big fat flakes against the window. The ground was covered with a couple inches of snow. Jon was at the grocery store; she hoped he came home soon. Those sidewalks could be mighty slippery until folks got around to shoveling.

She made her way back to her computer. It had become a bit of an obsession for her to check the weather in the Caribbean. She knew those storms cropped up quickly and the back end of them could be a problem, too.

She clicked on the *Jezebel*'s Web site and then to the journey section. The boat was moving again—like Vera had said. It was moving toward Grand Caymen, where Sheila was going to lead a scrapbooking-photography class, the one she had been planning to lead in Mexico.

Beatrice felt she was being a bit silly and obsessed by this scrapping cruise. *Get it together, woman.*

She clicked on her file that had the schedule for the week, leading up to the bazaar as well as the bazaar schedule. She printed four copies—one for each of the committee members. Even Elsie Mayhue, who was driving Bea to distraction.

In fact, there was an e-mail from her. Bea clicked on it:

I contacted all the local papers and we are set to go.

Okay. Did she want a medal for doing her job? Beatrice caught herself rolling her eyes, then heard Vera's voice chiding her. "Not everybody is as smart as you. You need to be patient with the rest of us."

Hmph. I'm eighty-three years old and I don't have time to be that *patient.*

Chapter 26

The crop room was open twenty-four hours a day, and some croppers took advantage of it. Sheila overheard one woman say to her husband that she'd been up since 3:00 A.M. cropping and had finished a whole scrapbook. The crop room was lovely, with floor to ceiling windows, so the scrappers' view was inspiring and the lighting was great during the day.

The classroom, however, was windowless. It was just a conference room, like so many conference rooms Sheila had visited. She was dressed in black slacks and a silky, flowing red shirt, with a blazer over it. Creative but profes0sional was the look she was after. Vera gave her a thumbs-up as she entered the room.

Sheila had capped the class at one hundred participants because the cruise organizers said they only had that many laptops for attendees.

Sheila was unveiling her One Journey digital scrapbooking and journaling system today. This was part of her entry into the competition and what she wanted to sell to David's Design. One Journey was a template for use with any number of digital scrapbook applications. Each participant had already selected the application she was using and Sheila would teach to each one. Most participants were using Photoshop Elements and My Memories.

As she considered her students, she was pleased to see both Heather and Theresa, not sitting together, but each with her own group of friends or colleagues. *Interesting, since Theresa said she didn't care for her designs,* Sheila thought. Was she imagining it or did Theresa just smirk at her?

Sheila looked in the other direction—the direction of the podium. Ms. Irons approached it.

"We are so pleased today to bring you our top prize winner, Sheila Rogers. We've found during this cruise that she's as delightful as she is talented."

Who found that? Sheila was finding it hard not to knit her brows.

"Sheila is a perfect example of a woman who puts family first, yet has found success. And we are so honored that she's here and able to share her scrap-journaling template One Journey. But before we do that I wanted to share with you what some of our judges said about Sheila's work.

"This from David of David's Designs: 'Grounded in classical tradition, with a nod toward the modern, and one of the freshest design eyes I've ever seen.' "

Cheering from the crowd jolted Sheila's heart into a near panic. *Really, he said that about me? These people are cheering for me? It was too much!*

"This from Memory Mama: 'Sheila's work is solid. Her style is fresh and original. Where have you been, Sheila Rogers?' "

"And this from our Allie—"

A hush came over the room.

" 'I love this woman's keen sense of design flow and color. But most of all, I love the heart and soul that goes into each one of her designs. Welcome to the big league, Sheila!' "

Much cheering from the crowd again as Sheila's face heated. She noticed that very same man she seemed to see everywhere. He was sitting next to Theresa. He wasn't going to bother her. Not now.

"And now, we give you Ms. Sheila Rogers," the voice from the podium said.

"Thanks so much," Sheila said. "Also thanks so much to all of the judges for their kind words." She messed with her mike a bit. "Thanks to all of you for coming here today. Can everybody hear me?"

"Yes!" several people yelled back.

"Good," she said. "The first thing I want you to do is to shake your body. Either stand up and shake or sit in your chair and shake your parts. Get all the kinks out."

Much commotion ensued.

"I'm the mother of four children. We used to call this getting the wiggles out."

Laughter, then the classroom settled.

"The next thing I'm going to ask you to do is quite . . . extraordinary. And some of you may find that you simply can't do it," she said.

This was a technique she'd learned from Cookie Crandall's yoga class.

"I want you to take five minutes and sit quietly. No talking. At all. There's a reason for this and I'll explain it after we're finished. Let's start. Now." She took a seat.

As in every class she taught with this technique, there were a few giggles, then sounds of people settling. As time wore on, the room stilled. At four minutes in, Sheila arose from her chair and walked back and forth in the front of the room.

"So," she said softly. "One of the reasons I like to start my class in silence is that it focuses your energy inward. The room's energy also shifts."

She heard sniffling. *Yes, there was always at least one woman moved to tears.* Silence was a luxury for some, especially women in the thick of doing everything for everybody in their lives. Silence was a gift.

"This kind of scrapbooking is about you. And believe it or not, this is something your kids will probably cherish more than the photos of themselves," Sheila said.

Her eyes caught Vera's. She was glazing over. *Honestly, Vera was the worst student.* She found it hard to sit still, let alone listen to a teacher. Sheila watched her and used her as a gauge.

"Let's move on to the first exercise and then we will take a break for those of you who need it," Sheila said. "Let's click on your screens." She waited a few minutes to continue. "Now, the first page has a space for your photo, which if you don't have now, you can load up later. It also gives you a prompt. 'I Am' asks you to list five things that you are. Mother, doctor, so on. This will get you going. Let's give that ten minutes or so and then we'll take a break."

After class, Sheila was approached by people for autographs and several participants told her how much they enjoyed the class. One woman, who was young, svelte, and blond, touched her arm. "Sheila, I want you to know how powerful and moving that was for me. I've never thought about scrapbooking about myself. And you've made it so easy. Thank you."

Sheila beamed. Even as the room thinned out, her friends still hung in there and gathered around her at the end. There were hugs from everybody.

"Just fabulous," Vera said, with tears in her eyes. "I'm so proud of you."

"Excuse me." A voice came through the

gathering. It was Matthew Kirtley, chief of security. "Mrs. Rogers, may I have a word with you?"

"Certainly," Sheila said. "What can I help you with?"

"Can you come down to the office with me, please?"

"I had planned on going to the pool," she said.

Ms. Irons approached him. "Now, I've told you to leave her alone. She's an honored guest."

"I just want to ask her a few questions," he said.

"Why don't you ask them here?" Sheila said. "What's this about?"

"It's about the untimely deaths on board this ship," he replied.

"I don't know anything about them, except what you've told me," she said, packing her things into her bag. Her friends stood motionless, watching over them.

"Can you remember anything else that might help out the FBI? We'll be docking tomorrow and they will have questions. I'm working on my report."

"I've told you everything I can remember. Everything I know," she said.

"There seems to be two links in the deaths. One is that they were both poisoned."

"And what's the second link?" Sheila asked.

"You," he replied. "You tripped over the first body and you were in the hallway when we discovered the second one."

Sheila didn't know what to say. Could he really

think she had something to do with these deaths? Her mouth dropped.

"There's something else, chief," Randy said. "Something you might not be aware of."

"What's that?" He turned to face Randy, who was glowing.

"Allie and Harold were seeing one another. Both were getting a divorce so they could be together," he said.

"We knew they were in the same room together, but privacy dictates . . . a little decorum," Matthew said with a lower voice.

"We've looked up some of this stuff on the Web," Paige said. "It's a bad divorce situation all the way around. But John, Allie's ex, is not on the cruise."

"But we have a list of nine men on board who are not attached to women, as we figured that they would be the most likely culprit," Randy said.

"Really? Where did you get this information?" Matthew said.

They explained how they had worked with Annie to come up with the list.

"It's a good idea," Matthew said. "Why didn't I think of that?"

"Well, you do have other things on your mind," Randy said, with a note of flirtation in his voice.

Sheila's cell phone rang and she stepped aside to answer. It was DeeAnn.

"So did you find the killer yet?"

Chapter 27

Annie checked on the brisket, the scent of which was filling the house. It was browning nicely. The boys and Mike were out for a while, so she decided to look up Harold Tuft's wife, Sharon. It was disappointing. She seemed to have led an exemplary life; no arrest records. But that didn't mean much when it came to murder—the human condition continued to fascinate. The woman she was writing about, Mary Schultz, who killed her father, was not someone you'd think of as a murderer. She'd never done anything illegal her whole life. She simply snapped one day and chopped her father to pieces.

Gruesome. And scary. How far was the woman pushed to lead her to that moment?

So Annie went back to her passenger list to see if Sharon Tuft was on it. There were three Sharons, but none of them were Tufts. Annie returned to her computer and tried to find a record of Sharon Tuft's maiden name, and there it was: Milhouse. Sharon Milhouse was on the passenger list. Annie's stomach clenched.

She picked up her cell phone to call Vera. She was unable to get through once again.

So she tried to text Vera instead.

Harold's ex-wife, Sharon Milhouse, is on the passenger list. Your killer?

Send.

Annie had no idea that it would be so difficult to reach her friends on this cruise. It was kind of maddening, but they'd be back by midweek, in time for Beatrice's Christmas bazaar and then for Christmas itself the following week.

Annie shut off the computer and grabbed her purse, remembering that she needed to pick up more potatoes. She bundled up in her coat, hat, scarf; it was cold outside and the last time she checked it was still snowing.

The cold met her with a punch when she walked out of her house. She lived close to the grocery store, about two blocks, but it was so cold that she thought for a moment about driving. But by the time the car warmed up, she could be at the store, so she walked, with the new-fallen snow soft and powdery beneath her feet. A smoke scent filled the air as she walked down her block. Several houses were using their fireplaces or woodstoves and smoke curled from their rooftops.

Annie wrapped her scarf tighter around her face. Dang, it was cold. One more block to go.

A halfhearted snowman was in the yard of the Jenkins family, which made Annie smile. This was not a good snow for building. It was soft and airy, giving off little sparkles when light hit it in a certain way. The skies were completely overcast—moonstone gray.

Annie smiled as an older couple passed her on the sidewalk, right before she turned into the grocery store parking lot. Walking down the aisles of the store, she heard someone call her name and turned to find Beatrice with several bottles of wine in her hand.

"How do?" Bea said. She looked distracted. Maybe annoyed. Annie was getting good at reading Beatrice.

"I'm good. Just picking up more groceries for tonight," Annie said.

"Oh yes, Hanukkah. Well, have a good one," Bea said.

"Thanks. How are you and what are you up to?"

"I'm okay. Heading over to this committee meeting. I'm hoping some wine will calm them all down," she said, and clicked her tongue.

"Good luck with that. What do you hear from Vera?"

"I talked with her a couple of hours ago. She seems worried about Sheila."

Annie nodded. "But what about the murder investigation?"

"Investigation?" Bea said. "There really won't be one until the FBI gets on board tomorrow. That ship's security team doesn't have their act together."

"I sent Vera the name of Harold Tuft's ex-wife,

Sharon Milhouse. She's on the passenger list," Annie said.

"What about the ex-husband?" Bea asked.

"He's in jail for embezzling from Allie's company, so he's not involved at all."

"Mercy," Beatrice said. "Do you think a woman could have killed them both?"

"If there's one thing I've learned over the past few years, and more so now that I'm writing about the Schultz case, it's that women are very capable of murder," Annie said.

"I think you're right," Bea said after a moment. "I've always thought there might be more of them out there than what we know. Women are smarter than men and don't get caught."

That statement sent chills through Annie.

Chapter 28

As Beatrice walked to the library, carrying her brown paper bag with wine bottles clunking against one another, she noted that the snowfall was picking up. It didn't look like a thing had been done to the streets or sidewalks to clear the snow away. Good thing she had her boots on.

Milhouse. Now, why did that name seem so familiar? She sifted through her brain. She couldn't think of one person whose name was Milhouse. Yet the name felt like it was one that she knew. Ah, well, chalk it up to old age. You couldn't remember everybody you met in eighty-four years of living.

Beatrice loved the library. It was one of the newest buildings in town, built in 1985. The old library was now an office building full of lawyers and architects. The new library was light-filled and bright; Beatrice never liked dark libraries, other than the fact that they held books in them.

Milhouse. Hmmm. So familiar.

She walked into the meeting room and everybody was there, for a change.

"Let's get this shindig going, shall we?" she said, and set the bottles of wine on the table.

After the meeting, two emptied wine bottles later, the women gathered their paper and pens and handheld devices holding their calendars and important numbers, chitchatting as they moved along. Beatrice hated the chitchatting. If she didn't love this town's history so much and feel so strongly about feeding the poor, she'd not be involved with this bunch at all.

As she walked out of the library, she was surprised by how much snow had fallen. As it was getting darker, the snow took on a blue cast. She glanced off to the right, at the heart of Cumberland Creek, which was snow-covered and twinkling blue.

"Hey, Beatrice," she heard a male voice say.

It was Detective Bryant. They said he'd gotten another job in Charlottesville and would be leaving town soon. She didn't know and she didn't care enough to find out.

"What?" she replied, pulling her scarf in closer around her neck.

His mouth twisted. "We need to chat."

"About what?"

"About this scrapbooking cruise."

"What? Why does that concern you?"

"I really can't tell you that right now," he said, his eyes not meeting hers.

"I mean, they are heading for Grand Caymen. You're in Cumberland Creek," she said, baffled.

"I know that, Beatrice," he said with a bite.

"Watch your tone, young man."

He smirked. "Yes, ma'am."

"What do you want to know?" They fell in walking together toward Beatrice's dusty rose Victorian home.

"I know someone won a prize—"

"It was Sheila," Bea said. "A very prestigious prize."

He nodded. "A prestigious scrapbooking prize?"

"Why, hell, Bryant, I don't know anything about scrapbooking, but they say it's a top honor."

"What's your sense of these folks, these, ah, scrapbookers? Is it highly competitive?"

Beatrice chuckled. "I doubt it. I mean, it's made of women who are making scrapbooks about their families. Why would it be competitive?"

"No, I'm not talking about those scrapbookers. I'm talking about scrapbooking as a business."

"What are you getting at, Bryant? What has happened?" Beatrice asked impatiently.

"All I can say is this cruise has more links to Cumberland Creek than Sheila Rogers," he said. "And now that there have been two murders . . . and then this other thing came up. I'm just trying to make sense of it."

"What other thing?" Beatrice asked.

"I can't tell you right now. But what I can say is that it leads back to Sheila. If you can, please tell them to be very careful."

"Careful about what?" Beatrice persisted.

"Look, Beatrice, I can't tell you," he replied.

"You can't expect me to tell them that without answering questions. Questions I can't answer," Beatrice said, "because you won't tell me."

"You're one of the smartest women I know," he said, after a few beats. "You must know that there are some things I can't share."

Beatrice warmed and smiled, allowing the tension between them to subside. She knew she was smart—but it was good to know he knew it, as well. But what he didn't have to know is that she wasn't going to give up so easily.

"Care to come in?" she asked him.

They stopped in front of her house.

"I have cookies," she said, and grinned.

"Oh man, Bea, you know I'd love to, but I need to get going," he said.

"Well, hold on, Bryant. I'll get you a bag—you can take some cookies with you. Spirit of the season and all that."

He twinkled. Bryant was a man who enjoyed food. Particularly sweets.

Beatrice went into her home and noticed Jon at the kitchen table. "I'm making a goodie bag for Bryant," she said.

Bryant was coming up behind her. "Oh man, it smells so good," he said as she pulled out the cookies and began placing them into the bag. "So rich."

"That's Vera's recipe. She loves her chocolate," Beatrice said, and handed him the bag. "Now you going to tell me what's going on?"

He grinned and raised one eyebrow. "I can't tell you anything," he said. "But I can tell you that you should check in with Steve Rogers." She let him have the bag of goodies. "He can tell you whatever he wants. He's a private citizen."

"Steve?" Beatrice's blood started to race. *What could Sheila's husband know?*

Chapter 29

"If I were a single man on a cruise ship and not scrapbooking, where would I be?" Vera said as she leaned back into her lounge chair. It was after lunch and they had all gathered at the pool, each one of them with outrageously expensive fruity alcoholic drinks in their hands.

"You'd think most of them would be scrapbooking. After all, this is a scrapbooking cruise," Sheila said. "There's a man I keep seeing everywhere. He seems unattached. He's been to every activity I've been to."

"The next time you see him, you should find out a bit about him," Paige said, fixing her floppy hat on her head.

"I most certainly will not," Sheila said. "I'm here for the scrapbooking, not the sleuthing. The only thing I care about as far as all this is concerned is getting my scrapbook back. I'd like to see them bring the murderer to justice, but that's not my business."

"You know, Sheila, you're right. None of us should be involved, least of all you. You need to focus on making connections for your career. Leave the rest up to us," Vera said.

"Oh Lord," Sheila said, and rolled her eyes. "Please leave well enough alone. Would you?"

A beautiful young woman walked by in a white bikini. Eric perked up.

"You know, if I were interested in women on this cruise, I think I'd be right here at the pool—or maybe at one of the lounges," he said.

"Ya don't have to ask me twice," Paige said. "I'm willing to circulate a bit and get out of the sun. I've had it. I want to get to the crop around five and I've got a couple hours to kill."

"I'll come with you," Randy said.

"No," she said. "You better stay here. I don't need my son tagging along while I work my magic." She winked before taking off down the deck.

Randy sat back in his chair, astonished. "Well, I never!" he mocked.

Vera laughed the loudest. "Stick around, Randy. Your mother is quite a character."

The ship jiggled around a bit. Vera grabbed on to Eric; the rest of them grabbed on to their chairs. Sheila closed her eyes for a moment. Her head still ached, though the drink seemed to be helping a bit. When she opened her eyes Vera was scanning the crowd.

"What are you looking for?" Sheila asked.

"I'm looking for single men," Vera said. "I think I found one. The guy over by the diving board. You see him sitting there?"

"Yes," Sheila said. "What are you going to do?"

"You just watch me," Vera said.

Sheila watched her old friend walk to the other side of the pool as Eric looked on, horrified. Vera, at the age of forty-four, was still a stunning woman, with her heart-shaped face, big blue eyes, and high cheekbones. As she walked by the man in question, she dropped her bag, with her things scattering everywhere. He rose from his chair to help. The next thing Vera knew, he was getting her a drink. She cozied up next to him, pulling her chair close to his.

"I'm not sure I like this," Eric said as he watched, his chest puffing out a bit.

"Calm down," Sheila said. "She's prodding him."

"He doesn't know that," Eric said. "I don't like how he's looking at her."

"You don't own her, doctor," she snapped. "She can talk to whomever she wants to talk to."

Silence. Randy scootched around in his chair with discomfort.

"I know you don't like me, Sheila," Eric said. "I've tried to ignore your snide remarks. Your eye rolling."

Sheila sat up as a sudden wash of embarrassment came over her.

"I think Vera has enough room in her heart for both of us," Eric said. "I'm not going anywhere."

She didn't know what to say. Her heart was thumping in her chest. Her face felt hot.

"It's not that I don't like you," she said after a

moment. "I'm not used to husbands and boy-friends hanging around. Mine doesn't. Bill didn't. There's family time—then there's girl time. I don't know why you're always hanging around."

His eyebrows knit.

"I don't mind having you around sometimes, but give Vera room to breathe. Allow her to have time with her friends," Sheila said.

"I'm sorry. I'm crazy about her," he said, and glanced in Vera's direction. "She's never com-plained about my tagging along. . . . In fact I think she's always invited me."

He looked crestfallen and Sheila wished she had never opened her mouth.

"She probably has invited you," Sheila said. "But you don't need to accept every invite."

Randy turned the page of the magazine he was pretending to read.

"You know I'm crazy about you, too," she said, reaching out and patting his hand. "Don't pay any attention to me. I'm probably being a selfish old coot. I love her, too. She's my best friend."

Sheila's cell phone buzzed. And then so did Eric's.

"We must be getting close to land," he said.

Sheila picked up her phone and read Annie's text: Harold's ex-wife, Sharon Milhouse, is on the passenger list. Your killer?

How odd. She'd known a Sharon Milhouse in college. Now, she had been an odd bird. Surely it could not be the same person she went to school with. A wave of panic gripped her as a memory of Sharon hit her hard. Sharon had been madly in love with Steve. In fact, she had been Steve's girlfriend when Sheila and he met. When they broke up, Sharon had tried to kill herself. Sheila had felt so sorry for her at the time, but later, when she and Steve started dating, she began to get death threats. They were never able to prove it, but everybody, including the local police, assumed it was Sharon.

The Sharon Milhouse of her college days on board the *Jezebel*? That was too much of a coincidence. Must be another one. Must be. Oh, she'd find out. Yes, she would.

"Are you okay?" Vera said as she approached the group. The boat rocked, making Randy spill his drink, just a little. He sat up to clean it. "You're so pale."

"I'm sure it's nothing," Sheila said.

"Is it your head?" Eric said.

She waved her hand. "I just got a text from Annie." She read it to them: "Harold's ex-wife, Sharon Milhouse, is on the passenger list. Your killer?"

"Sharon Milhouse?" Vera squealed.

"What? Who is she?" Eric asked.

Vera explained.

"I'm sure it's not the same one," Randy said with assurance in his voice.

"We need to find out. That woman was a hot mess," Vera said.

"What did you find out from the mysterious man from across the pool?" Sheila said.

"His name is James Spangler," Vera said. "He's an accountant from Oklahoma. This is his third scrapbooking cruise. Hard-core scrapbooker. He seems like a nice man," she said.

"Don't they all," Randy said, and sighed.

The shipped rocked harder, sending the pool water right over the edges of the deck. The life-guards blew their whistles. "Everybody out of the pool!"

Chapter 30

Since moving to Cumberland Creek, Annie had been forced to consider her spirituality, looking deeper into her life for meaning, not simply the outer trappings of being Jewish. So tonight, when she lit the menorah and sang the prayers, she felt it. A hush came over her boys. Their eyes were solemn. It gave her surprising joy. Oh yes, this was worth not going on the cruise.

After the dishes were done, Annie began to gather her scrapbooking things, but then sat at her table and wrote more in her new art journal instead. For the first time in many years, she felt truly inspired.

It was odd; she was a writer and in the midst of a book. But if she were honest with herself, that kind of writing had become a slog. It was a job. This, this opening up on the page through journaling and painting, it was inspiring and addictive. The next thing she knew, she was kissing the boys and Mike good night and heading off to meet DeeAnn at Sheila's place, where the group met every Saturday.

DeeAnn was standing out on the door stoop waiting for Annie.

"I know Sheila said we should do this, but I feel kind of weird about being here without her," DeeAnn said.

Annie shrugged. "I get it. Do you still want to go in and give it a go?"

"Well, now that you're here . . . I guess it would be okay," DeeAnn said.

When they entered the basement it felt very different without Sheila's music already playing, Vera's humming, and Paige's laughter. But it was more than that, really. Annie was jabbed once again with a pang of missing her friends.

"They will be back soon," DeeAnn said, and placed her things on the table.

Annie did the same. Then she reached over and turned on the stereo. The sound of Justin Timberlake filled the room.

"Love me some Justin," DeeAnn said. "Hey, happy Hanukkah, by the way."

"Thanks," Annie said, sitting down. "Look, Sheila left us snacks." Plastic bowls with lids sat on the table, filled with pretzels, chips, and nuts. "Wasn't that sweet?"

"I brought some cupcakes," DeeAnn said, and placed her container on the table.

"Ah, what kind?" Annie said.

"Peanut butter with chocolate icing. A new recipe," DeeAnn said.

After they settled into their scrapbooking and eating, Annie got up and reached into the fridge for a beer.

"So what do you hear from our friends?" DeeAnn said, looking up from her new scrapbook project. Her aunt had recently died and DeeAnn was working on a memory album that celebrated her mother's life.

"The last I heard they were making their way through the list of unattached men on the cruise," Annie said, sitting back down at the table.

"What? Why?"

Annie explained their working theory.

"I guess it's a good place to start," DeeAnn said. "It will keep them occupied, I suppose. But you know as well as I do that a woman could be the killer, especially if poison was used."

"I can see that. Harold's wife might think she has cause if her marriage was broken up by this affair."

Annie pulled out her scrapbook and her new art journal.

"But no man's worth a prison term," DeeAnn said. "What do you have there?"

"I've been working on this book. It's kind of a journal, I suppose," Annie said. She slid it across the table.

DeeAnn gasped. "Annie! It's gorgeous." She ran her fingers over the cover, where Annie had embossed a gold Star of David, which was surrounded by words scattered in every direction, providing a collage of sorts. It almost looked like graffiti. She opened the book to Annie's painted page.

"How did you do this?" DeeAnn asked.

"I used the boys' acrylics."

"There's a whole movement of art journalists now. Did you know that?"

"No. I was moved to do this. I love to scrapbook—but this seems like a more personal extension of it."

"It feels that way to me as well. I've never tried this. You're so talented," DeeAnn said.

"Speaking of talent, Bea says you're doing some baking for the bazaar," Annie said, cutting out a photo of her grandmother's menorah.

"Yep. Anything to help Bea out. She's taken on a lot with that bazaar. Nothing she can't handle, but still."

Annie grinned, thinking of Beatrice and the bazaar. "Should be fun."

The two of them worked without chatting for a

bit, listening to the music, pasting down photos and embellishments, and journaling.

"Where do you think they are right now?" DeeAnn said.

"Almost at Grand Caymen," Annie replied.

"I'll feel a bit better with them on land for a day or two," DeeAnn said.

"Yeah, me too," Annie said. "It's been a very strange cruise. The murders. The storm. Communication fading in and out." Annie took a deep breath and tried to settle her stomach. She tried hard not to think of all the dangerous possibilities on that cruise ship.

Chapter 31

Armed with a box of cookies, Beatrice rang the doorbell of Sheila and Steve's home. It was a nice home; Steve had done well, as had Sheila. Beatrice had rarely been to the front door of their home. She usually entered at the basement door, just like the scrapbookers.

When Steve opened the door, Beatrice was taken aback. She'd not seen him for at least a year. But he'd aged. Drastically.

"Why, hello, Beatrice," he said, with a smile cracking across his rugged, wrinkled face.

"How do?" she replied.

"C'mon in."

She entered their home. It was immaculate, as always. Sheila was not like her mother in that regard. Gerty hated housekeeping and it showed.

"Can I take your coat?" Steve asked.

Well, she hadn't planned to stay that long, but it might be nice to visit with Steve a bit. She felt a sudden warmth toward him. Besides, she wanted to find out what Bryant had been talking about.

"Okay," she said.

He took her coat and they sat together in the living room on the couch. The walls were decorated with photos and paintings done by their oldest daughter, Donna, a gifted artist.

"What do I owe this visit to?" Steve said.

"I figured you might be a bit lonely. And hungry," Bea said, and handed him the box of Christmas cookies.

"Oh," he said, excitement in his eyes. "Sheila's not doing any baking this year, so this is a treat."

"What do you hear from her?"

"Communication has been sporadic at best," he said, and scratched his chin. He needed a shave and a hot shower. "I've just gotten back from a trip."

"You take hiking trips in the mountains during winters?"

He nodded. "This was the last one of the season."

Steve had his own outdoor guide company

and led fishing, hunting, and hiking expeditions through the Blue Ridge.

"That's crazy," Bea said.

He laughed. "So they say. But it usually works out okay."

He opened the box of cookies and a look of pure joy washed over his face. Nothing like homemade cookies to bring a man to his knees.

"So you know about Sheila falling and so on," Beatrice said.

"I want her to come home," he replied, examining the cookies. "There's been what, two murders now? I want her home."

"I hear ya. Listen, I ran into Detective Bryant. . . ."

"Hmph," he said, finally picking out a cookie. "You won't believe what's happened. I came home, exhausted, right? And there was this creepy postcard in the mailbox."

"What kind of a postcard?" Bea asked.

"Someone had cut and pasted a note together. You know, like you've seen on TV or in the movies or something? It said 'Die, die, die, scrapbook queen.' And it has something on it. Looked like blood," he said.

Beatrice's heart raced. "Why would someone do that?"

"Good question. I wondered if she may have pissed someone off on the cruise, but Bryant wondered if she had any local enemies. There was no postmark on it. He thinks someone just shoved it in the box. I can't think of one person who doesn't love Sheila," he said.

Spoken like a man in love with his wife. Of course there may have been people who didn't like her. But who? Beatrice felt her brows knitting. "I'll give that some thought."

It was true that there was nothing to dislike about Sheila. Except of course for the scrap-booking craziness, which drove Beatrice nuts. It was a little over the top, with all the fancy embellishments and die cuts and so on. Memory keeping was one thing—hell, it was valid—but the way these scrapbookers went about it often rubbed Beatrice the wrong way.

But Sheila was one of those women who was always nice and polite and went out of her way to please people. A definite people pleaser. Other than Beatrice herself, she couldn't think of anybody who didn't like that type of person.

"Have you told Sheila about it?" she asked.

"Bryant asked me not to," he said, and then bit into a gingerbread cookie.

"Hmph. I guess I can see that, but she might know who it is." And so might the women in the basement, scrapbooking this very moment, if Beatrice calculated correctly.

"I best be going, Steve. If I think of anything, I'll let you know. Are you okay?"

"I was a bit shook up," he said, getting her coat and handing it to her. "But I'm all right now, I suppose. I am worried about Sheila. She's on the high seas with a concussion and a killer. I ain't happy about it."

"I hear ya. They will be home soon. Good night, Steve."

"Night," he said, and then shut the door.

Beatrice hightailed to the back of the house and peeked in the glass sliding doors. Yes, there was Annie and DeeAnn, both there with their scrapbooks in front of them. She opened the door.

"Bea, what a nice surprise," Annie said, starting to rise from her chair.

"You might not think so once I tell you why I'm here," Beatrice said, and then told them Steve's story about the postcard.

"I think we should tell Sheila," DeeAnn said. "I'd want to know, wouldn't you?"

"But she's having a rough time as it is," Annie pointed out.

"True," DeeAnn said. "But I can't think of one person who would do such a thing."

"Steve thought she may have stepped on someone's toes on the ship, butting her nose into the murder investigation," Beatrice said. "Bryant said it was unlikely."

"I agree. What are the chances?" Annie said. "I mean, who else on that ship even knows where Cumberland Creek is or even that it exists, let alone that Sheila lives here?"

The room quieted.

"A desperate person who thinks Sheila can finger them for murder would find out where she lives, right?" DeeAnn said.

"Yes, but that person is on the ship," Annie said.

"Unless the killer has a partner," said Beatrice.

Chapter 32

"Well, here we are, cropping on a Saturday night. Who'd have thunk it?" Vera said, as she sat down at the crop table. It was their table; they camped out there, claimed it for their own and were able to leave their things there while they moved about the ship.

"Where's Paige?" Sheila said.

"She'll be here," Randy said. "She needed a quick shower."

"What?" Vera said.

"I think she was a bit tipsy," Randy replied, with a grin. "I've never seen my mother tipsy."

Sheila stifled a giggle. Paige was tipsy a lot—almost every Saturday night in Cumberland Creek. Clearly Randy hadn't lived at home for years.

Sheila stood and pulled out one of her cutting boards from her bag. "I'm eager to see if she found out anything. The more I think about being on this ship with a killer, the more freaked out I get. Steve too. I spoke with him a few minutes ago. He wants me to find the closest airport when we hit land and come home."

"What? That's a bit crazy. This is such an important trip for you," Vera said.

"He's just worried," Sheila said, and shrugged. "I'm not going home. I'm leading a class tomorrow and I get my award tomorrow night."

Vera placed her photos on her paper, then switched them around again. She sighed.

"Where's Eric?" Randy asked.

"He said he needed a break from all the scrap-booking," Vera said. "I don't know where he is. He was in the room catching up on e-mails and some reading. He also mentioned a football game at one of the bars."

Sheila's eyes caught Randy's and then quickly looked away. She felt like a fool. Ashamed of herself for butting in.

"It's good that he can be honest with you about needing a break," Shelia said, and then checked out Vera's page. "I like that layout the best."

Vera nodded and reached for the glue dots.

"I love those glue dots," Randy said. "I never knew about them until this cruise. I can't believe how much I'm learning. And in one of the sessions I sat in the teacher talked about repositionable adhesives. Amazing."

"I love playing with those," Vera said. "But I did one whole book with the repositionable adhesive, then a year or so later had to go back and use the real stuff. I think it's not as good as the real stuff."

"Ah, something to keep in mind," he said, finishing up his page and sliding it into his book. He stood. "I'm off for my date." He turned to walk away, as Paige entered the circle. He kissed her cheek and left.

"You're looking a bit peaked," Vera said.

Sheila looked up from her page, filled with musical notes and violins and photos of her Jonathan. Vera was right. Paige did not look good. She had a green hue to her skin.

"I had a bit too much to drink," Paige said, and sat down. "And this ship has been rocking a lot."

"I've never known you to get sick from drinking," Vera said.

"There's a first time for everything." Paige looked over her page from earlier in the day. "Drinking and rocking around the ocean don't mix for me. Lesson learned."

"Poor dear," Vera said, and patted Paige's hand.

"So did you find out anything?" Sheila asked.

Paige nodded. "I met two of the men on our list. Hank and Colton."

"And?"

"I think it's safe to say that they are both here to get laid," she said, picking up her doily and placing it onto a red scrapbooking page. "Of course, that doesn't mean they aren't capable of murder."

"Did you get any weird vibes?" Vera asked.

"Yes," Paige said. "But they were weird vibes of another kind." She twitched her eyebrows and laughed.

Sheila giggled. "Okay, maybe we can take them off our list," she said. "I still need to find Sharon Milhouse. I left a note on the message board. I hope it's not the one I knew before."

"People can change," Paige said. "I wouldn't worry too much."

"Not that crazy woman," Vera said.

But then an odd feeling crept over Sheila once more. Someone was watching her again.

She scanned the area as Vera and Paige laughed about something. And then she noticed him—the man who had been watching her throughout the trip. She caught his eye and he sneered. She looked away. Her stomach flipped around in her body and then squeezed.

She reached for Vera.

"What?" Vera said.

"Hush," Sheila said, almost in a whisper. "That's the man I've been telling you about. The man with the orange shirt on and the glasses? Do you see him?"

Vera twisted and looked at him. "Should I call Eric? He looks kind of menacing. I can see why he worries you."

"What the hell is Eric going to do?" Sheila snapped. "Beat him up? What are we, in middle school?"

"Well, what should we do?" Vera said.

Paige sighed, long and deep, her forehead in her hands. "I can't help you. I just can't. I still feel sick."

Sheila thought a moment. "Let's keep our eyes on him. That's all we can do really."

"It looks like he's married," Paige said. "He has a ring on his finger. But I can't figure out which of those women he's attached to." She had the best and closest view of him. "There is something very strange about him. I agree that we should keep our eyes on him."

"What do you mean?" Vera said.

"I don't know what I mean," Paige said. "Something about him doesn't seem right."

"I agree," Sheila said, setting down her photos. "I think he's wearing a wig, for one thing."

"Yes!" Paige said. "But look around; there are a lot of men wearing wigs, even on this cruise. Women too. And let's not even talk about the fake boobs everywhere."

"But maybe this guy's bald. A lot of bald men wear toupees," Vera pointed out. "They are very self-conscious about their baldness."

"Which I've always thought ridiculous," Sheila said. "But it's not only the wig. It's his clothes, his stance, the way he's always watching me."

"Maybe he has a bit of a crush on you," Paige said. "You are one of the stars of the cruise."

Shelia laughed. "I can't imagine anybody having a crush on me."

She touched her head, which still ached. A crush? Oh my. She'd not had another man in her life for twenty-five years. Steve and she had married right out of college and started raising their family. If there was anybody who had a crush on her, she'd not have noticed. She was entirely too busy and focused on her family and scrapbooking. The thought of someone having a crush on her swirled around in her mind and she found herself giggling.

Chapter 33

Beatrice's theory about the killer maybe having a partner held no water at all, as far as Annie was concerned. Murder was a lonely business.

"If the killer has a partner—let's just say *if*—then the partner is in Cumberland Creek," DeeAnn said, setting down her scrapbook with a thud.

"Sorry, Bea, that makes no sense," Annie said. "Most killers don't work with partners, for one thing. For another thing, I doubt that Sheila has had time to butt in to any investigation on the ship. It pains me, but I agree with Bryant on this."

"Now, hold on," Beatrice said, after finishing one of the chocolate peanut butter cupcakes. "I know I've read about couples who kill."

"Yes, I've read about them, too. But let's not get carried away," Annie said. "Let's look at the facts."

"Sheila trips over a dead body on the ship," DeeAnn said. "Fact one."

"A woman she barely knows," Annie added, then sliced a photo in the cutter.

"The woman was poisoned," Beatrice said. "Then her boyfriend was poisoned."

"Both of them officially still married to other people," Annie said.

"That right there tells you this has nothing to do with Sheila," DeeAnn said, waving her hand.

"Other than the fact that she stepped into the middle of it, it has nothing to do with her," Annie said.

"So you think the note is some weird coincidence," Beatrice said.

Annie nodded. "The note came from someone in town."

"Who on earth?" DeeAnn said. "I don't understand who would write something like that to Sheila. I don't know anybody who doesn't like the woman."

They sat for a few minutes, listening to the music and scrapbooking, each with their own thoughts. Who didn't like Sheila? Annie had no idea. Now, if it was her getting the threatening note, she could think of several people, starting with any member of the Schultz family, who didn't like the fact that she was writing a book about the murder. Any of the people who had attachments to the New Mountain Order would also like to see Annie leave town.

"What are you thinking?" Beatrice interrupted her thoughts.

"Thinking about all of my potential enemies," Annie said, and grinned.

Beatrice shrugged. "Well, you and me both." She cackled.

"But not Sheila," DeeAnn said. "Oh, that's a fabulous page, Annie!"

Annie held up her Hanukkah book: blues and golds, candles and flames. She'd found some Star of David embellishments, which she used on the page where she had several photos of her boys lighting the menorah. She'd taken photos without the flash so the flame and the hands were the only things shown in the picture. The Star was at the center of the page with the photos on each pointed end. It did look pretty good, Annie mused. Her final touch was the overlay that said "Day 1" on it.

"I love the colors of Hanukkah," DeeAnn said. "What's the meaning behind them? Anything?"

"I don't know, really," Annie said. "Some say the colors come from the Israeli flag. The flag's blue stripes symbolize those found on prayer shawls that are worn at synagogue, bar or bat mitzvahs, and Jewish weddings. That's about all I know.

What about the red and green of Christmas?"

"Hell, who knows?" DeeAnn said. "I'm not a big fan of Christmas anymore. It was fun when my girls were small. Now, it's all about work. The bakery keeps me hopping right up until Christmas Eve. I swear if I was open on Christmas, I'd have folks coming in."

"I always thought that the blue and white of Hanukkah had universal association. You know, purity, peace, light. That kind of thing," Beatrice said.

"Sounds good to me," Annie said. "I'll take that explanation."

"Well," Beatrice said, getting up from her seat, "now that I've eaten all the cupcakes, I need to get home. It's late for me. And you two have been no help at all."

"Sorry, Bea," DeeAnn said.

"I'll feel so much better when they get home. I don't like any of this business. I don't like cruises and I don't like my daughter being on one. And this cruise's security is a big mess. I can't allow myself to think about it too hard," Beatrice said.

Damned fool of a daughter, sailing off on a cruise right before Christmas. Beatrice had told her not to go. But it was as if all sense had recently left Vera's brain. Her dance studio usually produced *The Nutcracker* every year, but not this year. Vera said she had been thinking of not doing it anymore and when the opportunity to go on a cruise for free came up, that settled it.

"It's a struggle each year," Vera said. "I've decided to focus only on recitals every year."

"For how much longer?" Beatrice had asked her.

"For as long as I can," Vera replied.

But Beatrice knew that Vera had been thinking of calling it quits. Her dance studio had never completely recovered from the Emily McGlashen episode. She had gone on a campaign against ballet and stolen many of Vera's students. Only a few returned after Emily's death. Many of them now made the trek to Charlottesville to continue with their Irish dance studies, leaving Vera and her beloved ballet in the dust.

But beyond all that, Vera was evolving once again. Beatrice watched, awestruck, as her daughter picked up the pieces of her life without her husband and with a new baby and more than simply survived, but flourished. She'd scaled down her business, but was still able to make a profit.

Then there was Eric, the new man in Vera's life, whom Bea approved of. Finally, after years of Bill being a pain in the ass, there was a man that Bea liked. She was surely glad that she'd never met Tony, the man Vera had dated briefly who lived in New York.

Beatrice never liked walking the streets after dark—even the streets in Cumberland Creek, which had relatively very little crime. Dark streets were no place for a lady, she mused. And there were not many streetlights in Cumberland Creek; people didn't want them. Once when she was walking in the dark, she nearly tripped over a cat that was lounging about on the sidewalk.

As she approached the corner of Ivy and Oak, there was a big streetlight that threw its light halfway down the street. She liked that. She walked by her neighbors' houses and noted many of them already had their lights out. It was late, even for a Saturday night.

She marched down the street to her front door and noted a man walking toward a car on the other side of the street. She had never seen him before; maybe he was visiting someone. She opened her gate and walked into her yard, deciding to sit for a moment on her front porch. The man was opening the door of some kind of fancy red car. *Ain't that something?*

She noted his black leather jacket—the way it shined as the little bit of light on the street played off it. She caught a glimpse of his face in a momentary slice of light. He had a goatee. Beatrice always hated facial hair. She twisted her mouth. He might have been a decent-looking man if it weren't for that damned beard. There was something about his stance that Bea didn't like either. He was trying too hard to be cool.

Her brain clicked into action as she remembered what Bryant had said earlier in the day.

"All I can say is this cruise has more links to Cumberland Creek than Sheila Rogers," he said. "And now that there's been two murders . . . and then this other thing came up. I'm trying to make sense of it."

She reached into her bag and jotted down the license plate number. Few strangers came to Cumberland Creek, though it was not unheard of, of course. But you couldn't be too careful.

She shrugged. He most likely was a visitor, but even so, it couldn't hurt to check him out.

One thing was for certain—she had his license plate number. That could be a very good thing.

"What are you doing out here?" Jon said as he walked onto the porch. "It's cold."

"It is cold. I never minded the cold," Beatrice said. "I love looking at the snow at night."

"Come inside. I made some hot cocoa," Jon said.

She smacked her lips together. "And that's why I love you so much. You make a mean hot cocoa."

As she walked into her home, the car pulled away. Its headlights briefly lit up the street. She tucked the license plate number into her bag. She'd call Bryant in the morning after a good night's sleep.

Chapter 34

Sheila tossed and turned. She couldn't get her last conversation with Steve out of her mind. He wanted her to come home, which was sweet and maddening all at once. He knew how important this trip was to her. He'd never even asked about her meetings. So frustrating! Would he ever recognize her need for more than a family? He mouthed it all the time. He seemed proud of her. But when it came to really taking it seriously, did he?

Up until this point, she had tried not to care. It didn't matter how he felt. She'd forge ahead. But what did that say about their marriage?

She sat up, flicked the light on, and sat on the edge of her bed. How to get to sleep? If she were at home she'd make herself some warm milk with cinnamon, nutmeg, and a drop of honey. Sometimes bourbon. But she'd drunk her weight in gold already and was not hankering for booze at all.

She could call room service—but the idea of a stranger coming into her room in the middle of the night unsettled her.

She glanced at the clock: 1:18 A.M. Which of the closest cafés or restaurants were still open? She dressed in her running clothes and headed out the door.

When she walked into the all-night café, she was surprised by the crowd. Didn't anybody sleep anymore?

"What can I get you?" the man behind the counter asked as she approached.

"Warm milk?" Sheila asked.

"I've got just the thing," he said. "Milk with vanilla and cinnamon sound good?"

She nodded. "Sounds delightful."

"Please have a seat and I'll bring it to you."

She searched for an empty table and, much to her surprise, she spotted Randy alone, eating. She sauntered up to his table. "Why, hello there," she said before she realized how upset he was. "Are you okay? Do you want to be alone?"

"Oh . . ." He waved his hand. "I'll be fine. Just feeling sorry for myself. Please sit down." He was eating a huge bagel with cream cheese. "I'm so hungry," he mumbled.

"I can't sleep," Sheila said. "I'm here for warm milk. I thought you had a hot date tonight."

He wiped his face with a napkin. "Hmph. I did. I'm no good at the dating thing. I was much better in a committed relationship." He took a drink of water. "Sometimes I miss him more than other times. Night time is hard. We used to, you know, talk about our days, our dreams. I miss the companionship."

Shelia reached out and touched his hand. "It will get better," she said.

Looking up, she spotted the creepy guy, sitting just beyond Randy. He was there with Rhonda from Life Arts, who draped herself over him in a most unattractive manner. Every now and then she kissed him or reached up and touched his face or hair. The man appeared completely disinterested.

"This dating business," Randy said. "I am reminded what a lousy judge of character I am. Whew, boy."

"What do you mean?" She turned her attention back to Randy. Rhonda and the creepy man were disturbing to watch.

"I thought Matthew was cute, sure. But I also thought he'd be interesting, him being a security chief and all that."

"Not interesting?"

"If you call crazy interesting . . ."

"What?"

"Yes. Very odd. I'm not sure how he holds it together to do his job. It's troubling," he said. "I've been sitting here and thinking things over. I can't think of a way to soothe myself about it. There's been two murders on board and the chief of security is nuts."

"Surely not," Sheila said.

He nodded vehemently. "Listen, I don't like to judge people. But that man is bat shit crazy."

It was a bit odd to be sitting here with Paige's only child, who looked and acted a good bit like his mother. He said things like Paige, with the same inflections. But this "crazy" business troubled Sheila. They sat next to a window that looked out over a clear night sky. She glanced out at the horizon, then back to Randy, trying not to watch Rhonda make a fool of herself in public.

"What exactly do you mean?" When the server brought her milk, she looked up and said, "Thank you." After the man left, her attention focused back on Randy. "Well?"

"I don't want to scare you," he said.

"As if I'm not scared already. And a bit beat up," she said, smiling and pointing at her head. "I think you should tell me."

He sat back in his chair. "Okay, but let's keep it between us, for now."

She nodded. What could it be that had him so troubled?

"He thinks he's a vampire," he said.

"What? Who?"

"Yes, the chief of security thinks he's a vampire," Randy repeated. "He was quite serious about it. Scared the bejesus out of me."

She was struck speechless. A vampire?

"What do you say to that?" Randy continued. "And that was my first date after breaking up with a brilliant, creative man. Just my luck."

"I—I—"

"Yep," he said.

Sheila took a sip of her milk. The warmth and

the sweetness comforted her as she mulled over the news.

"Needless to say, I told him I was not interested in dating a vampire—or even having a fling with him. But I did look up vampires on the Internet and there are people who claim to be vampires out there. People who actually drink blood," he said.

"Seriously?" Sheila said.

"Yes, some people are into this vampire lifestyle—and I hope that's what our friend is talking about. But there are also some serious psychiatric problems associated with people who claim to be vampires, people who crave human blood," he said, with a low voice.

"He reports directly to the captain," she said. "I can't imagine he hasn't picked up on this."

"Oh, he doesn't tell everybody, of course; it's a secret that he bestows on a lucky few."

"Aren't you the lucky one then?" Sheila said. Suddenly a giggle erupted from her. She couldn't even try to stop it. *Oh, it wasn't funny,* she told herself, *stop.* A man responsible for the safety of the ship might be bat shit crazy. *Not funny at all.* She tried to stop her laughter.

But Randy's eye caught hers and the next thing she knew, they were both laughing uncontrollably.

Tears ran down Randy's face. "Oh my God," he said, finally calming down. "What have we gotten ourselves into?"

Shelia took a deep breath and settled herself,

suddenly feeling tired. She took another sip of her milk. "I'm not sure," she said. "But I have a new goal: just to get off this ship in one piece."

Then it hit her with a startling thud. Her face must have reflected her thoughts.

"What?" Randy said.

"If the man thinks he's a vampire, then he might think he needs to kill to survive."

Chapter 35

Annie was putting the finishing touches on her manuscript. At least she hoped she was finished. She liked to let it sit a few days and then go back over it, fact checking and looking for grammar mistakes and spelling errors. Then she'd fix it up, let it sit a few more days, and go back over it yet again.

She drained her second cup of coffee. Should she have another? Hmmm. Probably not.

Her computer buzzed. Good thing she was at the kitchen table and not in her bedroom.

"Good morning, Annie." First a voice and then two faces appeared on the Skype screen: Vera and Paige, who looked awful.

"Good morning. You two are up early."

"Early breakfast today and off to explore Grand Caymen. Thank God we are going to be on land for a few days," Vera said. "Paige is sick."

Paige nodded and whimpered.

"Sea sick?" Annie asked.

"She'd been drinking and got sick and hasn't gotten any better. The waters have been a little rough."

"Sorry, Paige. You do look awful," Annie said.

"Thanks," Paige mumbled.

"What's up?" Annie asked.

"Listen, I read the text you sent to Sheila about Sharon Milhouse," Vera said.

Eric passed by in the background, then backed up and waved. He looked a bit tan and very relaxed. The trip was doing someone good. Annie waved back.

"And?" Annie said.

"And I'd like you to see what you can find out about her. I mean, even get Bryant involved if you have to," Vera said.

"Why?"

"She used to be nuts. I'm sure she still is. If that's the same woman, we need to know it." Vera took a breath and then filled Annie in on the background.

"Don't you think she'd be over Steve and Sheila by now? I mean, it's been twenty years," Annie said incredulously.

"I wish," Vera said. "There were some things that happened that Sheila never knew. Things we didn't tell her."

"We?"

"Bill, Steve, and I," Vera said. "We thought it was best to keep some things from her."

"Why would you do that? I don't understand."

"I don't want to go into this over the computer, but suffice it to say the woman was committed because of her actions. I'm not exaggerating her illness." Vera took another deep breath. "I think it would be best if we knew if she was on this ship."

Paige harrumphed, then said, "You know Sheila; things like this would wear on her. She's scared enough as it is. I mean, she's really not acting like herself. We're worried about her."

Annie thought a moment. "I promise to try to track down this woman. I'll text you to let you know what I find out. But if I find out anything, you're going to have to tell Sheila. She's a grown-up and she can handle it."

But she, Bea, and DeeAnn had decided not to tell her about the note left on the door of her home. "Wait," Annie said. "Maybe you're right. With her concussion and everything else that's going on, let's leave her out of it until she gets safely home."

"She's getting very paranoid," Vera said. "I don't think she's eaten more than a bite of toast since yesterday."

"Well, we all are," Paige said. "I spoke with a couple of the men on our list yesterday—Colton and Hank. I think we can cross them off the list."

"Same with the guy I talked with. He's a hard-core scrapbooker," Vera said.

"That leaves what—six other men?" Annie said.

"I'll get back to it when I feel better," Paige said.

"We'll keep our eyes open," Vera said.

Eric poked his head onto the screen. "We need to go ladies. Bye, Annie," he said.

"Bye," Annie said. The screen faded out.

Annie saved her file and decided to search around on the Internet for more information about Sharon Milhouse. Over one thousand of them lived in the US. How to hone that down? What was the name of Sheila's school again? Sweet Wood University.

Annie keyed in "Sharon Milhouse" and "Sweet Wood University."

Bazinga.

An article popped up from a Richmond newspaper's online archives:

> Sharon Milhouse, a recent graduate of Sweet Wood University, has been convicted of attempted murder of another recent grad, Steven Rogers.

Holy Shit! Did Sheila know about this? Or was this what Vera was talking about?

Annie's heart raced and she read further on. Sharon had been housed in the Richmond

Institution and would probably remain there for life.

Life? Maybe this Sharon Milhouse wasn't the one on the ship. It couldn't be the same one; the Sharon Milhouse who was married to Harold had certainly been a free woman. Unless . . . unless Sharon had gotten out early and married.

Damn, she couldn't get into those records. If they had to do with medical issues at all, Annie was out of luck. But maybe Bryant had access to them.

She hadn't seen him or talked to him in a while. He'd been seeing a young police officer from a neighboring town and was too busy to hang out with Mike—thank goodness—and there were no other recent murders in their little town. She hated to call the man. In fact, the thought of it turned her stomach.

She'd call Beatrice later. Perhaps Beatrice could call him and explain the situation. Perhaps. Bea didn't like him any more than Annie did. But at least she hadn't had the somewhat personal experience with him that Annie had. Experience she was quite ashamed of and wished she could erase from of her life.

Chapter 36

Beatrice poured the pancake batter onto the griddle. She made pancakes every Sunday morning, but today she added gingerbread spice to the batter and the scent was filling the kitchen as Jon walked in.

"What are you making? It smells divine," he said, coming up behind her and kissing her on the cheek.

"Gingerbread pancakes," she said.

"And Christmas music is playing. . . . Have you gotten into the Christmas spirit, dear?"

Beatrice harrumphed. "Lord knows I'm trying."

"Still worried about the cruisers?"

She nodded, flipped her pancakes, then told him about what Bryant had mentioned to her last night.

Jon grabbed a plate and set it next to Bea for the pancakes.

"Bryant thinks it's related to the cruise?" Jon asked.

"I think he's just grasping for anything. It was a creepy postcard."

"I think you all made the right decision to not tell Sheila. She has enough on her mind right now. More coffee?"

Bea nodded. "I'd like that."

Jon made another pot of coffee and Beatrice

scooped her pancakes from the griddle onto the plate.

"It's really strange—we can't think of who might have done something like that to Sheila," she said. "Maybe she gets on people's nerves about the scrapbooking. God knows it drives me crazy."

"Why? It's something that she loves, so why does it bother you so much?"

Beatrice thought it over a few minutes, fussing over her pancakes. "I don't mind scrapbooking. You know, keeping your family's memories in a book. I've made several of my own. Not with any of that newfangled stuff. It seems to me that folks go overboard with it. And Sheila has built her life around it. I get tired of hearing about it, I suppose."

"Hmmm," Jon said. "Maybe Sheila doesn't like to hear about quantum physics."

Beatrice laughed. "No, I'm sure she doesn't. But who does? I'm used to nobody being interested in my thing."

"I'm interested." He grinned.

"Yes, I know—" She was interrupted by the phone ringing.

Jon answered the phone and handed it to Beatrice. "It's Annie," he said.

"Sorry to bother you so early. I know you're probably in the middle of your pancake breakfast," Annie said.

"I'm just now making it. What's up?"

"I Skyped with Vera and Paige this morning and Vera was really concerned about this possible connection with Sharon Milhouse."

"Now, why does that name sound so familiar?"

"Maybe because she was convicted of trying to kill Steve Rogers."

Bea's heart jumped. "Oh my," she said, her mind flicking through the memories. "I do remember that."

"Anyway, they called to ask if I can find out anything about her. I was able to pull up old newspaper reports and criminal records, but she was sent to the Richmond Institution, which isn't even open anymore. And since she was determined to be mentally ill, I can't access those records."

"Neither can I. What can I do to help?"

"Can you call Bryant and explain the situation?"

"Oh, I nearly forgot; I need to call him about something else. So yes, I can call him. But why don't you?"

"I'd rather not. It's Hanukkah and I don't want to spoil my day. You know how I feel about that man. And it's not exactly a professional inquiry."

Beatrice suspected that she'd never really know what had gone down between those two. At first it seemed like they despised one another. Then he became a friend of Annie's husband and it seemed they reached some kind of friendly understanding about their relationship. Then it went sour again about the same time as Emily McGlashen's murder. Beatrice didn't like to pry. But it was the oddest thing.

"Well, none of us really like the man," Beatrice said after a moment. To say that he was abrasive would be putting it mildly. But Beatrice had seen traces of a real human being beneath his tough-guy exterior from time to time, like when Vera was having problems sleepwalking. "But he's a good cop. I think he might appreciate this information and might want to help out."

"I hope you're right. You know it may be nothing. But Vera is very concerned," Annie said.

"She should be," Beatrice said. "Sharon Milhouse was a total freak. If she's on that ship, knowing that Sheila is, too, there could be problems."

"Surely not," Annie said. "That was years ago. Besides, she's probably still in a hospital some-where."

"I'd not count on that," Beatrice said. "If she is the woman who was Harold's ex-wife, I'm sure she'd have killed both Allie and him and not batted an eyelash. She was that sick."

"Maybe she's gotten better."

"One would hope. But so many times I've seen that there are some people who are beyond help. I wish that wasn't the case."

Jon had taken over the pancake making and

now had a stack of golden brown pancakes on the table. Beatrice's stomach growled.

"I'll call Bryant later," Bea said. "I need to eat my breakfast."

"Later," Annie said.

Bea sat down at the table and recounted what Annie had told her on the phone.

"Sounds like a good lead," Jon said, cutting his pancakes up.

"Maybe," Bea said. "But if that's our Sharon Milhouse and she's on a ship with Sheila? Our friend is in very real danger."

Chapter 37

Poison. Murder. Vampires. It was all swirling around in Sheila's mind as she led a group of forty people off the ship to where a bus waited for them. Her legs felt strange and wobbly as she adjusted to ground after being on the sea for several days.

Paige's skin still had a slight green tinge to it and even with a few days of sun, her long legs were white and looked unstable. "Jesus, it's hot," she said.

Randy fanned her for a few minutes with his guidebook.

Eric's arm slipped around Vera, who was looking over the crowd. She appeared nervous. Sheila knew she was wondering if the killer was around.

Once again, Sheila found herself wondering how many of the passengers knew that the untimely deaths were actually murders and not accidents. The ship had never called them such in any of the announcements. But Sheila and her friends knew—only because she had tripped over Allie's body and then had the misfortune of witnessing Harold in the hallway.

Sheila looked right and left before she spotted the bus across the street. The port city of George Town was awash in color, noise, and scent, which was jarring after being on the sleek cruise ship for days, mostly colored in whites and shades of blue. Their bus was waiting for them right where it was supposed to be.

"Sheila Rogers?" The bus driver met her with an extended arm and a lush Caribbean accent.

She nodded. "Nice to meet you," she said, and extended her own hand.

Their schedule had changed again. The plans originally included three days here, but since they'd lost some time because of the storm, their stay was shortened to a day. And Sheila's prior research had all been done for a Mexican photo shoot, not Grand Caymen, so she was winging it. But she was able to sneak a bit of research in on the botanical gardens they'd be visiting during their photo excursion. It would make for fabulous scrapbooking material.

"Good morning, ladies and gentlemen," a tour guide said to them after they were all settled on the bus. "Welcome to Grand Caymen."

"Thank God it's air conditioned in here," Paige said in a low voice.

"Our beautiful island is seventy-six square miles and is home to fifty thousand residents," the guide said after everybody had settled and the bus began to move around the edge of the city.

It was even more beautiful as they left the city behind and drove along the coast. Sheila sat back and took in the view of white sandy beaches giving way to lush trees and rolling green hills.

A sudden image of Cumberland Creek came to her mind—she wondered if it was still snowing there. It was December, close to Christmas, and it felt unnatural to be here in the heat and the tropical weather.

"I love the heat," Randy said, as if reading her mind. "Doesn't bother me a bit. I could live in the tropics."

Paige sighed.

"I love the seasons," Vera said from across the aisle. "I couldn't live someplace where it was warm all year long."

"We'll be at the Queen Elizabeth Two Botanic Park in about fifteen minutes," the guide said. "This heritage attraction was officially opened on the twenty-seventh of February, 1994, by Her

Majesty Queen Elizabeth the second and named in her honor."

"This should be gorgeous," Randy said. "I'm so excited about this."

"One of the things the park is known for is our blue iguanas, a rare species. You should be able to get a view of them this morning. They like to sun themselves in midmorning," said the guide.

"They are in cages, right?" Vera suddenly asked.

"We have an enclosed habitat that provides a natural home for an adult male blue iguana, which can be seen by visitors."

Vera sat up taller and her eyes widened. But it wasn't because of the tour guide's statement. Sheila followed her eyes. It was hard to see because of the bus seat, but Sheila observed what Vera saw: the man who had been staring at Sheila throughout the trip. And he was with Theresa Graves, which was interesting, as he seemed a lot younger than her. Oh well, to his or her own.

But was he her husband? Sheila tried to remember if they had talked about her husband. A sourness formed in her as she remembered how discouraging Theresa had been and how David himself of David's Designs had no kind words about her. Sheila was fascinated by the competitive nature of these huge scrapbooking business owners. Couldn't everybody get along?

Vera's eyes met Sheila's and she tilted her head in the couple's direction. Sheila nodded.

When they disembarked from the bus, Sheila took over and led the group to the visitor center. They all had real cameras draped around their necks. She was happy that nobody was there with cell phone cameras. The guide from the center gave them a quick orientation and they were off.

First stop: the "color gardens."

The pink garden's collection consisted of rose and green caladiums, Anderson Crepe hibiscus, Cordyline morado, and exotic large bromeliads including Aechmea Victoria.

"Keep the sun in mind when you are shooting these flowers," Sheila said. "Make sure it's at your back."

"Like we don't know that," came a voice from the back, and a group of people giggled.

Sheila ignored the jab.

"We have about ten minutes here and then we move on through the rest of the colors," Sheila said.

Vera eyed her and then leaned in. "Did you hear that?"

Sheila nodded. "Who was it?"

"Theresa," Paige said, interrupting. "She's got a group of some of the most negative people I've ever heard. They are all laughing and joking, but I don't see them taking pictures."

Sheila shrugged. "You get all kinds," she said.

As they moved through to the red gardens, a

young woman asked her if she had ever made a garden scrapbook.

"I haven't," Sheila said. "I'm not much of a gardener. But I have customers who have made garden scrapbooks. Really lovely."

"I've made a few myself," the woman said. "I inherited this old rose garden with our house and I'm fascinated by the shapes and colors of the roses. The way at different times of the day the light makes the pink roses look almost orange, sometimes yellow."

"What an interesting observation," Sheila said.

"Not really," came that same voice, and then more laughter.

A shot of anger tore through Sheila. "If you'll excuse me for a moment," she said in her most polite voice to the woman, who had reddened.

Sheila made her way easily to the back of the crowd where Theresa stood with her gaggle of friends.

"Are you having a good time?" Sheila asked, concentrating still on trying to be polite, but allowing her eyes to shoot daggers.

Theresa's posture changed a bit—she wasn't expecting Sheila to seek her out, to face her. She didn't answer, but simply looked at the man standing next to her, the man who had been freaking Sheila out the entire trip.

The others looked in Theresa's direction, expecting an answer.

"Yes, of course," Theresa said.

"Good," Sheila replied as sweet as she could muster.

Theresa shot her a look of pure, unadulterated hatred.

What the hell had Sheila ever done to the woman?

An uncomfortable hush came over the group.

"Well now, Ms. Fancy Pants scrapbooking diva bitch, I think you should either shut your mouth or find another tour group who will put up with your nonsense. We're here to learn from Sheila Rogers," a voice said from behind Sheila.

It was the woman who had been discussing her roses. A stunned silence came from the group as Theresa reddened and huffed off in anger. Vera and the others applauded.

Sheila took the rose lady's arm. "Thanks so much," she said. "Now, let's get down to business, shall we?"

Chapter 38

Annie was cleaning up from a late breakfast when the phone rang.

"Hey," Bea said on the other end of the phone. "I talked to Bryant."

"And what did he say?"

"He said he'd check into all of it and get back with us."

"That's it?"

"Oh yes—he thanked me for the information about the strange man and car I saw last night. In fact, he seemed more interested in him than the note, really."

"You didn't mention that to me," Annie said, wiping the counter off with her dish towel.

Beatrice then explained what she had seen the night before. "Probably nothing, but with all the weird stuff happening, I thought it best to give Bryant the license plate number and let him know."

"I suppose so," Annie responded. "Will you let me know when he gets back to you?"

"If he gets back to me. He thanked me, was very polite, but made sure I knew this was police business."

"Typical," Annie said, but she knew he was right. Unless he needed more help from them, he had no obligation to fill them in on what was happening.

If she had time today, she'd try to sleuth around. But she was feeling a pull toward her art journal; if she had some free time, she wanted to work on it, along with her Hanukkah book. She was so thrilled that the scrapbooking supply businesses now carried many different kinds of Hanukkah materials. She loved the pieced-paper menorah kit she had purchased and the chipboard Star of David. And there was so much Jewish-themed paper that it was hard to choose. A few years ago, it was much harder to find anything relating to any other religion but Christianity. Cookie used to go off a bit about it—but Cookie was a Wiccan, an unconventional religion to say the least. Cookie sometimes used non-pagan paper and embellishments for pagan purposes. She relied a great deal on nature, celestial, and Halloween-themed papers.

Annie's heart sank. She still missed Cookie and wondered about her frequently. Whatever became of her friend who was wrongly accused of murder? She was probably one of the kindest people she'd ever met. Last year Bryant slipped her information that he knew that Cookie was fine and that was all he could tell her. That settled Annie's mind somewhat. She knew that Cookie had escaped from jail and was on the run—and that could lead to a number of dangerous situations. But she still yearned for her friendship and she knew the other scrapbookers did, as well.

"What are we having tonight?" Sam said, coming into the kitchen for a glass of milk.

"I'm making latkes," Annie said. "Would you like to help shred the potatoes?"

He nodded. "Yep, I'm a good shredder."

"I remember," Annie said. "So I can count on you?"

He nodded and took a long sip of milk. "Why do I have to go to school tomorrow?"

"It's only a few more days," Annie said, folding her towel and hanging it over the side of her kitchen counter to air dry.

"Yes, but it's Hanukkah," he said.

"We've talked about this. Maybe someday we'll be okay with you missing school for Hanukkah, but not this year. You've already missed more days than you should because of the flu. School is important."

"Someone trying to get out of school tomorrow?" Mike said as he walked into the room.

"Yep," Annie said.

"But I don't understand why we have Christmas off and not Hanukkah," her son said.

"You know what? I don't understand it either," Annie said. "But it's just the way it is."

She tried to shrug it off. Where she grew up, it was the same way, even in a heavily populated Jewish area. For children, school was the most important thing. Besides, her parents were secular and most of her friends' parents were, too. Hanukkah was not that big of a holiday for them.

"Poor boy," Mike said with false sympathy.

"How about a cookie?" said Annie.

Sam's face lit.

"Did someone say cookies?" Ben said as he came bounding into the kitchen.

Annie watched her three boys sharing cookies in her vintage kitchen. She'd miss this tiny kitchen if they ever saved enough money to move.

Later, after the boys got involved in a game with their father, she sat down at the computer and found an e-mail from Vera.

> Annie, can you find out anything about Theresa Graves? She's a big-time scrap-booker. But she's been heckling Sheila. And she's hanging out with a guy who's been watching Sheila closely. We are still in the gardens. I stopped by the visitor center and hopped on the computer.

Annie looked at her clock; the e-mail had been sent an hour ago.

Heckling Sheila? How odd. Sounded like another unbalanced sort was on the cruise with them. Poor Sheila. Why couldn't this scrapbook cruise have gone smoothly for her?

Annie clicked on the crime database and typed in "Theresa Graves." A number of hits came up. The woman had quite the record: domestic violence, DUI, a drug arrest, and . . . attempted murder. Attempted murder? This was the woman heckling Sheila? Could she be the person who'd poisoned Allie and Hank? And what would she have against Sheila?

Annie grabbed her cell phone and sent Vera a text message. She hoped Vera received it before it was too late.

Chapter 39

Beatrice was eating lunch when the phone rang. It was Detective Bryant.

"Well, twice in one day. Aren't I a lucky woman?" she said after answering the phone.

The detective laughed. "I need to ask you some questions."

"Shoot."

"What do you remember about Sharon Milhouse? About that time in Vera's and Sheila's lives?"

"Not much really," she said after a moment. "It was such a busy time, with the girls graduating and so on. And I'm sure you know I didn't know half of what went on. But I do remember Sheila getting death threats and thinking they were from Sharon."

"Did anybody prove that?"

"Not that I know of. But then again, Sharon was carted off to the Richmond Institution. So it was dropped. Ever find out what happened to her?"

"She's out," he said after a minute. "I was trying to place her in Cumberland Creek, thinking maybe she left the postcard in Sheila's mailbox. You know, maybe she was trying to settle an old score."

A chill traveled up Beatrice's spine. "Where's the woman now?"

"I'm working on that. She's not easy to find, which troubles me. I have no idea if this Sharon Milhouse on the cruise is the same one or not. I'm waiting to hear back from their security team," he said. "Hell, she may be right here in Cumberland Creek for all we know."

"Let's hope not," Bea said. "Very few people have scared me in my life. But I remember the vacant, strange look on that woman's face and it frightened me."

"If she's on the cruise, it could be a coincidence, right?" Bryant said, as if he was talking to himself.

"I'm not sure I believe in coincidence—or at least not as most people seem to see it," Beatrice said after a momentary pause. She was reminded of what Albert Einstein said: "Coincidence is God's way of remaining anonymous."

Does the unexpected only seem like a coincidence because we are unaware of the complex order behind it? Beatrice often pondered the "coincidence of a higher order," which was based on connections that science was now beginning to discover.

"I believe in a certain order behind most events," Beatrice said.

"We're in agreement about that," the detective replied. "But every once in a while, something does happen that appears to be unexplainable."

"In the short term, perhaps," Beatrice said. She

took a long sigh. So many questions to be answered in the universe and she was running out of time. She'd never answer all of them by herself. "So will you let me know what you find out?"

"It depends, due to the nature of privacy acts and investigations and so on. We'll see. But I appreciate your help. When you talked to Steve, was he able to think of anybody who doesn't like Sheila?"

"No. Sheila is well liked. But I can't imagine that *everybody* likes her. There has to be someone . . . besides that Sharon from so long ago. That's a long shot."

"But it's all we have on the note," Bryant said. "A long shot."

Beatrice finished her sandwich after they hung up. From time to time, she really liked Bryant. But other times he was nothing but a pain in the ass and seemed like he had no compassion.

But when she had been poisoned, he'd helped her out—and thank goodness for that or else she might be dead right now. But he hadn't been very polite when he was questioning her about Cookie. In fact, he was downright rude. *Hmmm.* But maybe he had been frustrated. He knew something was going on and he couldn't quite put his finger on it. She smiled. He was right—even though she still had no idea what was actually going on with Cookie and her escape. The more the detective tried to understand it all, the more it confounded him. She knew how he felt.

She checked out her Christmas tree and noticed a gap in the trimming. She rose from where she was sitting and moved some ornaments around. Flipping on the stereo, she slid in a Christmas CD. It was Christmas, damn it! And she was going to get into the spirit of things and not dwell on Cookie. Nor did she want to dwell on what had happened on that cruise ship—or what could still happen. There was nothing she could do about it from here.

Maybe all she needed was a few cookies. That should do it; nothing like gingerbread cookies to bring on the Christmas spirit. She resisted smacking her lips together.

Chapter 40

Sheila immediately knew something was wrong when the bus driver pulled up to the bus stop, which was right next to the dock where the *Jezebel* was sitting. Shiny black cars and about twelve young men wearing dark clothing and sunglasses greeted them. She and Vera exchanged an anxious glance as they got off the bus.

Matthew was in the midst of it. "Mrs. Rogers," he said, stretching his hand out to her. She backed away and cringed—the man thought he was a vampire. The more she thought about it, the more plausible it seemed that he could be the murderer of poor Allie and her boyfriend.

He noticed her shrinking away and tilted his head. "Mrs. Rogers, I'm not going to hurt you. FBI agents are here and want to talk with you. I told you they were coming."

"Me? Why me?" she managed to say.

Vera's arm slipped around her.

"Because you were the person who discovered Allie's body," Matthew said slowly, as if she were two years old.

"May I please come with her?" Vera asked.

Matthew glanced at one of the young men standing nearby. He must have been an FBI agent. He looked like he was about eighteen. How old did an agent have to be?

"Certainly, you can come with her," he said. "Please follow me."

He led them back onto the ship and two of the young men followed.

Paige, Randy, and Eric waved as the two of them looked over their shoulders one last time before boarding the *Jezebel*.

Grace Irons, the woman in charge of the scrapbooking cruise, joined them once they were on the ship.

"I'm so sorry for this inconvenience," she said.

"No worries," Sheila said. "I'm sure it won't take much of my time. I don't have much to say, really. But if I can help find out who killed Allie, I'm happy to share what I know."

The group walked through the marble foyer with a huge cascading crystal chandelier hanging from the ceiling, then off to one of the side corridors to a room with a shut door.

"Mrs. Rogers," Matthew said, opening the door and gesturing for her to enter. She did, followed closely by Vera.

A few people were already there, including a woman who smiled at Sheila and Vera as they sat down. Introductions were made. The officer in charge, a ruddy-complexioned man named Ron Pereles, asked for Sheila to tell them about the morning she tripped over Allie's body. She recounted her story.

"Mrs. Rogers," Agent Melinda Walters spoke up. "What were you doing up and running at that time of day?"

She shrugged. "I run every day."

"But not yesterday or today?" she asked.

"I haven't been feeling up to it." Sheila pointed to her head. "Mild concussion."

The officer nodded.

"Did you think it was odd that Allie wanted to see your scrapbook again the night before she died?" Pereles said.

She thought a moment. "I was just so honored that she wanted to take another look at it. I've admired her for a very long time. So, at the time,

I was flattered. But thinking back, I suppose it was odd."

"How so?"

"I mean, I'm sure she had other things to do besides look at my scrapbook, which she had already seen once before."

"I thought the same thing," the agent replied.

Agent Walters cleared her throat. She held a pencil in her hand. Nobody else seemed to be taking notes. "Mrs. Rogers, can I ask you about Harold? When was the first time you saw him that night?"

"I saw him earlier in the bar. Then later in the hallway, after he had died."

"What was he doing in the bar? Drinking? Eating?"

"He was having a drink with Theresa Graves."

"You all should talk to that one," Vera said.

"Excuse me?" the agent said to her, obviously charmed and trying not to smile.

"She was heckling Sheila during her photo class, rather loudly. Something ain't right with her," Vera said. "And our friend Annie said she has a record."

The agent smiled and crossed his arms.

"People don't heckle on my scrapbooking cruises," Grace Irons said.

"She did. You can ask anybody who was there," said Vera, as if it were the juiciest bit of information.

"I don't believe it!" Grace said, then looked at Sheila. "Is this true?"

Sheila felt the blood rush to her face as she nodded. "It was so embarrassing. I don't know what made her do it."

"What was that woman's name again?" Agent Walters asked.

"Theresa Graves."

"She was seen talking with Harold right before he was killed?"

"Yes, she said they were friends," Sheila said.

"What else did she say?"

"Well . . ." Sheila took a deep breath and mentally sifted through that night. "They both had been crying. He didn't look well at all and she said he was very upset because of Allie's death. They were . . . close friends. But he left when I arrived."

"How long were you with Theresa?"

"Maybe an hour. We had dinner and I left."

"And who is Annie?" Agent Walters asked. She was one of those women who made the other women in the room feel inadequate. Drop dead gorgeous, with a tight-cropped short haircut and a face right out of a magazine. Plus, her intelligence was easily sensed.

Sheila explained.

"Mrs. Rogers, please take my card, and if there's anything else you can remember, please call," Walters said, and handed her a card. "In the meantime, your discretion would be appreciated, ladies." Sheila noted the beautifully manicured, clean, short fingernails.

"Well," Vera spoke up. "We may have some other leads for you."

It was like a scene out of a TV show. All of them stopped what they were doing and looked at Vera. Sheila elbowed her.

Vera waved her off and went on. The woman loved an audience—and she had one. "Since we knew it was a murder and had been talking to our friends back where we live in Cumberland Creek, Virginia, we came up with a plan, you see, to try to find out who the killer was."

"Why?" Agent Pereles said. "Why would you do that?"

"For one reason," Vera said.

Oh, she's good. And she's loving every minute of this, Sheila thought.

"For our own safety," Vera concluded.

"Why would you think you're not safe? I don't understand," the woman agent said.

"Well, the security on this ship is mighty lax, if you ask me. They told my mother that Sheila was killed—"

"Yes, yes, we know about that. It was a mix-up with the report."

"I still don't know how that happened," said Matthew Kirtley—the first time he spoke during the entire meeting.

"So we decided to come up with our own list of

suspects. Knowing that most killers are men," Vera said, ignoring him.

Sheila took a closer look at Matthew. He appeared so normal. *How could he think he's a vampire?*

"Is that right?" Agent Pereles smiled.

"Everybody knows that," Vera said. "Now, we narrowed it down to the men who are not traveling with their wives."

"Why is that?"

"Most killers don't travel with their wives," Vera said.

Sheila noted that the agents were stifling laughter.

"So, we've been looking for these guys and found a few," Vera went on.

"What was your name again?" Agent Walters asked, carefully taking notes.

"Vera Matthews," she said. "Do you need that list from me?"

"No," Agent Pereles said. "We'll be able to get that information. But thanks so much for everything."

Vera grinned wide. Sheila rolled her eyes.

The gentlemen in the room shifted around like they were getting ready to leave.

"One more thing," Vera said. "There's this person named Sharon Milhouse on board."

"Yes?"

Sheila paled and bit her lip.

"I have no idea of it's the same person we knew in college, but we knew a Sharon Milhouse who tried to kill Sheila's husband and also sent threatening notes. She was sent to the Richmond Institution. We've seen her name on the roster, but we can't seem to find her. I've been leaving her messages," Vera said.

"Why?" Agent Pereles asked.

"We need to know if it's the same person, don't you think? If she's on board and has a history—"

"Thanks so much, Mrs. Matthews. We'll take it from here," Agent Pereles responded.

"There is one more thing," Detective Walters said. A few of the ship's crew stepped forward with scrapbooks in huge see-through plastic bags. Six scrapbooks thudded as they were dropped onto the table. Sheila sucked in a breath.

"Which one of those books is yours?" Pereles said.

Sheila stood and walked over to the other end of the long table and felt her throat clutch as she spotted her beloved book.

"That one is mine," she said, first pointing to it and then starting to reach for it.

"Can't let you have it yet," Pereles said. "Sorry. We only needed you to ID it for us. Thanks so much. You can leave now, ladies." His tone was cold and dismissive.

"Wait. When will I get it back?" Sheila said as she was being shoved out the door.

"We'll get it to you when we're finished with it. It's evidence."

"Evidence?" Sheila managed to say before the door shut. She looked at Vera and lifted her arms and shoulders in a huge shrug. "Evidence? In a murder case? My scrapbook?"

Vera laughed. "Crazy!"

Sheila wrapped her arm around her best friend since childhood. She couldn't imagine a life without her—even if she loved to "perform" everywhere she went.

"At least we know my scrapbook didn't go overboard!" Sheila said.

Vera stopped walking and grabbed Sheila by the shoulders. "Now that we know it's on board, maybe we can swipe it."

"Yeah, right," Sheila said. "Nobody says 'swipe' anymore, by the way, old woman. And nobody is going to take that scrapbook away from the FBI."

Chapter 41

Annie walked down the aisles of the grocery store, heading toward the bread. She popped three loaves into her cart. "Three loaves? Are you feeding an army?" a friend had once said to her when they were shopping together.

"My boys eat a lot of sandwiches," Annie had explained. Truth is, they'd go through that bread in less than a week, which was why she was here on a Sunday afternoon. They had run out of bread and milk. No matter how she tried to plan for groceries, they ran out of something before week's end.

Annie loved the fact that the grocery store had recently expanded its hours and was now open on Sundays, which turned out to be a great day to shop because not many people shopped on Sundays in Cumberland Creek.

Christmas music played in the background. By this point in the season, Annie was pretty sick of the music. She turned the corner and headed for the dairy section and ran right smack into Steve Rogers, Sheila's husband.

He laughed. "Where are you going so fast?"

"Just to get milk," she said, and smiled. "I don't think I've ever seen you here before, Steve."

"I hate this place. Sheila usually shops," he replied. He looked forlorn and Annie was torn between feeling sorry for him and wanting to shake him.

"They'll be home soon," Annie said, starting to move her cart around Steve.

"I hope so," he said. "With all the stuff going on, I'm very worried."

"What do you mean?" Annie asked.

"Sheila was questioned by the FBI today. Imagine," he replied.

"That means nothing, Steve. They're investigating. Of course they need to talk with her. She discovered Allie's body," Annie said, moving her cart beyond his so that they stood beside one another. She placed her hand on his shoulder. "I know you're worried. I am, too. But Sheila can handle herself."

"I know that," he said, after a minute. "It's just . . . it all seems so weird. The note. The murders."

"Yes, I'll give you that. And now this business about Sharon Milhouse."

Steve paled. "What?"

Annie realized nobody had told him about Sharon. "I'm sorry, Steve. We've been trying to figure out who could have killed Allie and were looking at the passenger list. . . ."

"Sharon Milhouse is on board?" he stammered.

"We're not sure it's the same person that you once knew," Annie said. He didn't look good; his eyes widened as he paled even more. Beads of sweat formed on his forehead. Was he going to have a heart attack standing there in the grocery store? "In fact, Bryant said it's a long shot. A very long shot," she added.

"She's still in the Richmond Institution, right?" Steve said, after a moment.

Annie shrugged and glanced away. She wished she had not told Steve all of this. He was coming undone. Yet, she couldn't quite lie to him. That wouldn't be fair. "Bryant's looking into all of this.

You should call him," she said, starting to walk away.

"Damned right I will. I want my wife to come home. Now. I want her to get on a plane and leave the cruise and come home where she belongs," he said. Something about his voice made Annie spin around to look at him. Was it just her safety he was concerned about or was it something else?

"Steve," Annie said, "you can't mean that. So there was a little trouble; Sheila will be fine. And think of all the people she's meeting. All of the opportunities she has laid down at her feet right now. She's so talented. Finally, she's being appreciated for it."

With each word, Steve reacted as if she were pinching him instead of talking to him. He resembled a beleaguered child standing there, with his shoulders drooping.

"You'll be fine," Annie said, and gave him a playful punch. "Gotta run, Steve. If you need anything, give us a call."

"Thanks, Annie," he said as she moved toward the milk.

Oh boy. What was that all about? Was Steve unhappy that Sheila was off pursuing her dreams? He'd always seemed so cool and supportive about everything. But this was the first time Sheila had left home on business. Usually he was the one traveling through the mountains with his outfitting company. One thing was certain: he didn't like his wife being gone. But Annie was uncertain how much of that was worry because of the murder, or maybe disdain because Sheila had the audacity to leave her family for a few days. Oy.

Sheila and Steve had been married for a long time. What—twenty-some years? Had four kids. And Sheila had always stayed at home, but also built her scrapbooking supply business. She'd always done it from home. This was new, this traveling around with successful scrapbookers. Could Steve be insecure after all those years of marriage? Or was he just being an asshole?

Good thing she didn't tell him about Theresa Graves. He might be hopping the next plane to the Caribbean to fetch his wife. What was a woman like that doing in the scrapbooking world? Annie shrugged. Scrapbooking attracted a wide variety of people—that was for sure. And why wouldn't it? Once you got over the overwhelming quality of it—where to start? I'm so behind! I know nothing about design!—it was fun and felt very rewarding to capture your family's memories. Sheila had gone into some local prisons and taught some scrapbooking classes and she said the classes filled up every time.

"Everybody has a story to tell," Sheila liked to say.

Annie thought about Mary Schultz, the woman she was writing about. She definitely had a story to tell. She needed to get that book done and out of her life. She'd been dreaming about her again.

Sad dreams. Scary dreams. Mary's life was both sad and scary.

As Annie placed her bread and milk on the counter to be paid for, she thought about human frailty. And how sometimes it turned into ugliness and violence.

Chapter 42

"You've never seen such a beautiful garden, with all of these wild-looking flowers. I can't wait to show you the pictures," Vera said over the phone to Beatrice. "Then we came back to the ship and Sheila was questioned by the FBI."

"Thank goodness the FBI is finally there. Maybe they can get to the bottom of what's happening on that ship," Beatrice said. "And let's hope those agents have it more together than the ones who visited me the other day."

"They seemed to be real professional. But they kept Sheila's scrapbook."

"Why?"

"It's evidence."

"Really?"

"Well, I think it was in her room and everything. Maybe that's why, but we laughed and laughed about Sheila's scrapbook being evidence," Vera said, and laughed a bit more.

"Now, that is funny," Beatrice said, grinning

widely. "Have a good time at the awards ceremony tonight. And try to be careful."

"I feel so much safer knowing the FBI is here," Vera said.

"I understand that, but remain vigilant. Have you all talked to any more of the men on your list?"

"No. We haven't been able to find them yet. It's a huge ship. We were lucky to find who we did. We'll keep at it, though."

"Just make it a policy to stay away from single men on the ship. That ought to do."

"On more than one level, I'm sure," Vera said, and paused a beat. "I'm more concerned about Sharon Milhouse."

"Anything ever come of that? I mean did you find her? Is it the same one?"

"Nothing. The thought of her being on this ship freaks me out. But now the FBI is on it."

"Just a possibility that she'd be there, anyway—a very remote one, statistically speaking," Beatrice said.

"Oh Mama, you and your statistics," Vera said, and laughed. "But this time I like those odds. That woman scared me half to death. Steve too. Sheila didn't even know the half of it. But one morning Steve woke up with her in his bed. Completely naked, smeared with blood. Another time, she showed up in one of his classes with a gun. It turned out to be a fake. So many other stories. I'll fill you in when I get home."

"So what's on the docket for today?" Beatrice changed the subject.

"We're shopping this afternoon. We're heading back to Florida tomorrow. They shortened our land time to a day. We really want to take a look around. Then tonight is the award ceremony. Sheila's as excited as could be."

That thought warmed Beatrice. "The scrapbooking queen is excited? Imagine that," Beatrice said, and harrumphed.

"She's been offered several different jobs since she's been here."

"Jobs? Where? In Cumberland Creek?"

"No, I don't think so. Most of the companies are somewhere else, but she's talking about freelancing. One minute, Eric. I'm on the phone with Mama."

"Go ahead and go. Don't spend too much money shopping," Beatrice said, and hung up the phone. Well, Sheila had been offered some jobs. How fabulous was that?

Beatrice had no more than hung up her phone than it was ringing again.

"Hello," she said.

"Hey, Bea, it's Elsie."

"Yes? What can I help you with?"

"Well, I had some questions about the bazaar."

"And?"

"We've gotten three more vendors and one wants a specific table."

"It's our policy that we don't allow that. It's first come, first served that morning. You know that," Beatrice said.

"I know, but I'm trying to appease them."

"Blame it on me. You can tell them I'm a Grinch. I don't mind."

"If they are still interested, you're sure there'd be space?"

"Oh yes, plenty of space," Beatrice said, rolling her eyes. Lawd, the woman was driving her mad about the space issue. "I think I've told you that now about a million times. You need to relax about the damned space."

"Well, I'm sorry, Bea," she snapped. "I want everything to go smoothly. I don't want vendors coming back to us with complaints about space."

"Look," Beatrice said. "It's a charity event. If any of them complain about anything, then shame on them."

Elsie was silent for a moment, then laughed nervously, more like a twitter really. "You're right, and if any of them complain, I'll tell them just that."

"We need to keep reminding ourselves and the vendors that we are trying to raise funds for the hungry. We have plenty of hungry people right here in our area. That's why we are doing this—not to show off our products or whatever. People need to get a grip. It's friggin' Christmas," Beatrice said.

"Friggin' Christmas indeed," Elsie muttered.

Chapter 43

When Sheila woke up the next day, she was surprised to find that she'd fallen asleep in her evening gown. After spending half the day shopping in Grand Caymen and the evening at the awards banquet, she'd stretched out on her bed to unwind before getting ready for bed. Hmmm. And here she was. Completely dressed and made up. She struggled to get out of bed and glanced at herself in the mirror, laughing out loud. What a mess!

And last night she'd looked the prettiest she had ever looked, except for maybe her wedding day.

She had sat at the head table with all of the big designers and talked about design, trends, paper versus digital, and how many exciting changes were happening in their field. When the time for the award came, Sheila's heart had raced. She'd be speaking in front of two thousand people, those in the huge dining room and those in the other dining rooms who watched from monitors.

"We have a very special guest this evening. Sheila Rogers, who is the winner of our Creative Spirit Award, has been scrapbooking for thirty years. She has a successful home-based scrap-booking business and, I might add, she maintains a weekly crop along with running her household.

Did I mention she has four children?" Grace had said.

The audience had applauded.

"We've already told you about her design skill. You all know how talented she is. She's being honored tonight for those impressive skills, yes, but also her passion and determination. Thanks for coming aboard, Sheila!"

When Sheila stepped onto the small stage, after adjusting to the lights and the camera, she glimpsed herself on some big screens in the back of the room. She beamed. She cut a fine figure for a woman in her midforties. She blew a kiss at the crowd and they roared.

"Thank you all, thank you!" she said. "Thank you from the bottom of my heart." She was glistening in her dress and happier than she could remember. But the tears started then—and she'd never been a pretty crier. Soon, mascara was running down her cheeks and she became a snotty mess as she was whisked away by one of the nice young servers.

Now, she glanced at the clock. Did she have time for a run? She didn't have to meet the others for another two hours. She reached for her workout clothes. She would at least try.

Coming back from her run, she passed by Harold's room, which had a huge plastic sheet draped over the door. A person in a white suit with strange-looking head gear passed by her and entered the room. They must have found the source of the poison in Harold's room! That was sort of a relief.

After her shower, Sheila headed to the breakfast buffet, where all of her crew were already waiting. Some had plates already piled high with food. Randy's plate had huge Belgian waffles with whipped cream and strawberries. Goodness, the man could eat.

"Where've you been?" Paige asked.

"I'm only a few minutes late. I went for a run," Sheila said.

"Trip over anything?" Paige asked with a grin.

"Not this time—thanks for asking," Sheila shot back at her.

"You feeling okay?" Vera said, coming up to the table with a plate with an omelet and hash browns on it.

Sheila shrugged. "Not quite one hundred percent, but I'm getting there. You?"

Paige made a wavy hand gesture indicating she was so-so.

Sheila surveyed all the food and couldn't help but think of the poison possibilities. She told the others what she'd noticed earlier.

"I was hanging out in the kitchen last night," Randy said. "Turns out there was a lot of investigating and testing the food that we didn't know about. At least the food is perfectly safe. They knew within hours that it wasn't food poisoning."

"How did they know that?" Vera asked.

"They have a safety inspection team on board. The food testing is rigorous."

"Where did the poison come from then?" Paige asked.

"Evidently something in Harold's room," Sheila said, and turned her attention to the buffet. Suddenly she was ravenous.

"We were just talking about the crop before you arrived. It's going to be so much fun!" Randy said, then took a huge bite of waffle.

"I love Christmas-themed scrapbooking," Vera said, and sighed. "And I love Christmas since Elizabeth has come along. It's so much fun playing Santa."

"Love those dolls you bought her yesterday," Paige said.

"I want to capture each moment," Vera said wistfully. "Like my mama says, it's futile to try to stop time. But I say I can try to at least savor it."

"You can," Sheila said. "That's what we scrappers do."

Later, when the group entered the cropping room, it was like walking into a Christmas wonderland, complete with a Santa and elves. A live string quartet was playing Christmas music and there was fake glittering snow strewn about the room. Sheila was seized by a pang of home-sickness. Backdrops displayed quaint little towns decorated for the holidays. Cumberland Creek could have been one of those places. The cruise had created a winter Christmas scene for everybody here when Vera and the others already had the real thing at home waiting for them. Sheila shook it off as they arrived at their tables and set eyes on all of the wonderful crop goodies waiting for them.

"Welcome to the Scrap Your Christmas Crop," said the woman in the front of the room. "Do you know what one of the biggest challenges to scrapbooking your Christmas is? That's right. Someone said it over there." She pointed off to the left. "It's time. Well, we have a few pointers for you today as you scrapbook. Just a reminder, folks. I know some of you came from breakfast, but we have Christmas goodies at the food table. The tables will be full all day long."

Sheila had known that immediately, as when she walked into the room the scent of gingerbread, chocolate, and mint greeted her. But good Lord, she couldn't eat another bite after that breakfast.

"I think I'll spew if I eat one more thing," Vera said. She was already at work on a page. She was using one of the freebie papers, which was crimson, patterned with Christmas stars.

"You and me both," Sheila said. "Oh, I love this mulberry paper." She ran her fingers over the textured paper. She reached into her mini file folder and pulled out a photo of all four of her kids sitting in front of the Christmas tree and felt the gnawing of missing them.

"The first thing to do is decide what kind of scrapbooking you want to do. Are you adding a page or two every year to a Christmas scrapbook, or are you scrapbooking the entire season leading up to it?" their instructor said as people studied their photos and papers, some of them plunging into their layouts already.

"Okay, so that would be a bit mad," Paige said. "To scrapbook the whole season? Who has the time for that? I'm lucky to get done my two or three pages every year."

"I always thought it would be a fun challenge," Sheila said. "There are several bloggers out there who offer classes starting December first every year. They send you prompts and other fun stuff."

"I guess if you told yourself 'I'm going to sit down every day and do this,' it might work out," Vera said, holding up a glittering card stock snowflake and placing it on her page.

"If you're going to scrapbook the entire season, you need to be organized by December first. That means you have all of your supplies gathered and you have an idea of what time every day you'll give yourself to accomplish your goal," the teacher said over the speaker.

Paige groaned. "Who are these people? Do they not have lives? Jobs?"

Sheila placed her photo on green card stock.

Yes, she liked the green as a background color for the photo. She sliced the card stock and glued the photo to it. Now, what kind of paper would work best? She sorted through the new paper they were given and found an interesting red paper with a wreath pattern on it. She placed the photo in the middle of the page and then sorted through all of the embellishments they were given. Buttons. Snowflakes. Candy canes. Stickers. Card stock.

"Can I get you some coffee or hot chocolate?" a server asked.

Sheila looked up at a server dressed as an elf. "Coffee, please," she said, then noticed something odd about the table where the creepy guy had sat for every crop. It was completely empty. An irrational shiver traveled through Sheila.

Chapter 44

Beatrice stood along the wall of Elizabeth's preschool. The school was in the basement of the local Methodist church, even though it didn't have anything to do with the church. She smiled as the other adults lined up behind her. She was always the first in line to pick up Elizabeth. She couldn't wait to spend the afternoon with her grand-daughter.

When the teacher opened the door, she smiled at Beatrice. "Elizabeth, your grandmother is here," she said, and Elizabeth came out of the room, already dressed for the winter day, holding a crayon drawing she had done in class.

"Let's go home, Granny. We have some cookies to bake," Elizabeth said as she hugged her.

Beatrice's old heart melted a little every time Elizabeth hugged her.

"Okay, let's go," Beatrice said as they left the warm building and ventured into the cold for the block and a half walk home.

"How was your day?" Beatrice asked her.

"Good," she said. "We colored. I like to color."

"Me too," Beatrice said, and reached for her hand.

They walked up the first slope of the sidewalk and stood a minute to look at the white mountains against the blue sky.

"Mama's mountains," Elizabeth said.

Beatrice cackled. "Well, that's a nice way to think of them."

As they made their way, Beatrice noticed a man walking toward them. He was either new in town or perhaps just visiting. She'd never seen him before. But he looked odd—something about the way he held himself. Beatrice held Elizabeth's hand tighter as the man's gaze traveled to the child. Beatrice held her head up and said hello as he walked by. He nodded in return.

That reminded her to telephone Bryant to see if he'd found anything out about the stranger she had seen the other day. He probably wouldn't tell her, but she had to try.

The man who had just passed gave her the creeps. She couldn't say why. Maybe she was being paranoid, but she didn't like the way he looked at Elizabeth—almost like he knew her. She had learned throughout the years to trust her instincts.

Oh well, she noted as she followed the sidewalk toward home, he wasn't following them. He had gone on about his merry way. She sighed.

After they arrived at her house and were settled in, and before they started the cookies, Beatrice called Bryant.

"How can I help you?" he said.

"Did you ever find out who that strange man was?"

"Which strange man are we talking about, Beatrice?"

"The one I gave you the license plate number for."

"Oh, he was just some guy staying at the new B and B over on Magnolia."

"Of course!" she said. "I should have thought about that." Her old friend Lydia's house, which had been bequeathed to her daughter, Elsie, was now a bed and breakfast. There was much fuss in the neighborhood about it.

"I guess the parking was full until later and he was moving his car," Bryant said.

"Well, don't I feel like a fool," she said.

"Well, don't. He was a stranger in your neighborhood. And you'd just learned about the note left in Sheila's mailbox. Makes sense."

"Did you find out who did that?"

"Nope," he said with a clipped tone. He was either unhappy that she asked the question or unhappy that he hadn't found the answer.

"I'll let you get to it then."

"Beatrice, keep your ear to the ground. If you hear or see anything odd, please let me know," he said.

"Okay," she said, and hung up the phone. Oh bother, maybe she should have told him about that odd bird of a man she ran across today—but then she chided herself. She could get paranoid over this thing. The world was full of strange people, even in Cumberland Creek. Lawd. If she thought about all the strange characters she called her friends, that could give her a start.

There was old shifty-eyed Max Kruegar, one of the sweetest men she'd ever known. But he'd never look you in the eye; in fact his eyes always shifted around so it appeared he was up to no good. If someone saw him on the street, they might turn around and call the cops.

Oh, and then there was Penny, who had this odd giggle; every time she said something, she'd follow it with a giggle. It didn't have to be funny. In fact, most of the time it wasn't. She giggled out of nervousness because she was so shy. Someone might think her a crazy person escaped from the local hospital.

Then of course, there was her: Beatrice Matthews. She'd heard what people said about her. Most of it was true. She was quarrelsome and opinionated. At one point in her life, she had a relationship with the ghost of her husband and she believed you could manipulate time. Brilliant, but strange, people said. Hmph. She guessed she should settle down a bit about looking for strange people. What could you tell from the way someone looked, anyway?

Chapter 45

Sheila, Vera, Paige, Randy, and Eric stood on the deck of the *Jezebel* and took in the sea and sky one more time before heading to the airport.

"I'll never forget the way the sky looks here. The color, the light," Sheila said. "I'm so glad you all came." She wrapped her arm around Vera. "You too." She wrapped her other arm around Eric. "Stick around, Eric, for more craziness."

She was so thrilled that they'd made up last night while Vera was in the powder room.

"I've been thinking," she said. "I hope you'll accept my apologies for what I said the other day. I'm really happy that you are in Vera's life."

"I'd like to apologize, too," he said to her, leaning in and grinning. "I'll try to be aware of girl time." He kissed her cheek.

"Thanks for bringing us along," Paige said to Sheila. "It was . . . an experience. But I really can't wait to get home."

"Oh, I know. I miss Lizzie and Mama and the mountains and the snow," Vera said. "But this has been a once in a lifetime trip. Of course, we could have done without the murders."

Sheila grimaced. "I hear ya."

"You know, I wish I could have continued with my investigation, talking with all the single men," Paige said. "I felt so ill. But it was fun pretending to be single for a while."

"Mother!" Randy said.

She shrugged and walked toward the elevator. "Your mother still has it going on," she said, looking over her shoulder. "Deal with it, Randy!" She laughed and Randy grinned.

"Well, all right then," he said, grinning and following her.

Once at the airport, the group navigated their way through security and on to the plane without much ado. Within a few hours, they were back to Virginia, with its snowy mountains welcoming them from the air, offering their own beauty and light. Sheila once again found herself amused by travel—a few hours ago she stood on the deck of the *Jezebel* overlooking a beautiful glassy sea.

Now they circled the Blue Ridge Mountains, waiting for clearance to land.

She should have been thrilled to be getting home. A part of her was, of course, but she still had lingering strange feelings about the cruise. She supposed she'd get over it at some point, but tripping over Allie, finding out she was murdered, being questioned by the FBI, them keeping her scrapbook for evidence—it was a lot to process. Not to mention that the name Sharon Milhouse had come up. That brought back horrible memories that she hadn't thought about in a long time. Of course, it had to be another Sharon. The Sharon she knew was sick and in the Richmond Institution. Or at least that was the last she'd heard of her.

"So which job are you going to take?" Vera said.

"I won't be working for Theresa Graves, I can tell you," Sheila responded. "After all that heckling. And she was standing there with that weird dude."

"Wonder what happened to him," Vera said. "I didn't see him at all after we left the island. Maybe he stayed there."

"As long as he's away from me, I don't care where he is," Sheila said.

"I just have to say wow, my eyes have been opened to the scrapbooking industry," Paige said. "It's so competitive. Who would have thought?"

Sheila thought a moment. "I suppose you have

that in every business. Allie seemed to be the type to pay it forward. She loved my designs and seemed like she was really interested in helping me along."

"It's a shame what happened to her," Randy said. "I hope they find her killer."

"Now that the FBI is involved, maybe they will," Vera said.

Except for Randy, who had to get back to his job in New York City, the group had a two-hour drive from Dulles International Airport to Cumberland Creek, where their families all waited with bated breath.

When Steve opened the door to their home, Sheila fell into his arms and unraveled. It was too much. Too much. All of this: the excitement, the murder, being away from home. She enjoyed being respected for her work, but she hadn't realized how much she missed home and her husband until that very minute.

"So glad you're back," Steve said.

Jonathon came running through the hallway and attached himself to both of them. "I missed you, Mama!"

Two of their other kids were sitting at the kitchen table and barely rose to give her a hug. High schoolers. They were way too cool to make a fuss over their mother. But Sheila could see it in their eyes. They were glad she was home, too.

She surveyed her house. Things looked pretty

good. The boys had kept up with the housework, though, of course, the place still needed a good vacuum and dusting, and she didn't even want to look at the laundry or in the pantry. She knew Steve hated grocery shopping.

"I missed you, babe," Steve said to her later as they readied for bed. "How are you feeling?"

"I'm feeling better," she said. "I missed you, too."

Steve was already in bed and he lifted the blanket and nodded for her to snuggle up. Which she did. Quite happily.

Chapter 46

Annie tossed and turned most of the night. Mary was still on her mind and she dreamed of her and her father. The one person involved with the case that she hadn't talked with was Mary's mother, who refused to talk to her. Period. But Annie dreamed of her, too, the woman whose husband abused her daughter. What must she be going through? Then her dreams shifted to Hannah. Young and sweet and leaving for New York City. Talk about leading the lambs to slaughter.

After the boys had gotten off to school and she was clearing away the breakfast dishes, Paige called her.

"We're ba-ack," Paige said in a sing-song voice.

"How are you and what's been going on in Cumberland Creek?"

"I'm fine, and Cumberland Creek has not been the same since you all left," Annie said. It was true—at least for her. She was glad they were off the ship and home. Now they could put the murders behind them and get on with life.

"Did you get your book done?" Paige asked.

"I'm polishing it a bit before I send it off to the publisher," Annie said. "Did they solve the murder?"

"No," Paige said. "The FBI talked with Sheila and Vera and that's the last we heard of it. Now how about that strange postcard in Sheila's mailbox? Did they find out who left it?"

"No. The trouble is Steve and Sheila were both gone when it was left. When he came home, the postcard was in the mailbox. They have no idea how long it had been there, only that it wasn't there when either one of them left."

"Maybe it was there longer than they knew," Paige said.

"Steve's been working with Bryant on this," Annie said. "I'm sure he told him that." She placed the last dish in the dishwasher. "How was the cruise, other than the murders?"

Paige sighed. "It was good to get away with Randy. I'm hoping he comes home. He's thinking of changing jobs. I think he wants to leave the city."

"That would be awesome," Annie said. "How would Earl feel about that?"

"I'm not sure," Paige said. "We're making progress."

"Did you learn any new scrapbooking techniques?"

"Oh yes. I'm sure we'll get to that during the crop this Saturday," Paige said. "It was really scrapbooking overkill." She laughed.

"How is Sheila?" Annie asked after a moment.

Paige paused. "I really don't know. She seems fine. But she has definitely been spooked by all of this. Imagine tripping over a dead body. Any dead body, let alone a woman you respect and admire. Then the concussion put a damper on the next few days. I could tell she wasn't feeling well. But she still managed to get a few job offers."

"Freelance?" Annie said. That, of course, is what Sheila had been hoping for. But Annie had warned her about it—people often had misconceptions when it came to freelancing. It was not as easy as it sounded and some of these work-for-hire contracts—at least for writers—were bad news. She hoped that Sheila hadn't signed anything yet.

"I think she's going to work with David's Designs. She'll have to make monthly trips to New York, but most of her work will be done from home," Paige said.

"David's Designs? Wow," Annie said, sitting

down at the kitchen table and fingering her new art journal. She loved this. It had become a ritual every morning to sit and work on this journal. She was producing something totally new for herself. It was so satisfying. And she was also keeping up with her Hanukkah scrapbook. She would have a lot to share with her friends on Saturday night.

After Annie and Paige said good-bye, Annie worked more on her art journal. This time, the word she painted on the page was "Home." Traditional images of home and hearth played through her mind. But she drew waves. Waves upon waves.

When she was finished with her page, she went to her computer and checked e-mail. She noted that her request for the death report of Allie had been sent. She shrugged internally; now that her friends were home, she wasn't certain she cared about the murder that much. But the report might be interesting to look over. She clicked on the pdf file and printed out the two reports.

Then the phone rang. It was a call from the boys' school.

"Mrs. Chamovitz?"

"Yes," she replied, thinking, *What now?*

"This is Beverly Adams, the school nurse. Ben is sick. He has a very sore and red throat and a temperature," she said. "It may be strep. It's going around the school."

Poor, sweet Ben. And damn, there goes my day,

she thought. "I'll be right there to pick him up. Thanks."

After she dressed, she called their pediatrician for an appointment. Annie found herself hoping it was strep because antibiotics could help and within twenty-four hours her kids often bounced back. She hated for him to be sick at Hanukkah.

As she was leaving her home and thinking about the holiday, with snow coming down and all of her neighbors' homes decorated, she once again thought about Hannah and made a mental note to send her a care package when she got to New York. Or maybe even visit her, if she could swing it.

When she finally saw her boy in the nurse's office and how sick he looked, fear rolled through her. He was green. What had happened? He'd been healthy when she sent him off this morning—at least she thought so. This had come over him so suddenly. He stood and fell into Annie's arms. And then threw up all over her.

Chapter 47

It was lunch time before Vera came padding down Beatrice's stairs and into the kitchen.

"Good morning," Jon said.

"Hmph, it stopped being morning about an hour ago," Beatrice said. "Good to see you're still alive."

"Thanks," Vera mumbled. "Do I smell coffee?"

"Yes, indeed. Sit down, Vera," Jon said.

"We just finished lunch. Plenty left," Beatrice said, and pointed to the chicken noodle soup she'd made with the leftovers of the previous night's chicken dinner.

"Oh, that looks good," Vera said. Jon brought her a bowl of the soup and her mother brought her a plate of biscuits. The two of them sat down at the table with her.

"You look great. Very tan," Jon said.

Vera smiled. "Thanks. I feel pretty good except I'm worried about Sheila. She's not herself."

"Of course not. A concussion is nothing to mess around with, then add to it all the trauma. . . ." Beatrice said.

"Have they found out who killed that poor woman and her lover?" Jon asked.

"I don't think so," Vera said. "But you know there were some very strange goings on. Mmm. The soup is so good. It almost feels, I don't know, cleansing, after all the food I've gorged myself on."

"What do you mean by 'strange'?" Beatrice asked, leaning in a bit closer as she placed her elbows on the table.

"Well, the security guy thinks he's a vampire, for one thing," Vera blurted.

"What?" Jon and Beatrice said at the same time.

"Apparently, he told Randy this. You see, they went on this date."

Beatrice didn't know how to react to this. Of course the man must be certifiably crazy. She couldn't find words.

"Nonsense," Jon said after a few beats. "There's no such thing as vampires. If the man was serious, you must report this back to the company. He's not right in the head."

The words "no such thing as vampires" rolled around in Beatrice's old brain. That's what people always said about ghosts, too. And she knew they existed. Her husband's ghost had been with her up until a few years ago. Even now, though she couldn't see him like she used to, sometimes she still smelled him or felt him close to her. But vampires? That was a different matter. She remembered reading about people who thought they were vampires. Wasn't it a syndrome? Yes, she remembered—it was called Renfield's syndrome.

"But like Sheila said, if the man thinks he's a vampire, he may think he needs to kill," Vera said.

"Did you tell the investigators all of this?" Beatrice asked.

"I didn't know it at the time. I did tell them about Theresa Graves," Vera said, and dipped her spoon back into the bowl.

"Who?" Jon asked.

"She was a woman on the cruise. She's a big-time scrapbooker. Sheila had a meeting with her. And anyway, she came to our photo class on the island and she and this creepy guy heckled Sheila," Vera said. "So I told the agents about it. They seemed pleased. They wrote it all down."

"Heckled Sheila?" Beatrice said. "What?" It seemed that not everybody liked Sheila after all.

"Very juvenile," Vera said.

"And just plain weird. Why would a grown person do such a thing?" Beatrice said.

Vera shrugged. "You know, I asked myself that a lot on this cruise."

"I told you they were nothing but trouble," Beatrice said.

"I know you did. But we're home safe and sound. So at least there's that," Vera said, and took a large drink of her coffee.

"Between the weird security chief and the backbiting competitive scrapbookers, not to mention the juvenile ones, and all of the drinking, it was quite an eye opener. My God, the excess. And then the mention of Sharon Milhouse made me feel, I don't know, creeped out, or something," Vera said. "I'm so ready for a peaceful, relaxing Christmas break."

Jon and Beatrice exchanged looks of concern.

"What?" Vera said. "What else is going on? Don't tell me there's been another murder!"

"No, now calm down," Beatrice said. "Sheila

doesn't know this yet, but when Steve came home a few days after they both had left, he found a threatening postcard in their mailbox."

"What kind of threat? I mean, what did it say?" Vera said, her brows knitting.

"'Die, die, die, scrapbook queen,'" Beatrice said.

Vera gasped.

"There was something else on the note. Bryant is checking it out and the forensics team in Richmond is looking at it. It may have been blood," Beatrice said.

"Blood?" Vera paled.

"I've talked with Steve and Bryant about it. We're all wondering who would have it in for Sheila."

"Bryant? You talked with Detective Bryant?"

"Hmph. More than I wanted to," Beatrice said, sitting back and crossing her arms. "But he hasn't been too cocky these days."

"That's suspicious in and of itself," Vera said. "Does Sheila know about any of this?"

Beatrice shrugged. "I don't know if Steve's told her about it yet. But we decided not to tell her while she was on the cruise. Thought she had enough to think about."

Vera thought a moment. "Maybe so," she said. "As far as I know, Sheila has no enemies. Unless it's someone from afar that we know nothing about. I mean, I know everybody she does. I can't think of anyone except Sharon and that was so many years ago."

"I suppose Bryant is looking for her," Jon said.

Beatrice nodded. "I hope he finds her, too."

Vera's spoon clanked on her bowl as she scooped up the last of her soup. "I'm sure he will. I'm sure she's somewhere far away and there's nothing at all to worry about. I'm putting it completely out of my mind. It's Christmas and a joyful time of the year. I'm going to do my best to give Lizzie a good one."

Beatrice stopped herself from rolling her eyes at her only daughter. Try as she had over the years to vanquish the Scarlett O'Hara streak Vera had, it had never gone away. Sometimes she could almost see her daughter as Vivien Leigh, putting off today what she could do tomorrow.

It had served Vera well most of her life. This time Beatrice wasn't so sure.

Chapter 48

Sheila had just finished hanging all the Christmas wreaths in her windows. She stepped out into the front yard to see if she had them all straight. She had a very good eye for straight. The wreath that hung in Jonathon's bedroom window seemed a bit off. She went back in, walked up the steps to his room, and fixed the wreath. When she came back down, Steve was sitting on the couch reading the newspaper. One of the great things about his business was that he sometimes had a lot of time on his hands and could spend a lot of it with her.

"What are you doing, hon?" he said.

"Working on my wreaths," she said.

"Ever hear of a day of rest?"

"You know me better than that," she said, leaned down and kissed him. "Be right back."

She went outside again, welcoming the cold. Being in the Caribbean sun had felt unnatural to her. She walked to the edge of her yard and looked at her house. Each wreath in each window appeared fine. But something was off. She stood there a moment, trying to put her finger on what it was. Her house was the same, but it also somehow looked different. It wasn't simply the Christmas decorations she had added. Something was missing. Her old butter churn was gone!

She took a deep breath. Maybe Steve had done something with it.

"Steve?" she yelled toward the house.

It was a butter churn she had found at a yard sale a few years back. She had painted it and sat it on her front porch. It had been sitting there for years. She started to walk toward the house and a dark figure caught her eye as it moved around the corner. She caught a glimpse of the face—it couldn't be! It was the creepy man from the cruise! She was certain.

What was he doing here? Well, damn if she wasn't going to find out! He was on her turf now. She started to take off after him when her husband came out onto the porch.

"What?" he said.

She kept moving.

"Where the hell are you going?" Steve chased after her.

All her years of running were going to do her good. She'd catch him and force him to tell her what he wanted with her. Why was he in Cumberland Creek?

"There's a man," Sheila said. "I just saw him."

She ran to the end of her street, her heart thrumming, blood rushing. Where did he go? She scanned Ivy Lane. Nobody was out. A car passed. She didn't recognize the driver.

Steve caught up with her and grabbed her shoulder. "What's going on?"

She explained about the creepy man on the cruise and how she'd seen him.

"Here?" he said. He seemed incredulous. "Did you get a good look?"

Mrs. Blackburn came walking down the street and smiled at them. "How do?" she said.

"Did you see a man dressed in a long dark coat?" Sheila asked.

"No," she said. "I've not seen anybody out. Right before supper for most folks, I guess. Merry Christmas, if I don't see you before."

"Same to you," said Steve.

Damn! thought Sheila. *Where did he go?*

"Sheila, let's go back in the house and talk about this. I don't see anybody at all. Are you certain you saw someone?"

She nodded as he led her back to their house. She stopped in front of it.

"Steve, what happened to my butter churn?" she said.

"Your what?"

"My butter churn. You remember, I painted it green with daisies down the front of it. We had it sitting on the front porch for years," she said.

He looked off toward their porch. "I don't know," he said. "I didn't even know it was missing."

"Someone took my butter churn? Right off the porch?"

"We haven't been home," he said. "Maybe we should have secured it elsewhere. I didn't even think about it. Bryant asked me if anything was missing and I told him no."

"Bryant?" Sheila said.

"Sheila, I've been waiting for the right time to tell you this. Let's go inside. Seems like you've got something to tell me, too. Who is this man you think you saw?"

Sheila took a deep breath and told her husband about the man on the cruise ship.

Steve reddened and looked like he was about to explode, but then took a deep breath. "Sheila, I'm so glad you're home. I didn't like you being gone. Not one bit," he said, and hugged her.

She didn't tell him that she'd almost accepted a job that would require her to travel to New York City once a month. Oh, she wanted that job so bad she could taste it. Working for David's Designs would be a dream come true.

"What's on your mind, Steve? What is it that you need to tell me?"

He then filled her in on the postcard.

She watched her husband's mouth form the words. And though she heard what he was saying, it somehow refused to sink in.

Die, die, die, scrapbook queen.

"Sheila?" he said after a few minutes.

Her chest pressed heavy against her lungs. She gasped for air and fell back on the couch. "Who?" she managed to say.

"We just don't know," Steve said. "Bryant sent it to the crime lab in Richmond. I didn't realize anything was missing. I better call him. Are you okay?"

Sheila nodded. But she wasn't certain she was. What was happening to her well-constructed and controlled life? She'd done everything that was expected of her and more. She was a good wife and mother, a volunteer in the classroom and community, and she had built a good business based on good products and a solid reputation. She thought she was well liked. But lately she wondered. And it had all begun when she won that scrapbooking contest. She was in the news—everywhere—and some people seemed genuinely pleased for her. Others had developed an attitude with her, like they thought she had gone beyond her upbringing. She had caught the looks and heard the chatter. She tried not to pay attention to it. But now it seemed she would have to. Some-one had stolen her butter churn and placed a threatening note in her mailbox. She would have to fill out a police report.

Beyond all that, no matter what Steve believed, she was certain she'd seen the man from the *Jezebel* walking down Ivy Lane today.

Chapter 49

"That's crazy," Annie said when Vera told her that Sheila thought she saw the creepy man from the cruise. "Don't you think?"

"Stranger things have happened," Vera said. "But I do think it's a stretch, even though the man seemed to be infatuated with Sheila for most of the cruise. I mean, he stared at her. Then all of a sudden he was with that Theresa, who was heckling Sheila. Then we never saw him again."

"Maybe he wasn't infatuated. Maybe he didn't like her at all," Annie said. "And we know Theresa doesn't like her."

"Well, whatever; Sheila noticed it and it made her uneasy even before she tripped over Allie," Vera said.

"How is Sheila's head?" Annie asked.

"Still bruised. But she said she was feeling better. I tell you, Annie, I'm so glad to be home. First the murder, then the storm, then the heckling."

"But what about the rest of the cruise?"

"Eh," Vera said. "The food was good. And so was the scrapbooking. I've been using doilies and making some great patterns on my pages. We also learned about gels, chalks, paints. It was fun. And it was awesome seeing Sheila get that award. She was glowing that night, you know? All these years of hard work . . ."

"I'm sorry I missed that. But you all took pictures, right?"

"Of course. By the way, Annie, happy Hanukkah."

"Thanks. We've had some wonderful evenings. My Hanukkah scrapbook is filling up."

"I can't wait to see it. You are coming on Saturday?"

"Yep."

"Mommy!" Ben cried. He had been sleeping and awoke suddenly.

"I gotta go," Annie said, and turned to find her son walking toward her, drenched in sweat. He didn't have strep, but the doctor thought it could be the flu and they were still waiting for the test results. He fell into her arms, burning with fever. She glanced at the clock—it was time for another round of ibuprofen.

"Sit down, sweetie," Annie said. "I'll get you some water and some medicine."

He curled up on the couch. By the time she brought the water and pills to him, he was softly snoring. Poor boy. She gently shook him awake to take the pill, which he did before promptly falling back asleep. She grabbed the throw from the back of her couch and wrapped her boy up in it.

Her phone rang again. It was the school nurse. Sam had come down with the same thing, apparently. "I'll try to get there soon. But I need to find someone to stay with Ben."

"Understood. We'll keep him in here on the cot until you come for him. He's not going anywhere," the nurse said.

Beatrice and Vera were out of the question. That afternoon was Elizabeth's Christmas concert at her preschool. DeeAnn was working. She called Sheila, who said she'd be happy to come right over.

When Annie opened the door, she was surprised to see Sheila looking so pale—and the bump on her head was still there, quite visible.

"Thanks for coming, Sheila," Annie said. "I shouldn't be long. Your bump is still there?"

Sheila nodded. "It's much smaller than it was, believe me."

"I can't wait to catch up," Annie said. "But I've got to run."

"I'll be here," Sheila said, and stepped forward into the foyer. "Don't worry about us."

"Okay." Annie turned to leave and then shut the door. She heard the clicking of the lock. Odd. Sheila must still be a bit spooked.

But as she headed to her car, she spotted a man walking by her house and looking it over with some interest. Annie's reporter instincts kicked in.

"Can I help you?" she said, her eyes locked on him. He looked up at her, surprised. He shook his head and shrugged.

She walked toward him. "Do you need some help? Directions?"

He kept walking. "I'm going for a walk, enjoying the day," he said, and then moved quickly away.

Annie stood on her sidewalk and watched him disappear around the corner. Who the hell was that? Was that the man Sheila thought was her creepy guy from the cruise? He *was* creepy—soft looking, with watery brown shifty eyes, and wearing a ski hat, long black coat, and boots. This man did not belong in the neighborhood. Waves of fear rolled through her as her heart thumped against her chest.

She took a deep breath. In the meantime, she had to pick up Sam from school and get back home to tend her two sick boys. But if this was the man Sheila had witnessed wandering the streets earlier, Annie could see why she was freaked out.

Soon she had both of her sick, feverish sons home, each in his own bed with a bucket next to him. *Please, God, don't let them throw up again.*

She walked out to her living room, where Sheila was perched, watching television and eating fresh rum cake that she had brought over with her. Annie told her about the man she'd observed.

Sheila's jaw dropped. "I told them! I told all of them. He's here! I know that's him."

"Just a minute, Sheila. Stop and think. Why would he be here, in Cumberland Creek?"

"I have no idea . . . unless he wants me . . . wants me for some perverse reason," Sheila said, dropping her cake onto the plate.

"He came all the way from Florida so he could stalk you?" Annie said, trying to calm Sheila. But she knew stalkers had done worse and gone further for their victims. Annie sat back and lifted a cup of tea that Sheila had made to her lips. She was pleased that it was still warm.

Sheila's shoulders dropped. "I suppose it does sound a little crazy. But if that's not him, the guy really looks like him. I saw him for five days straight on the cruise. He was at the next crop table over. Almost every time I looked up, he was staring at me. It wasn't like, I don't know, a nice stare. It was full of hatred."

"Why would the man hate you?" Annie asked.

"I've asked myself that question," she said, and

253

flung her arms up. "But people are crazy. Look at what happened to poor Allie. I don't know why anybody would want to kill her."

"But you didn't know her that well, Sheila," Annie pointed out. "Who knows what she was really like, what she was involved in, and so on?"

"Whatever it was, she certainly should not have been killed for it," Sheila said. "I was shocked by the competitive nature of some of these big scrapbookers. But I really can't see any of them as killers."

Annie nodded in agreement, then said, "But come to think of it, if there's one thing I've learned over the years it's that human nature is so complicated. I'm usually surprised to find out who killers actually are."

"You know, that's true," Sheila said. "Sometimes it really is the boy or girl next door."

Chapter 50

Beatrice marveled at her granddaughter's rendition of "Silent Night." The child could sing. Where did she get that from? And what's more, to have the courage to stand up in front of a whole church full of mostly strangers? My, my, my. Tears pricked at Beatrice's eyes. Jon knew it; as if by psychic connection, he placed his arm around her in a comforting gesture.

She leaned into Vera's ear. "We need to get her voice lessons."

Vera waved her off and smiled. But Beatrice would see to it. Yes, she would.

She mentally checked off all the things she had to do before tomorrow's bazaar. She thought she had it under control. But that Lizzy. Oh, sweet Lawd, what she did to Beatrice's old heart. Her brain couldn't think quite clearly enough right now. She was swimming in a glowing sea of grandmotherness.

After the show, the preschool had cookies and drinks for the family members. As Beatrice took in the crowd, she noticed only a few families she didn't know. But everybody looked at least a little familiar. She was certain if she asked some of the folks she didn't recognize, she'd at least know their people.

"Nice tree," Jon said, tilting his head in the direction of a completely white tree with red ribbons tied around it.

"I prefer natural trees," she said. "Who ever heard of a white tree? Besides I like my Christmas to smell like Christmas. And that includes having a live pine tree."

"I like any color tree, especially my pink one," Vera said, coming up beside her mother.

"Hmph," Beatrice said. "Where's Elizabeth?"

"She and Eric are getting more cookies. You know, I think she likes him."

"Too bad that Bill couldn't make it," replied Beatrice.

"I know, Mama, and it's getting to be more and more like that. He doesn't seem interested in this kind of thing. He had to administer a test or something today. Last day of classes."

"Hmph. Well, it was sure a nice little concert," Beatrice said, not wanting to dwell on the missing father of the year.

Beatrice and Jon then said their good-byes and went home. As they were walking, tiny little flakes of snow began falling.

"Just lovely," Jon said. "I love the snow here."

"Me too," Beatrice said.

When they rounded the corner, she noticed a couple of men standing at her gate. One had his hands on his hips and was looking up and down the sidewalk.

"I know who that is," she said.

"Now, Bea, let us comport ourselves," Jon said.

"Comport? The FBI comes to my house with false information—"

"Hush, my love," Jon said, holding up his finger to his mouth. "It wasn't their mistake. It was the cruise security error. Be nice."

They walked up to the gate and opened it.

"Can I help you?" Beatrice said.

"I'm—"

"I know who you are," Beatrice said. "What do you want?"

"We wondered if you have the time to answer a few questions," one of the agents said.

"I do—but not much. It's a few days until Christmas, you know."

Jon moved ahead and unlocked the front door, letting the group stream in to Beatrice's Victorian house.

After they were situated in her living room, one agent asked her if she had kept the death report she'd received the day they delivered it.

"No, sir. I threw it in the trash where it belongs," she said, trying not to be too bitter or brusque sounding, which was a challenge to be sure.

"Have you put the trash out for the local authority?"

"Yes, he came yesterday and carried it all away."

"I was afraid of that," one of them said.

"Did you happen to read it at all?" the other man said.

Beatrice thought a moment. Did she? "No, I don't believe I did. What's the problem?"

"There may have been some discrepancies on the two reports. We're following up, investigating Ahoy Security," one explained.

"It's about time someone investigated them. Do you know the chief of security thinks he's a vampire?" Beatrice said.

One man coughed; the other's jaw clenched as if he was trying not to laugh.

"No, ma'am, we did not."

Chapter 51

Sheila had just sat down on her couch when the doorbell rang.

"I'll get it," Steve yelled in at her.

She heard the sound of the door opening. "Detective Bryant," her husband said. "How can we help you?"

Bother! What was he doing here? She only wanted to sit and enjoy her Christmas tree.

"Can I talk to Sheila?" she heard him say. Damn, she'd had enough questions and lawmen to last a lifetime.

"She's right in here," her husband said.

"Sheila," Bryant said.

"Detective Bryant," she replied. "Please sit down. Can I get you anything? Water? Soda?"

"No, I'm all right and I'm here on business, actually."

"What kind of business?"

"I need to ask you a few questions about this Allie person who was on the cruise you were on."

"What? I thought this was behind me. I'd rather not talk about it."

He pulled out a photo. "Is this your scrap-book?"

"Yes, it is. Am I ever going to get it back?"

"You've got more to worry about than getting your scrapbook back," he said.

Steve sat down next to Sheila and put his arm around her.

"I do?"

"After you left Florida, an FBI agent died," he said.

Sheila, stunned and wondering what this had to do with her, said nothing.

"They ascertained quickly that he had been poisoned the same way the other two victims had been. With ricin. Have you ever heard of that?" Bryant asked.

"I may have," Sheila said after a moment.

"It was in the news a few times," Steve added. "But what's this got to do with Sheila?"

"They finally figured out the murder weapon used on Allie and Harold because of this agent collapsing from the same thing," Bryant said.

"Weapon? You said it was poison. I don't understand," Sheila said, flustered.

"Your scrapbook is filled with ricin. As far as we can tell, anybody who touched it has been killed," Bryant said.

Sheila gasped. "What?" Her favorite scrapbook! The one she poured her heart and soul into! The one she'd been so hungry to get back! How could it be poisoned?

"How can that be? Sheila handled it and she's fine," Steve said. "Right, honey?"

She nodded. "I made it right here in my base-ment. But I sent it off to the judges and didn't see it again until after I boarded the *Jezebel*."

"Did you touch it after you were on board?" Bryant asked.

Sheila thought a moment. Did she? It was in a plastic envelope. Did she take it off before she gave it to Allie?

"I, ah, can't remember," she said.

"What do you mean you can't remember?" Steve said.

"Well, I . . ." She swallowed hard. "It was wrapped in a plastic sleeve or envelope or something. I don't remember if I took it out or not before I handed it to Allie."

"Think, Sheila," Bryant said.

"I'm fairly certain I never took it out of the envelope," she said.

"Fairly certain?" Bryant prompted.

She nodded, her heart racing and sweat starting to prick at her forehead.

"You don't look well," Bryant said.

"Well, I—" she started to say.

"Look, I know this is harsh news for you," he said. "My job is not an easy one sometimes, Ms. Rogers. But I have a search warrant for your house and a crew outside to perform the search."

"What are you looking for?" She couldn't think. Her thoughts swirled around in her head. None of them made sense.

"We're looking for ricin," the detective said.

"In my home? You think that I . . ." She trailed off as Steve placed his hand on her leg.

"You're more than welcome to look through our home. You won't find any poison here," Steve said. His voice was flat and strong. It was soothing to Sheila.

"You can say that again," she said.

"And yet your scrapbook was loaded with it." Detective Bryant stood. "I'm sorry. I need to let them in."

Sheila watched as Bryant opened the door and a group of people dispersed throughout her home, decorated to the hilt for Christmas.

Chapter 52

"Depending on the route of exposure, such as injection, as little as five hundred micrograms of ricin could be enough to kill an adult. A dose of that amount would be about the size of the head of a pin. A much greater amount would be needed to kill people if the ricin were inhaled or swallowed," the voice on the other end of the phone reported.

"What about touching it?" Annie asked. "What about through the skin?"

"You'd get a nasty redness, maybe a rash. But how people get poisoned, of course, is touching it and then eating with their hands. Or licking their fingers as they flip pages or something. Then it's a matter of time."

"How long?" Annie asked.

"Depends on how strong the dose is. I've seen people who have died within two or three hours. But they ingested a huge amount of the stuff."

"Okay," Annie said. "Thanks, Frank."

"No problem," he said. "If you have any other questions, give me a call."

Ricin.

Annie could hardly believe that the police had searched Sheila Rogers's home for ricin. Of course, they didn't find anything. And of course, Sheila was a nervous wreck, although relieved that they didn't find poison in her home.

Annie began leafing through a pile of mail and papers.

Here were the death reports she wanted to see. Both of them: the first one and the final one. She sat them side by side on her kitchen table and compared them. Only a few differences existed in them: the names and addresses being the biggest. The type appeared the same; one wasn't aligned with the form boxes as well as the other. Maybe the printer was off a bit.

But something else was off. She looked at each from the bottom up, comparing the two documents. She had learned to look at documents like this from the bottom up from a professional proofreader. It scrambled your brain enough to make you pick up on things rather than your eye slipping over it.

There. There it was.

Sheila Rogers: time of death 5:30

Allison Monroe: time of death 5:38

Odd. That was an awfully big disparity between the two reports.

Could be a typo. God knows the ship's security team was careless. But she didn't have to be careless. She picked up the phone.

"Bryant."

"Hey, it's Annie," she said.

"I know that," he clipped. "What can I do for you?"

She explained the discrepancy she found. "What do you think?"

"I think Ahoy Security has more explaining to do. I'm going to check into them a little further. You know, I have those same reports and didn't notice that. Thanks."

"What does it mean?" Annie persisted.

"I don't know," he said. "I don't know if it means anything different from what we already know, which is that someone messed up the report."

"I think it means something else, but I'm not sure what," Annie said.

"When you figure it out, let me know," he said, and paused. "It's not really my case or my business, but I keep thinking there's a link between the threatening note and this. And I don't think Shelia Rogers is a killer."

Annie breathed a mental sigh of relief. You could never tell about Adam Bryant. He went about his job in a cold, calculating manner most of the time. He was not easily read. When he didn't don the detective mask, in his personal life, he had no control over himself.

"Does the FBI?" Annie said.

"I have no idea what those guys think. I imagine they are investigating Ahoy as well. I might be able to find out. But I do know that Sheila is a person of interest, not a suspect. At this time."

Annie's stomach twisted.

"Frankly, I don't think anybody would be paying that much attention except that one of their guys was killed. One of their own," he said.

"But that Allie woman was a pretty famous scrapbooker," Annie said.

"Famous scrapbooker? What the hell does that mean to most people?"

"But she was the one killed. Maybe the others were accidents."

"Or maybe the scrapbook was really meant for Sheila," he said. "Maybe someone wanted to kill her."

Annie sucked in the air. Why hadn't she thought of that possibility? "Who would want to kill Sheila?" she said more to herself than to him.

"Maybe the same person who left the note? Nobody dislikes her? How can you go through life and not make an enemy or two?"

"Well, apparently she did—that Sharon Milhouse."

"Yep, but I lost her. I can't find her anywhere. She was released earlier this year. Her husband is now dead, so we have no idea what went on there. Nobody knows where she's at. I've called her caseworker, left several messages. Maybe I'll give her another call."

"Can you let me know? We're so concerned about Sheila. She's taking this so personally," Annie said. The more she thought about it, the more she thought it was ridiculous that Sheila might have been the intended victim.

"I can't make any promises," Bryant said. "But I will try."

The phone call left Annie with a feeling of lightness. She and Adam had really sorted it out and it hadn't gotten personal. Maybe there was hope that they could put the awkward feelings behind them and have some sort of professional relationship.

When she thought about the fact they had almost had an affair, it made her cringe. It also made her grateful that she was strong enough in her commitment to Mike that she could stop herself from acting on that base attraction to Adam Bryant.

Chapter 53

Beatrice's craft bazaar to fund the local food bank was in full swing. The ladies on the committee all behaved—much to Beatrice's surprise. A steady stream of customers came into the church hall and paid their five dollars or left a bag of canned goods at the front desk. Either way, the food bank would profit. Each of the vendors paid fifty dollars to set up and was giving the food bank 40 percent of the profit.

She took a break after collecting at the front door for a couple of hours and walked down the neat aisles of card tables aligned side by side. There were Christmas quilts, wreaths, and candle holders. Glittering homemade ornaments hung from Elsie Mayhue's tabletop tree. Crocheted ornaments were lined neatly on the table next to Elsie's, and next to that was a table of homemade cards and carved frames.

Beatrice had a dulcimer player sit on the podium and play music; the sounds of the strings soothed the crowd—or so it seemed. The scent of bayberry filled the air as Beatrice walked past Becky Richmond's homemade candles. Beatrice never cared for smelly things like potpourri and strongly scented candles, but she did like bayberry very much. It reminded her of Ed, who had loved bayberry soap. The thought of Ed spread warmth through her. She would always love and miss him. Always. But there was enough room in her old heart for Jon, who, by the way, could not stand bayberry. Such was life.

Jon was surrounded by a group of women who were gathered around Sally Krestly's table, looking over her lace. She was an amazing talent.

Jon held up the lace to the light. "Extraordinary," he said. "Look at this!"

"Gorgeous," Beatrice said.

She moved along to Mariah Skylar's table, full of herbal crafts, mostly from her own garden. Lavender soap. Rosemary wreaths. Rose bath salts. Lilac sachets in homemade muslin bags. Mint tea. Beatrice found it all very charming. It reminded her of home and her cousin, Rose, who was an herbalist.

"Just wonderful," Beatrice exclaimed.

"Why, thank you, Mrs. Matthews," Mariah said.

The Skylars were mountain folk. Beatrice had known the family for years. They were good, solid, and kept to themselves.

"Rose taught me a few things," she said.

Beatrice warmed.

"Ms. Matthews, can I see you a moment?" A woman came up beside her and pulled her off to the side.

"I asked if we could have the first spot and was told we could," she said.

"I'm sorry, whoever told you that was wrong. We can't make promises like that. First come, first served. Or in this case first spots."

The woman crossed her arms and glared at Beatrice.

"It looks like you're doing a fine business though." Beatrice pointed out her table, full of homemade jellies and jams in glistening glass jars, as the dulcimer played "Silent Night" in the background.

"Yes, but we could be doing better. Placement is everything," she said.

"Who told you that? Product is everything. Besides, we're all here for charity, right?"

The woman looked down. "You know," she said, "I grew up hungry. And I wanted to help as best I can. It's an awful way to live, not knowing where you're going to get your next meal."

Beatrice's heart melted and she wrapped her arm around the young woman. "You're doing just fine," she said. "Now, you better get back to your table."

The woman walked over, stood behind her table and started answering a question about her blackberry jam.

"We have both," Beatrice overheard her say. "We have the kind with sugar and without."

Jam without sugar? Who would want that? Beatrice mused as she moved along through the aisle and spotted the table of baked goods that her committee was manning. DeeAnn had really come through and they were selling a lot: brownies, chocolate chip cookies, gingerbread, pumpkin bread, and scones. Oh Lawd, the lemon poppy seed scones! Beatrice needed to scoop one of those up now.

Jon was close on her heels. "Do you want a scone? I do."

"Yes, indeed, I do," she said.

Beatrice spotted Sheila and Vera the next aisle over, at the table where the handmade rag dolls were lined up. Vera was purchasing one. Oh, Lizzy was going to love that doll. Christmas with a child was the best kind of Christmas. Beatrice never really minded the holiday, but since Lizzy had come along, quite unexpectedly a few years back, her Christmases had been pure magic. Only four years ago, she had given up hope of having a grandchild. Then Vera went and got pregnant right as her marriage was breaking up. After a brief stint of living on her own, Vera had moved back in with Beatrice. And it was working out. Now that Vera and Eric were getting so close, Beatrice wondered if her daughter would be getting married again.

Sheila and Vera spotted Beatrice and sauntered up to her.

"Well, if it ain't the scrapbooking queen looking like hell on a Saturday morning," Beatrice said to Sheila. But the next thing Beatrice knew, Shelia fell into her embrace and wrapped her arms around her. "I love you, too, you old bat."

Despite herself, Beatrice blinked back a tear. "Glad you two are home safe and sound."

"We're home, all right, but I'm not sure how safe we are," Sheila said. "I swear I think creepy guy is here."

"Who?" Beatrice asked.

Vera explained. "I think that bump on her head has scrambled her brains."

"Now, wait a minute," Beatrice said. "I noticed a strange man a few days ago when I was walking Lizzy home from school."

"I'm sure it's just someone here for the holidays," Vera said. "Can't people visit this town without arousing suspicion? Don't freak Sheila out even more."

Beatrice took a good long look at Sheila. Eh, she appeared to be okay. Her disheveled self stood looking back at Beatrice, with her hand on her hip, as if to say "what are you looking at?"

Chapter 54

"Well, here we are on a Saturday night, three days before Christmas, like none of us have anything else to do," DeeAnn said, as she slipped her scrapbook out of her bag and onto the table in Sheila's basement. This was her spot. The spot she sat in every week to scrapbook and visit. She then pulled a tin of cookies out of another bag. "Sugar cookies," she said. "You know, sometimes I think there's nothing better than a simple sugar cookie."

"Oh yes, especially with tea," Sheila said. "Anybody want some hot tea?"

"I think only booze for me tonight," Paige said after a moment. There were murmurs of agreement. Sheila poured the wine and Annie dumped a bag of pretzels into a plastic bowl as Paige laid out pumpkin squares and brownies.

Paige took a sip of wine and sniffed. "Lord, it's been a week like no other. It's like one minute you're in the tropics and the next home where it's colder than a witch's you-know-what. No wonder I've gotten a cold."

"I guess that's better than being sick on the ship," Sheila said, and smiled. "Paige had one too many and spent the night heaving."

"And part of the day, as well. Drinking and sailing? Not a good combination," Paige said as the others giggled and started scrapbooking. "What do you have there, Annie?"

"This is my Hanukkah album. I need to finish it up," Annie said. "But this is the book I'm most excited about." She pulled out her new art journal.

"What is that?" Sheila said, leaning across the table.

"Oh my God, these pumpkin bars are a-mazing!" DeeAnn said. "I want the recipe." Then she turned her attention to Annie's journal. "Wow. Annie, you're an artist."

Sheila surveyed the book. "She certainly is," she said. "I love this page." Sheila ran her fingers over the flowers that Anne had painted. She had written the words "Nourish your spirit with inspiring things. My inspiration: poetry, my boys, brownies, my friends, my pink kitchen."

"I'm having a lot of fun with it. Don't know what's gotten into me," Annie said.

"Art journaling is the new craze," Sheila said. "I've been reading about it. Haven't quite taken the plunge yet."

"Wow, love this one, Annie!" DeeAnn pointed to the next page. "What's in my head?" was scrolled across the page along with a black and white photo of herself in the center. She had printed out words and then cut them apart and glued them around the photo to create a frame of words.

The word "murder" stood out.

"Why is murder in your head?" DeeAnn asked.

"At the time I was thinking about the book I'm writing and about the murders on the ship," Annie said. "Unfortunately there's a lot of murder in my life." Annie wilted. "I'm so glad I'm almost finished with this book."

"Me too, Annie," Sheila said. "I haven't had as much experience dealing with murder as you have. But it's unpleasant. I never want to trip over another dead body!"

Paige began to giggle nervously. "Only you, Sheila. Only you."

The rest of them giggled, too. It served to clear the air. Who wanted to talk about murder on a Saturday night?

"So, Sheila," Annie said, "do you have a new job?"

"Well," she answered, opening her laptop. "I think I'm going to accept the position with David's Designs. It's a freelance job, but I'll have to go to their offices once a month."

"How exciting!" DeeAnn said. "What did Steve say about it?"

"I haven't told him yet," Sheila said.

An uncomfortable silence settled over the room.

"What?" Vera said, looking up from her page. "Why not?"

Sheila shrugged. "He missed me so much and keeps going on about how he didn't like me being gone. I haven't found the right time to approach the subject."

Everybody went back to scrapbooking. DeeAnn was working on a Christmas cookie page. She had a cut-out green bowl with a spoon sticking out of it and a recipe card coming out of the top. She was working on the blank space where she'd place the photo at some point.

"I think you need to tell your husband soon," DeeAnn said when she noticed Sheila was looking at her page.

"I think you need to make the frame red, not green," Sheila replied.

"Steve's going to be okay with it," Vera said. "No need to make a big deal out of it."

Sheila's stomach sank. She was a modern woman, an artist. Why did it matter to her so much what her husband thought of this change?

"If this is something you want to do, I'm sure he'll support you," Annie said.

"It's just that—"

"You've been home all this time," Vera said. "That's where he is most comfortable. But I've known him as long as you have. He's going to be okay with this. He believes in you."

Vera focused on her snowflake page. A photo of Elizabeth and her first snowman was in the center of the blue and white page. She had layered the background of the photos with silver paper and a bit of lace.

"I guess I've had other things on my mind," Sheila said, handing Vera the blue-checked washi tape.

"Like what?" Annie said, and bit into a brownie.

"Like creepy guy from the cruise being in Cumberland Creek," Sheila said.

The room hushed.

"Oh, for God's sake," Vera said. "I'm sure whoever you saw resembled the creepy man. Anyway, why would he come here?"

"I saw him," Annie said. "Or at least we think it

was the same guy Sheila saw the other day. He was walking along Ivy. I asked him if I could help him and he said he was simply taking a walk."

"Y'all need to remember there's a new B and B in town. Lots of guests stay there," DeeAnn said. "You can't go around accusing people just because they are not from around here and look a little strange."

Annie laughed. "That's true. And now there are those new apartments for rent over on Ridge Avenue. I suppose we will be seeing more and more new faces."

Sheila wanted to relax. But the creepy guy on the ship was so unsettling, and so different, that he was hard to shake. Whoever the person was who had caught her eye the other day gave her the same feeling. She felt the hair on the back of her neck stand.

Chapter 55

It had been a while since Annie had walked into the Cumberland Creek Police office. They had made some improvements. It looked brighter, though not exactly cheery. Of course, Mondays were rarely cheery, no matter how brightly lit.

The woman at the desk looked up at Annie from behind thick glasses. "Ms. Chamovitz?" she said.

Annie nodded.

"They are expecting you."

"Thanks," she said.

When Adam called and asked her to come in with the reports she had, along with any of the other research she'd done, at first she thought he was joking. But he was dead serious.

She walked into the room and introductions were made. Two FBI agents joined them.

"We'd like to start by having a look-see at the reports you have," the redheaded Agent Woods said.

"Look-see"? Who says that? Annie had to stop herself from rolling her eyes—or at least asking him where he came up with it.

She pulled out the papers and set them on Bryant's desk.

"She's right," Bryant said. "Different times."

"And of course different names. But why the time change?" the other man, Agent Rodriguez, said. He pointed to the report with the earlier time. He pulled out their reports. His had identical times on them.

"Someone tried to cover their mistake," Bryant said, shrugging.

"Well, sure. But I don't think that's the whole story," Annie said. "You'd think they'd be extra careful on the second report since they'd already sent a false report of Sheila's death."

All four of them sat in silence.

"The more we dig into this, the stranger it gets,"

Woods said. "We may never really know what went on that day. Or the hours leading up to it."

"We know the scrapbook had ricin all over it," Rodriguez said.

"That's about all we know. We can't find any evidence that Ms. Rogers had any of that substance in her home," Detective Bryant pointed out.

"She could have gotten rid of it," Rodriguez said.

"Wait a minute," Bryant said. "I know this woman. Why would she kill Allie? She had no motive."

"Jealousy?" Agent Woods said with a tone of uncertainty.

"Gentlemen," Annie spoke up. "I think we're getting off topic here. We know Sheila didn't kill them."

"Or at least there's no evidence to support that," Woods agreed.

"Okay. What we don't know is where the ricin came from and why there appears to be a time discrepancy here," Annie said.

"I think I have it," Bryant said. "Or at least one possibility."

They all looked at him in expectation.

"The only thing that makes sense is at first someone wanted us to think Sheila was dead, or—"

"Or," Annie interrupted, "someone thought she would be."

"Okay," Woods said, and sucked in air. "It's a stretch, but it's a possibility."

"Well, yes, the book was in her room. How did it get there? Who had it before then?" Bryant asked.

"The judges of the competition," Annie said.

"We've already talked with them. Well, almost all of them. I'll check on that last one—Theresa Graves."

Annie recognized the name. "She has a record. I checked her out."

"Why would you do that?" Bryant said.

"She was heckling Sheila on a cruise where a murder took place," she said as she felt the breath almost escape out of her body. It was Sheila the killer was after. Sweet and kind Sheila. How could someone want her dead?

She jumped up out of her chair.

"Annie!" Bryant said. "Hold on. Where are you going?"

Her heart was racing so fast that she thought it would pound out of her chest. "I need to get to Sheila."

"What do you hope to accomplish?" He was standing next to her now. "This is just a theory."

"Yes, but it's the only thing that makes sense, isn't it?" she managed to say. "Someone filled out the report thinking Sheila would be dead. Someone on that ship. Someone with access to the security office. It makes sense."

"So much about murder doesn't make sense," Rodriguez spoke. "The fact that this one piece of information makes a kind of sense means nothing at all. We still don't have a strong case."

"Besides, if you go and tell Sheila, she will be more of a mess than she is now," Adam said, reaching for her arm. "Don't go yet."

She glanced at his hand on her arm, pulled herself away from him, and sat back down. Her legs were actually shaking. How could she not have thought of this possibility? How could none of the other scrapbookers thought of it? Or the ship's security? They were all looking at who killed Allie and Harold. Nobody realized it might have been a foiled attempt on the life of Sheila Rogers.

Chapter 56

Morning was Sheila's favorite part of the day. She loved her run; the hour or so she took to clear her mind and get her body moving was like meditation or prayer for her. But this morning she was excited that Donna would be home for the week. Her daughter, who had given them such fits as a teenager, was now a star student at Carnegie Mellon University, where she was majoring in design. She was getting good grades and applying for internships, doing everything she should be in order to keep up that scholarship.

Rusty, Sheila's oldest son, was sitting at the kitchen table when she walked in, his earbuds in his ears, listening to music. He looked up, smiled, and nodded. He planned to go to the local community college and major in business, wanting to join Steve's company. He was a great guide and knew the mountains almost as well as his dad. It was a solid plan. Sheila liked that.

Steve was in the living room with Gerty, their fifteen-year-old daughter, watching the morning news. She waved at them as she ran up the stairs to get her shower.

Sheila was feeling better today. After a few days at home, in her own bed, surrounded by most of her family and friends, she felt more at ease. She had even talked herself out of thinking the man she spotted the other day was the creepy guy from the cruise. She had a doctor's appointment today, as a precaution, to check her over post-concussion. After that, as far as she was concerned, good riddance to bad vibes about the cruise. She had plenty of time to talk to Steve about the new job opportunities. David's Designs was giving her until the end of January to sign on.

Showered and dressed, Sheila was ready for her and Steve's day of last minute Christmas shopping. Christmas was still two days away, Sheila told herself; no need to panic.

"Hon, you ready?" Steve called up the stairs.

"Yes, yes. I'm looking for my purse. I don't see it up here."

She came down the stairs.

"Do you need your purse?" Steve said.

"Yes, I do," Sheila said.

"I don't see it in here, Mom," Rusty called to her.

"Let me think," she said, sifting through her memories of the past few days. When was the last time she had seen her purse? "Ah-ha," she said. "It's in the basement."

Steve rolled his eyes. "I'll meet you in the car," he said, and leaned down to kiss her.

Sheila looked over at Gerty. "We'll be back soon, honey. Call your dad's cell if you need anything. Mine is probably dead."

She descended the basement stairs, flipped on a light switch, and gasped. Her uber-organized scrapbooking room had been tousled. What the hell?

Papers were splayed all over the floors, embellishments scattered everywhere. Her eyes traveled along a path of red paper to her glass sliding door, where there was a crumpled heap at its edge. There was someone in her basement, lying on the floor!

She backed up the stairs, her legs trembling, heart pounding against her rib cage. *This could not be. This could not be.*

Backing up, she smacked into a body coming up behind her, causing her to scream.

"Mom?" Rusty said. "You okay?"

She swallowed and tried to breath, which took way too much coordination than what she had at the moment.

"Get your father," she managed to say.

"What's wrong?" he said, and started to go down the stairs.

"No!" she said. "Get your father."

"Mom?" Gerty was off the couch now and headed toward Sheila.

"Get back, both of you," Sheila hissed. "There's someone in the basement." She closed the door behind her.

"I'll call nine-one-one," Gerty said.

Rusty was out the door to get his father in a split second. Steve came back in the house, bewildered and holding his keys, jingling in the sudden silence. Then came Gerty's voice: "Yes, that's the right address."

"What is it?"

"There's someone in the basement," Sheila said.

"In our basement?"

She nodded.

"What are they doing?" Steve asked. He was moving toward the gun cabinet.

"Just . . . just lying there," Sheila said between breaths.

"The police are on their way," Gerty said. "Mom? You okay? You don't look so good."

"Get your mother some water," Steve said, opening the cabinet and getting one of his rifles out. "Sheila, please go and sit down. I'm going downstairs to see who the hell is in the basement. I think you all need to wait outside on the porch."

"No!" Sheila said. "Let the police deal with it, please."

"I'm not going anywhere," Gerty said, sidling up to her mother.

"They will be here any second, Dad," Rusty said. "Please put the gun away."

The four of them stood in the dining room, with the gun cabinet door swinging slowly back and forth, creaking. Gerty held a glass of water. Rusty stood with his hands at his sides, pleading with his father. "Please, Dad."

Steve held the rifle with both hands. He was trembling with fear and anger as he looked at his family. Finally his eyes found Sheila's. "Okay," he said. "But if they are not here in five minutes, I'm going downstairs. I have a right to protect my family. Sheila, I'll put the gun away and you go outside and wait with the kids, please."

The room sighed with relief when Steve put his gun back in the cabinet and looked at his watch. They heard sirens in the not too far off distance.

Gerty handed Sheila the water and led her mother to the porch, where they both sat down on the lawn chairs. Rusty and Steve followed behind.

Sheila drank from the glass. Water. Glass. Daughter. Son. Husband. She tried to focus. But it all blurred and then melted together as she oozed back into the wicker chair pillows.

"Sheila!" she heard her husband say before she closed her eyes.

Chapter 57

Beatrice and Jon were walking back from the grocery store when they noticed the police cars and ambulance at Sheila and Steve's home. Beatrice dropped her bag of groceries and ran toward them.

"Bea!" Jon said, picking up her bag, as well as holding on to his own, following her as best he could.

Beatrice didn't bother asking the group of neighbors gathered what was going on; she barged through the line of officers and onlookers.

"Ma'am," one officer said, stepping in front. "You can't go in there."

"The hell I can't," Beatrice said.

The officer was visibly taken aback. "What's the relationship?" he said.

"Very good personal friend. She's like a daughter to me," she said. She looked at the officer. How old was he? Sixteen? She took a closer look. "I know your mama, boy."

The officer grimaced.

"Now step aside," Bea said.

Bryant came to the front door, which was open, and nodded to the officer to let Beatrice come up the front porch stairs. Jon followed with the bags of groceries. "He's with me," she told them.

"What's going on?" she said to Bryant, who shook his head in resignation.

"Beatrice, I'm glad you're here. Sheila has passed out. The medics are looking after her. I'm sure she'd like to see you," Bryant said.

"You're here because Sheila has passed out?" she asked, confused.

"No, I'm here"—he lowered his voice—"because there's a body in the basement."

"What? Who?"

He lowered his gaze. "We're not sure yet, Beatrice. The crime techs are down there now. After they're finished we'll search for ID."

He stepped aside and let Beatrice and Jon enter the house. Sheila was on the floor, her husband and children close by while the medics talked with her, took her pulse, and so on. Annie sat on the couch and her eyes found Beatrice's. Annie was pale and her eyes held fear.

"What's going on? Why are you here?" Beatrice said, and sat next to her.

"We were in Bryant's office when the call came in," Annie said.

"We?" Beatrice said.

"The FBI officers and myself. I think they are downstairs," Annie said.

"Bea?" Sheila said when she saw her. "Beatrice!" She was still groggy.

"I'm here," Bea said, feeling a sudden welling of emotion. "I told your mother I'd keep an eye on you. I guess I haven't done a good job of that."

"There's a body in my basement," she said, amidst the activity around her, ignoring what Beatrice said. "Can you believe that?"

"Can you please be quiet?" the medic said. "Don't talk. Save your energy. Please." He listened to her heartbeat.

"She passed out after she came up here and told her husband and kids to call the police," Annie said to Beatrice.

"She discovered the body?" Beatrice asked.

Annie nodded. "From what I've been able to piece together, she was looking for her purse and thought she left it in the basement."

A couple of uniformed police officers left the room after muttering something in the medic's ear.

"Okay," the medic said. "We're going to sit you up. Nice and easy."

One of the medics and Steve helped Sheila to sit up on the floor. Steve kept her propped up.

"You okay?" he said.

Sheila nodded. "I think so."

"Let's just sit here a while," the medic said. "You've had quite an exciting morning. We need to get those clothes off you, dear."

Sheila looked at the young woman like she was daft.

"Looks like your bad luck followed you home," Beatrice said.

Sheila's eyes and mouth narrowed as she looked at Beatrice.

"It's a precaution, but there was some poison found on the premises," the medic said. She looked at Steve and continued. "You all need to take your clothes off and place them in a plastic bag. It would be a good idea to shower."

Steve whispered something in the medic's ear. The medic nodded. Sheila gasped.

"Rusty, please go get a few trash bags," Steve said.

"Why would someone even be in our basement?" Gerty spoke up. She had been sitting in the chair next to the Christmas tree, taking in the scene. "You wouldn't go in a basement to rob people."

"Was it a robbery?" Annie asked.

"What else?" Steve said.

Annie started to say something, then appeared to change her mind.

"Anything taken?" Beatrice asked, after a beat.

"Not that I know of, but I haven't been downstairs," Steve said as he and Sheila took the empty trash bags that Rusty had handed them and the family left the room to shower.

The rest of them sat in silence as the medics busied themselves filling out reports, gathering supplies, and the police moved through the house and talked to one another via walkie-talkies. Soon, Sheila and Steve and their children came back down the stairs, all with wet heads from the showers. Funny what these situations did to break down social mores; Sheila would not have been caught dead in public with wet hair on an ordinary day. Here she was, in front of half of Cumberland Creek as well as the police and EMTs.

Detective Bryant walked back into the room. "The site has been secured, finally. We can't bring the body out yet until we get hazmat in here. Sheila and Steve, do you think you can look at the body to see if you know the person? I have a photo here on my phone."

"Why would we know the person?" Steve questioned.

"Just bear with me," Bryant said. "It will rule out a lot of possibilities if you know them."

"Well, okay," Steve said after a moment. "I'll take a look, but I don't think Sheila's up for it."

Beatrice took her in. Her coloring was coming back and her brows knitted together.

"You're damned straight I'm going to take a look at the body," Sheila said.

Steve wrapped his arm around her and Rusty stood on her other side.

"Do you think she can wait until later to view the body?" Beatrice asked Bryant.

"If she needs to, but it's better as soon as possible. It will help the investigation," he said, looking at Annie. Something was exchanged in their looks—Beatrice was certain there was more going on here than a robbery. She decided to sit tight and observe. She watched as the two FBI officers who had been to her house last week entered the room and then walked out the door.

"Come outside. I think this picture will show better."

Sheila and her husband and son walked out onto the front porch. Annie got up from the couch and followed. Jon sat with their bags of groceries on a chair next to Gerty. They were chatting.

Bryant pulled out his phone and showed it to Sheila.

"It's him!" Sheila screamed. "It's the creepy guy from the cruise!"

Beatrice shot up from the couch and ran to the porch.

Sheila fell back into Steve's arms.

Annie placed her hand on Bryant's shoulder and leaned into him. "That was the same man I saw the other day," she said.

He nodded.

"What the hell was he doing here?" Beatrice asked.

"Can't really ask him that, can we?" Bryant looked up at her with a smirk.

"Always a smart-ass, ain't you, Bryant?" Beatrice said.

Chapter 58

"Is that the vic's wallet?" Annie asked.

"It's a wallet all right," Bryant said. "But it doesn't belong to the vic."

"Who does it belong to?" Annie asked.

"I can't tell you that. C'mon, Annie, you know that. Thanks so much for your help earlier, but I got this now."

"Wait a minute, Bryant," Beatrice spoke up. "Maybe we know this person and can help."

He shook his head. "You've got to believe me on this one, ladies. You can't help. Not now. You know there's protocol here. We need to inform family and so on."

Annie watched him walk away. Just like him to pull her in, ask for help, then not give them any information. She made a mental note to not be so helpful next time.

"Sheila, do you feel up to coming down to the station and giving me a statement?" Bryant asked.

She nodded. "I can do that. I was going to go shopping."

"It won't take long, I promise. Wait a minute." A medic interrupted and whispered something in Bryant's ear. Then he turned to the group.

"How long were you in the basement? How close did you get to the body?" the medic asked.

"I went all the way into the basement," Sheila replied. "I didn't get close to the body at all. When I noticed the mess, and . . . and then I saw him, I backed up the way I came in."

"Okay, we think it's best you go to the hospital first. Just to be safe," Bryant said. "I'll get your statement there. That won't be a problem."

"Okay," she said, still pale, her voice not quite as strong as usual. Steve's arm wrapped around her. He hadn't left her side.

"In the meantime, nobody goes in the basement until our crew says it's okay," he said.

"Please be watchful, ladies. I've got my guys on the ground and I've got a couple of roadblocks set up. Our vic wasn't alone in the basement," Bryant said quietly to them, as if he didn't want his colleagues to hear him, then turned and walked away.

A few hours ago, Annie had been sitting in his office and helping him with the FBI investigation. They had almost concluded that the ship's murder might have been aimed at Sheila. Perhaps this guy had planned to finish the job. But he had been waylaid.

"Adam," Annie called out as she followed him.

He kept walking, but she was on his heels.

"Listen, Adam, can you at least tell me how this guy died?"

He stopped and turned to look at her. A uniformed officer came up to him and got his signature on something.

"Annie, we still have to run the tox tests to be sure. But it looks like poison," he said.

"What kind of poison?" Annie said, her stomach jumbled, her pulse racing.

"Definitely ricin," he said. "We found a bag on him. And there was a spoon of it stuffed in his mouth."

Her jaw dropped. "You mean . . ." What were the chances of the same poison that was used to kill the victims on the ship being found on this man? Annie's reporter intuition was pinging.

"What I mean is it looks like someone killed this person with ricin and they wanted to make sure he was quite dead," he said. The way he spoke was odd. Usually so self-assured, he stumbled around the words. "He was quite dead. Are you going to be writing about this?"

"No," she said. "I haven't been called to cover it. I already told my editor I'm on deadline for my book. So I'm out of circulation."

"Okay," he said. "Let's keep this little bit of

information to ourselves. I don't want people to panic. Understand?"

Annie nodded. But her brain took over and began to leap to all sorts of conclusions.

"Sheila?" Annie asked.

"Let's hope she didn't touch anything down there," he said with a serious tone.

A welling of fear ripped through Annie.

He slipped into his car. The FBI agents were already inside. One was on his cell phone. The other was looking straight ahead. Annie watched as the car pulled away before she turned toward her friends.

The red lights on the cop cars no longer spun and flashed. The paramedics were beginning to leave. A calm started to descend on what had been, a few hours ago, constructed controlled chaos with law enforcement professionals performing their duties.

"What on earth is going on here?" Annie turned to see Vera approaching up the street.

"Mama, you okay?" She ran up onto Sheila's porch and grabbed her mother. "Are you okay?"

"Unhand me, Vera Matthews. I am fine," Beatrice said. "It's Sheila who's going to the hospital."

"Hospital? Why?" she said, looking around for Sheila.

"She found a dead body in the basement and passed out. It's a safety precaution," Beatrice replied.

Annie hoped she was right.

"A dead body!" Vera said. "What on earth is going on? Why does she keep tripping over dead bodies?"

"It is odd," Jon said. "I was thinking the same thing."

"You ain't heard the best of it," Beatrice said. "The dead body in the basement is the creepy guy from the cruise."

Vera gasped. "What has Sheila gotten herself into?"

Annie was starting to wonder the same thing. Someone had it out for Sheila, and either wanted to kill her or frame her for murder. And with the same substance that was used to kill Allie and Harold. But why? What could a little middle-aged scrapbooking woman have done to elicit such hatred?

Chapter 59

Sheila and Steve lay in the same hospital room. Their kids had been taken to a "safe house" where they could clean up even more and change into new clothes. Nobody was allowed in or out of their home until there was a complete inspection and cleaning of the substance.

"If you for some reason got the ricin on your clothes, you should be safe now," the doctor explained. "But if you breathed the substance in, we won't know for a few more hours. After having a good look at both of you, I'd say that didn't happen. But we need to be certain, you understand."

"What kind of symptoms?" Sheila asked.

"You'd be having a hard time breathing, maybe coughing or fever," the doctor said nonchalantly.

"I feel fine," Steve said. "I'd like to go home."

"Me too," Sheila said. "We're expecting our daughter anytime to come home from school and we had planned to shop and—"

"I'm sorry, folks. I know it's the Christmas season and all that, but we have to follow CDC guidelines. You could have ingested a lethal substance. I'll be back in a little while," he said before leaving the room.

Steve flicked on the TV. "Might as well relax," he said, and flipped the channel.

"Nothing relaxing about that," Sheila said, crossing her arms.

"What do you want to do?" he snipped at her.

"Let's sit in silence. Or talk. How about that? Let's talk."

"About what?" Steve said, shutting off the TV with the remote and sitting up on the edge of the bed.

"I was offered a job," she blurted out.

His head tilted in, as if he hadn't heard right. "A job?"

Sheila gazed at the cheap prints on the wall.

Flowers and puppies. As if that could make the fact that you might have been poisoned okay. As if that could make the fact that your husband wasn't going to like your news—not one little bit—better.

"What kind of a job?" he asked.

"I'd be freelancing for a design company, designing scrapbooks," she said. Her heart fluttered in her chest.

"Does that mean you'd be working from home?" he asked.

A nurse poked her head in the door. "Can I get you some water?" she asked.

Steve nodded.

"Yes, please," said Sheila.

"For the most part," she continued once the nurse had left. "I'd have to go in to the office once a month or so."

"Where's that?"

"New York City," she replied quietly.

Several minutes passed. Time seemed to stretch and the room seemed to stand watch over them.

"Is that something you want to do?" Steve finally asked.

"I'm not thrilled about going to New York City, but other than that, yes. I'd love to do this. I loved the people and I've respected their work for a long time. It's like a dream come true for me," she said, tears welling for the first time since she started considering the offer. It was. It was a dream come true. And she wouldn't be able to stand it if her husband did not support her one hundred percent. It would hurt too much.

He moved over to her bed, squeezed in next to her, and held her hands in his. He brought them to his lips and kissed them. "I love you, Sheila. We'll make it work. I'm so proud of you."

Her heart exploded; tears, sweat, and snot streamed down her face. He handed her a tissue.

"Lord, woman, clean yourself up," he said.

"Here, here, no fraternizing." A nurse walked into the room with a pitcher of water and some glasses. She laughed.

Sheila and her husband toasted her new job with their ice cold water, both in their hospital gowns, with the winter sunlight streaming through the windows.

"Mom? Dad?" A voice came from the hallway.

"In here, Donna." Sheila sat up straighter.

Her daughter's eyes lit with excitement and fear. "What's going on, Mama? Daddy? They wouldn't let me into the house."

Sheila leaped up out of bed and hugged her daughter, as did Steve.

"Sit down, Donna; we'll explain," Steve said.

"Unbelievable," Donna said after they got done talking.

"Indeed," Sheila said, then surveyed her daughter. "You look tired, honey. How's school?"

Donna looked away. "It's intense, Mom."

"Are you going to be okay?" Steve asked.

"I think so, but I really need this break. No art. No design. Just bad TV and junk food. That's what the doctor ordered," she said, and laughed it off. But Sheila knew there was more to the story. Donna would tell her in her own time.

Sheila sighed. Donna had always been a challenge. Their firstborn was also their most stubborn and complicated. But once she found art and had a goal of becoming an artist, all of Donna's troubles seemed to fall away. The boys. The drugs. The bad grades. For some kids, that's all they needed—a passion—to straighten them up. That was the case with Donna. None of their other kids had given them any problems—so far.

"Where is everybody?" Donna asked.

"In a safe house. They promised us they're okay."

"God, I hope you weren't poisoned," Donna said, looking at her parents.

"I think we're lucky that your mom didn't touch anything," Steve said. "She didn't get close to the body. Or trip over it or anything." He grinned and Sheila playfully hit him on the shoulder.

Sheila sighed and a hint of a smile appeared on her face. "My new goal in life is to not find or trip over any more dead people."

Chapter 60

After putting the groceries away, Jon and Beatrice sat at the kitchen table mulling over the day's events. The kettle went off and Beatrice got up to make some tea.

"At least your bazaar went well. It was an astounding success. How much money did you make for the food bank?" Jon asked.

"Over five thousand dollars," Beatrice replied. "And a truckload of food!"

Jon stirred sugar in his tea while Beatrice pulled out a plastic container full of sugar cookies. She placed it on the table.

"Mmmm," Jon said. "You are going to make me fat!"

"Hmph," Beatrice said, as the front door opened. Vera and Annie walked into the kitchen.

"Quite a day, heh?" Annie said.

"Tea?" Beatrice offered.

"I'll get it, Mama," Vera said, and poured them some tea.

"You look troubled," Beatrice said to Annie.

"I'm trying to figure things out," she said, reaching for the cup of tea as Vera handed it to her. "I mean, it's pretty clear someone has it in for Sheila, but who? And why?"

"All I have to say is thank goodness she's at the

hospital where they can watch over her," Vera said, sitting down at the table.

"Indeed," Jon said, then bit into a cookie.

"The only person I've ever known to not like Sheila was Sharon Milhouse. But she was crazy. Then there was the woman on the cruise—what was her name? Theresa Graves—who heckled Sheila."

"Maybe they're connected in some way," Beatrice said.

"Bryant said he couldn't find Sharon Milhouse anywhere," Annie said. "He called her parole officer and hasn't heard back from him."

Beatrice took a long sip of tea.

"You know, it occurs to me that maybe we're looking in the wrong place for her," Vera said.

"What do you mean?" Beatrice asked.

"I mean she was in the Richmond Institution. Maybe her most recent records are medical, not criminal," Vera said.

"Vera! That's brilliant," Annie said.

"You don't have access to medical records, do you?" Beatrice said to Annie.

She shook her head. "No."

"I know someone who does," Vera said.

"Now, wait a minute," Beatrice said. "It might not be fair to ask your boyfriend to do that for you."

"Can't hurt to ask," Jon said, shrugging.

"I'm going to give him a call and see what he says," Vera said, and left the room.

Beatrice dunked her cookie in her tea. There was nothing like a tea-soaked sugar cookie.

"I don't know how much sense it makes that Sharon Milhouse would be our killer," Annie said.

"I agree," Beatrice said after a moment. "But none of the rest of it makes sense. What links Sheila to the other murders except the scrapbooking competition? And none of those people are local." Beatrice's brain suddenly kicked in. Her eyes widened.

"What?" Annie said.

"I know Bryant has roadblocks up, but what if the person who killed the man in Sheila's basement is still in town?"

"Hiding out in the open?" Annie said.

"If I were hiding in the open, where would I be?" Jon said.

"You know, I hadn't mentioned this before, but I've been seeing a lot of strangers in the neighborhood. I mentioned it to Bryant, who reminded me about the new B and B," Beatrice said.

"Well, let's go," Jon said.

"Now, hold on," Annie said. "It's a good idea, Beatrice. But we can't all go traipsing over to the B and B and demand a guest list."

"Oh, who needs to bother with that?" Vera said. "They have a guest book right there in the foyer."

"Like our killer would sign a real name in the

guest book," Annie said. "What did you find out from Eric?" she asked as Vera reentered the kitchen.

"He says he can't do it."

"Why?" Beatrice said.

Vera waved her hand. "Confidentiality issues or some such nonsense."

"Bother," Beatrice said. "You had to hook up with a decent guy."

"Oh well," Vera said, shrugging.   ·

"I'm happy to go over to the B and B and look around. I've been over there once before and it looked beautiful, but Elsie was getting some work done and invited me to come back and look when everything was complete," Jon said.

"Yes, she's taken quite a shine to you." Beatrice elbowed him.

"Sounds like a great excuse to me," Annie said, standing. "I'm going, too."

Beatrice stood and began making up a gift bag of cookies. "Take this bag over with my holiday greetings."

"Sure thing, Beatrice." Jon went into the hallway and slipped his coat on. Annie tightened her scarf.

"It's cold out there," Beatrice said. "I hear snow is predicted."

"Just in time for Christmas," Vera said. "Lizzie will be thrilled."

"Now, be careful over there," Beatrice said.

"What do you mean? We're only going to see who's staying there," Jon said. "Don't worry."

"Yes, but don't forget—you are looking for a killer. A devious one at that. One who appears to have followed Sheila from the cruise to Cumberland Creek," Beatrice said.

"Maybe the killer is afraid she knows something," Vera said. "Maybe that's all it is."

"All?" Annie turned around. "That's plenty for a killer who's frightened someone can finger them."

Beatrice felt a cold chill run through her. That Annie. She had a way of setting them all straight.

Chapter 61

"Here's what I'm thinking," Annie said to Jon as they walked along the sidewalk. "You distract Elsie by chatting with her and I'll look at the guest book and take some pictures on my phone. That way we can all look over the names later to see if any ring a bell. How does that sound?"

"Great plan," Jon said. "I think I can do that."

They walked up the sidewalk to the big sky blue gingerbread house. The only other house in the neighborhood that could compete with it in size and age would be Beatrice's Victorian. The old iron gate creaked as they walked through it.

Jon rang the doorbell and Annie readied her

phone in her hand. She didn't want to be fussing with it when the time came to snap the photos.

Elsie answered the door. "Why, hello, Jon, Annie. Please come in."

"Merry Christmas," Jon said, and handed her the goodie bag Beatrice had made up for her. "From Bea."

"Oh, isn't that sweet!" she exclaimed. "Now, Jon, I know you'd like to see the new dining room. I'm so thrilled with the color, the floors, everything. Come on inside."

Annie hung back in the foyer and headed for the guest book. She decided to work her way from the newest guest signatures to the last.

"Oh my!" she heard Jon exclaim. "What is the word for this color?"

"Chartreuse," Elsie said.

"Did you choose the drapes? Impeccable."

"I did," she replied.

Jon laughed and their voices lowered as they moved further into the house.

Annie took the first photo without reading the names. She felt like she'd have to move quickly and couldn't take the time to read the names, even though she desperately wanted to.

Click.

Her bag slid to the floor.

Turn the page. *Click, click, click.*

"Where did you ever get those prints?" Jon asked from afar.

Elsie's answer was quieter. Annie couldn't quite hear her.

Click, click, click.

Annie's heart was racing. She would hate to get caught. How would she explain it?

She turned the page.

"The floors are remarkable. Who did you say did them, again?" Jon asked.

Click, click, click.

Annie turned another page.

"What are you doing?" The voice sounded from behind Annie and she gasped, slipping her phone into her pocket.

She turned to face a woman she didn't recognize.

"Excuse me?" Annie said.

"I asked you what you were doing," the woman said. She was full of authority, even though she was thin and wiry. Even Annie could have knocked her down.

"Annie . . ." Jon poked his head into the room. "You simply have got to see what Elsie has done with this room."

"Sure," Annie said. "Friends," she said vaguely, and pointed in the direction of Elsie and Jon, then gave a little wave to the woman as she walked into one of the tackiest rooms she'd ever seen in her life. She smiled and nodded, disappointed because she was certain she didn't get to photograph all the names—but at least it was something to get started with.

"Would you like to stay for tea?" Elsie asked.

"I really need to get going," Annie said.

"Me too," Jon said. "Thanks for asking though. Can I take a rain check?"

"Absolutely. You too, of course, Annie," she said.

"Sure thing," Annie replied, thinking there was no way on God's green earth that she'd sit down to tea in this overdecorated room. She'd lose her appetite. There was something to be said for the simplicity that her old friend Cookie Crandall used to talk about. She'd leave the tea and the B and B visits to Jon.

After Elsie saw them out and they were halfway to Beatrice's house, Jon asked if she had gotten what they went there for.

Annie nodded. "Not all of the names, but those within the past few weeks, I'd say. And of course if our killer is there, we don't know what name he or she would be using. So I don't know if this exercise will do much good."

"It's worth a try," Jon said.

When they turned the corner, there stood the woman who had caught Annie riffling through the register at the B and B. Annie smiled nervously and nodded at her.

"I'm sorry," the woman said. "I'm going to have to ask you for your phone."

"Excuse me?" Annie said. "My phone? Why?"

"I saw you taking photos of the guest book.

That's private information," she said, her chin quivering in anger. Or was it fear?

Jon laughed. "She was not taking pictures of the guest book. She was taking photos of the wallpaper for me."

The woman looked confused. "But I could have sworn—" She stood in front of Annie.

"Step aside," Annie said. "I'm not giving my phone to you, in any case."

The woman stood her ground. "I can't have people lurking around the place I'm staying. You understand."

"We live here. Elsie is my friend. We were just visiting," Jon said. "I don't understand why it's your concern." His French accent was pronounced now. Beatrice always said she could tell when he was upset or stressed. It would thicken.

Annie's hair pricked on the back of her neck. Little pings of intuition zipped through her body. *What did this woman have to hide?*

Annie walked around her and motioned for Jon to do the same. She turned around one more time and noticed the woman watching them walk away, her hound dog cheeks stiff with outrage.

Chapter 62

Later, after roughly ten hours of observation, Sheila and her husband were escorted to the safe house, where their children were also harbored.

"This is the safe house?" Sheila exclaimed, when they pulled up to the house at the end of a cul-de-sac. "This is where Cookie Crandall lived!"

"It's empty and it's ricin-free," Detective Bryant snapped. Once inside the small house, he gestured toward a young woman with long stringy hair and glasses, standing in the kitchen doorway. "This is Vicki Crane," he said. "She is your caseworker."

"Hello," she said, shaking their hands.

"Caseworker?" Steve said. "Why?"

"Procedure, any time people are removed from their home," the detective said, and walked off as his cell phone beeped.

"What's going on here?" Sheila said, noticing her kids were sitting at the kitchen table—the only furniture in the place.

Vicki shrugged. "Your home isn't safe for you yet. So you'll need to stay here. I've arranged for more beds and clothes to be brought in. The beds should be here any minute. We'll bring some food in, as well."

"When can we go home, Mama?" Jonathon found his mother's side and slipped his arms around her. "It's boring here."

"We'll be bringing a TV in soon, as well," Vicki said, and smiled. "Maybe you can go to the library and get some books and things."

Jonathon looked horrified. He hated the local library.

"How long do you expect we'll be here?" Steve said. "I thought this was going to be a few hours."

"Oh no, sir. Ricin is very dangerous. We need to make certain it's completely gone before you can move back in," she said.

"That's just great!" Steve said. "First, my wife stumbles on a dead body in our basement, then we're told we can't go home. Jesus. Merry goddamn Christmas." His hands were on his hips.

Detective Bryant came back toward them.

"Any luck with the road blocks?" Steve asked him.

"No," Bryant said. Unshaven and baggy-eyed, Bryant was a mess. He sighed. "Nothing. No word back yet from the health department either. I'm afraid you're going to have to make yourself comfortable here."

Sheila's heart raced. "But it's Christmas in two days," she said. "Will we be home in time for Christmas?" She couldn't imagine celebrating it anywhere else but her home, with her tree, her fireplace, and her things surrounding her.

"I doubt it," Vicki said. "I'm sorry. You may be here for Christmas."

Sheila sighed and walked away from the group, toward the big window on the back wall. She remembered this place. When Cookie was in jail, a group of them had come here to gather her things. It was spare then; now it had a table and some chairs in it, which is where three of her children were gathered playing cards. She couldn't imagine spending the holiday here. But she looked over at her kids at the table and realized it didn't seem to be bothering them at all. They seemed to be having fun. Jonathan was a bit bored, but maybe that would be resolved when the TV arrived.

She gazed out the window at the mountains. This was the view that Cookie had every day and it was the view that Annie had talked about. Annie had said she'd been back to this house several times since Cookie had left. She found peace here. Sheila didn't understand it—the place kind of freaked her out. Why would someone want to live with no furniture or no decorations at all?

The detective came up beside Sheila. She spotted him reflected in the window.

"Mind if I ask you some questions?" he asked.

"Probably not," she said, turning to face him. "What now?"

"I know you've been through a lot the past week or so, but I'd like to ask you about Sharon Milhouse."

She swallowed hard. "Why?"

"Her name keeps coming up as someone who might be a danger to you, and I need to verify a few things."

This didn't make sense. Sharon Milhouse! Why now?

"I've got a lot to think about. What does she have to do with anything? That all happened so long ago."

He looked away from her and pulled out his notepad, flipped through it. "You said there was a Sharon Milhouse on the cruise," he said.

Her heart jumped. "I know that."

"I have no way of knowing if it was the same one. Er, at least not yet. There doesn't seem to be any recent photos of her," he said. "But there's something else you should know."

"What's that?" she managed to say.

"A Milhouse has been checked in at the B and B since Tuesday."

Chapter 63

"Oh shoot, Jon!" Annie said as they started walking up Beatrice's sidewalk. "I forgot my purse. I'll go back and get it."

Beatrice was standing on the porch. "Well, go on, the both of you. I'll have something to eat for you when you get back."

"Jon doesn't need to go with me," Annie said.

"It's getting dark. In case you need reminding, there's a possible killer on the loose," Beatrice said.

"I can't believe I left my purse. I hardly ever carry one," Annie said, and handed her phone to Beatrice. "Please keep hold of my phone."

"What? Why?" Beatrice said.

"I took pictures of the guest book and there was a woman who caught me and was livid," Annie said as she turned to go.

"Yes," Jon said, following her. "She was so angry she followed us and tried to get the phone from Annie."

"She must be hiding something," Beatrice said, more to herself that anybody else since Jon and Annie had already rounded the corner.

"What's that, Mama?" Vera poked her head out the door.

"Annie asked me to keep her phone while she went to pick up her purse. She left it at the B and B," Beatrice said.

"Mama?" Vera said, coming outside and standing beside her. "You don't look good. Is everything okay?"

Beatrice didn't reply. There was a familiar stir of worry in her, and she tried not to pay attention to it.

"Mama?" Vera said again, and placed her hand on Beatrice's arm. "Come inside and let's see what Annie has on her phone."

That snapped Beatrice out of her trance and they walked inside the warm house together. They sat down on the couch and clicked on Annie's iPhone to see the names listed in the book.

"I don't recognize any of these names," Beatrice said.

"Annie was probably right when she said the killer wouldn't use his or her own name," Vera said.

Elizabeth came bopping into the room, looking for her crayons.

"Under the coffee table," Vera said.

"Okay, Mama," she said, and plopped down on her stomach onto the floor with a coloring book. She started coloring a page with Santa Claus on it. She was making his suit purple. *So creative,* thought Beatrice.

"Now, here's a name I recognize," Vera said. "How odd."

"Who's that?"

"Theresa Graves," Vera said. "She's a big-time scrapbooker who interviewed Sheila for a job, then turned around and heckled her at the photography–scrapbooking session. What would she be doing here?"

"Look at the name underneath," Beatrice said, pointing.

"Sam Milhouse." Vera's breath nearly left her. "Could it be? I mean Sharon's husband? A son?"

Beatrice nearly jumped off the couch and ran to

her phone. Bryant—she had to find him. Jon and Annie were heading toward trouble right this very minute.

"Cumberland Creek Police. What's your emergency?" the voice on the other end said.

She didn't know what to say or how to explain what was happening succinctly enough.

"State your emergency please."

"May I please talk with Detective Bryant? I think there's a killer staying at the B and B."

"Who is calling?"

"Beatrice Matthews."

"Ms. Matthews, this is an emergency line. I will connect you with Detective Bryant's office," the operator chided.

"But this is an emergency," Beatrice said to nobody, as she was already in phone limbo land.

"Detective Bryant's office," came a calm and welcoming voice.

"This is Beatrice Matthews on Ivy Lane. I'd like to speak with him," Beatrice said.

"Hold on, Ms. Matthews, let me see if I can find him." *Hold on? Hold on?*

A moment later the line picked back up. "I'm sorry. He's unavailable," the ridiculously calm voice said.

"What do you mean?" Beatrice said, her heart thudding against the walls of her chest.

"He's out of the office on a call, Ms. Matthews. Can someone else assist you?"

Flummoxed, she said, "I don't know. You see, he's the one I know. He's the one who would know what I'm talking about. I think Jon and Annie Chamovitz are heading for trouble. They went over to the B and B and I think there's a troubled person over there."

The woman on the other line laughed.

"Well, Mrs. Matthews, if that's the case, they are going to get a snoot full of police attention in the middle of the trouble."

"What? Why?"

"Because as far as I know, that is where they went."

"They?"

"Detective Bryant took a team over there."

"For what?"

"I don't know the answer to that question, Mrs. Matthews. And even if I did—"

"I know, I know, you couldn't tell me anyway," Beatrice said, and hung up the phone.

Chapter 64

When Annie and Jon walked up to the bed and breakfast, she could have sworn a curtain moved. Probably that nut job of a woman who wanted her phone. Well, she didn't have it. Even if the woman searched her—and what kind of crazy thought was that?—she wouldn't find her phone. It was safely in Beatrice's hands. In any case, she girded her loins in preparation for seeing that woman again.

When Jon and Annie walked in, the door closed and locked behind them. Annie turned quickly and here stood the woman, stone faced, holding Annie's bag in one hand and a gun in the other. "I knew you'd be back," she said with a strange, twisted grin.

"Put that thing down!" Jon said with such a thick French accent that Annie wasn't quite sure that was even what he said.

"Listen, Frenchy, in this country, the person with the gun is the boss. Now both of you head for the dining room," she said. "And put your hands where I can see them. Not a word from either of you, or I will start shooting."

No. This could not be happening. Annie raised her hands as her eyes searched for a weapon. There was no way she could get to anything without being shot. Her head was throbbing, pulse racing.

"What do you want?" Annie said.

"I want your phone, then I want you to sit down in that chair. Your French friend there is going to tie you up for me."

"Absurd. I will do no such thing," Jon said.

The woman lifted her gun and pointed it at Annie. "I'll shoot her if you don't."

"Do what she says." A small voice came from behind her. Annie turned her head. "Elsie?" She

316

was tied up, and sitting in the opposite corner. There was a dim light coming in from the kitchen, but the dining room was dark. Annie couldn't see if there were others behind Elsie. She knew there were other guests. Where were they?

"Where are the other guests, Elsie?" Annie asked.

"Gone Christmas caroling," the woman said, and shoved Annie in the chair. "Won't they be surprised when they come back?"

Annie didn't answer.

"Give me your phone," the woman demanded.

"I'm sorry. I don't have it." She patted the outside of her pockets. "Check if you like."

She did. Annie was surprised at the strength of her touch. And by the way her body was reacting to it. She shivered from fear and disgust. What was going on here? *Is this the woman who tried to kill Sheila? The woman responsible for maybe three deaths? For spreading poison in Sheila's basement?*

"Where is it?" she hissed.

"I left it at Bea's," Annie said. Her mouth was dry with fear.

"Tie her up with that rope on the floor there."

Jon stood and looked at her, as if he didn't understand. He trembled, scared. Poor old soul.

"Move it!" she ordered.

Jon did as he was told. But he didn't tie the rope tight enough.

"Tighter!" the woman demanded.

Annie's arms already ached. Her underarms sweated profusely; she felt the moist heat as air entered the spot between her jacket and her arm. Jon yanked at the rope until her wrists were raw. "I'm sorry," he said.

Annie nodded. Now that she was tied up, what could she do? What was this woman capable of? Rule one, if you are kidnapped or held against your will, is to talk to the person. Try to reason with her.

"I'm not sure what you want. Maybe we can give that to you," Annie said, her voice shaking.

"Hmph," the woman replied. "What I want is gone. Nothing you can do about that. I killed him. Her. Whatever the hell he or she was."

The woman's face contorted, horrified. "I thought, finally, that I could be happy."

"We've all been there," Annie said, each word an effort now. Her body had been taken over with shivers. What did she mean "he or she"? This woman wasn't making any sense.

The woman was still pointing the gun at Jon. He was so pale that Annie thought he'd pass out any minute.

"But there's no man worth going to prison for," Annie said, fighting off a sudden, overpowering sleepy sensation. How could she be so tired? Concentrate.

"Hallelujah!" Elsie shouted from the corner.

"I know that!" the woman said. "I took care of it. Thought it would be all right until you came along, Ms. Reporter."

"Look," Annie said, fighting to keep her voice from shaking. "Just let us go and we'll forget all of this ever happened. Really. Just go back to where you came from, let us go, and we'll call it even, okay?"

The woman began to sob like a child. "I don't know, I don't know . . ." She kept repeating it. She was having a breakdown right before their eyes. But she still held the gun on Jon. "I thought he was so perfect. One cheating husband. Another man who turns out to be a disguised woman!" She held the gun up higher, still pointing it at Jon.

The look on Jon's face was scary, something between frightened and resolved. He was gathering courage to make a move. Annie hoped she was wrong about that assumption. But his jaw hardened. Annie held her breath.

"I don't follow," Annie said.

"Sam! Sam's real name was Sharon. She used me to get to Sheila's scrapbooks. And to get into the security office on the ship. Fool! She dressed up as a man to fool me. I'm a fool!" she raged.

"Cumberland Creek Police!" came a voice from outside, toward the front of the house. "Come out with your hands up!"

The woman was shaking now. The gun still pointed at Jon.

"I'll shoot him!" she yelled. "Don't come in. I'll shoot him."

"The hell you will," Jon said, and lunged for her. At the same time her weapon fired. Jon fell to the floor with a thud.

"Jon!" Annie screamed, trying to get to him, rocking her chair forward, as the front door came flying open.

Later, Annie wished she had passed out, wished she didn't remember the sordid details with her trained reporter's eye. The details that would haunt her forever. She'd never forget the look on Elsie's face as the woman turned to her and shot her straight in the shoulder, then the sound of the chair and her body falling over. The scent of the discharge. Blood everywhere. And Annie's hands tied behind her back. She could do nothing.

She watched the police and medics as they swooped in over Jon and Elsie. One of the medics nodded at the other. They were both still breathing. Both still alive.

She watched as the formidable shooter was escorted out of the bed and breakfast, looking sheepish and deflated.

Detective Adam Bryant found Annie in her chair and didn't say a word. The look on his face spoke volumes. He untied her hands, himself shaking, his jaws taut with emotion held back.

"Christ, Chamovitz," he finally said. "What am I going to do with you?"

It was then that she reached for him as he lifted her from the chair. She wilted into his arms, right when her half-crazed-with-worry husband walked into the room.

Chapter 65

This was not the Christmas Sheila had planned. Every year she served her family dinner on her great-grandmother's fine china, trimmed her tree with special ornaments full of family memories, took great care with her decorations, and found great joy in still playing Santa for her children. She embraced the ritual of it: leaving cookies out for Santa, food out for his reindeer, filling the stockings, all of it. But this year, she'd have none of her time-honored rituals. This year, the oven she was using barely held a turkey breast, let alone a whole turkey complete with her chestnut dressing, her great-grandmother's recipe.

But here were her friends and family, squeezed into Cookie Crandall's little house. Bedraggled, but there, determined not to let the Rogerses have a bad Christmas.

"Everybody needs a ham for Christmas," Beatrice said, as she placed the Virginia ham onto the table. Sheila knew better than to argue with her. Besides, she didn't have the fortitude. This holiday was a mess.

"Thanks," Sheila said.

Annie set corn and mashed potatoes on the table, next to the ham. She said, "Okay, so many Jewish people would have a problem with this." She laughed.

Beatrice and Elizabeth had strung popcorn on a "Charlie Brown Christmas tree," which they brought with them, and Vera had also tied red ribbons on it. Vera always had a ready supply of ribbons. Paige had brought an extra set of blinking white lights and some ornaments. They managed to fashion a bit of Christmas spirit from their hodge-podge items.

Jon was still pale and jumpy, but he tagged along with a wounded shoulder and broken arm.

"I came all the way from Paris, France, to Cumberland Creek to get shot by a lunatic scrapbooking woman," he said. And they all laughed. "But I'm still alive." He lifted his glass and was joined by the others.

Lunatic was right, thought Sheila. If only she had known that Theresa Graves was so disturbed. Well, how would she? The police told Sheila that Theresa had been freshly divorced and when she met a "man" a few weeks before the cruise who was everything she wanted, she fell head over heels. He treated her like a princess and didn't even pressure her to have sex. But her new boyfriend, "Sam" Milhouse, had secrets. He wanted vengeance and would have it by finally killing Sheila Rogers. Theresa had been questioned by the FBI and then figured it out. Sam had used her to gain access to Sheila's scrapbook. Theresa was the last judge to see it.

All of the clues the FBI had gathered pointed to Theresa—thanks to her involvement with Sharon Milhouse. Theresa herself was beginning to figure it out when "Sam" suggested they leave the cruise and go to Cumberland Creek to a little bed and breakfast, take some time and get themselves together. When Theresa finally did figure it out, after another visit from the FBI, she turned what was originally planned as a surprise attack on Sheila in her basement into Sharon's vengeful murder. She had tied "Sam" to the chair in the basement and force-fed her the ricin. Sharon Milhouse's cruel disguise as a man had sent the already troubled Theresa over the edge.

"I know it's strange, but I feel kind of sorry for Theresa," Vera said. "She was hoodwinked."

"Yes, she was," Sheila said. "Can you imagine dating someone all that time and finding out that he was really a she?"

"Let alone that she was a cold-blooded killer using her for access," Eric spoke up.

"I'll never understand why Sharon hated you," Steve said to Sheila.

Neither could Sheila, but at this point she didn't care.

"You can't understand something like that," Beatrice said. "She was ill."

"Funny how the damaged folks find each other. I mean, for Theresa to kill Sharon and leave her in your basement . . ." Vera said, shrugging.

"I don't feel sorry for Theresa at all," said Beatrice. "She's exactly where she belongs, in prison."

"On another note, that turkey was some of the best I've ever had," Annie said.

"Thanks," Sheila said. "It was hard to get used to the smaller oven in Cookie's kitchen, but I managed."

In fact, as Sheila looked around the table, where all of the adults were gathered over glorious food, she felt that she had managed very well indeed. The kids were all at the kitchen table and the college kids were in the living room. They were all managing Christmas.

It was unlike any she'd ever had. She felt a shift in her mood.

"I don't know why I thought it was so important to celebrate Christmas in my own house, with my own decorations and tree," Sheila said. The room quieted. "I think your generosity . . ." Her voice cracked. She cleared her throat. "This is the best Christmas I've ever had."

Steve's face was bright red with emotion. His arm circled around her shoulders.

The small house on the cul-de-sac was

brimming with light, food, and emotion. Sheila bit into the mashed potatoes and said a little silent prayer of gratitude. In fact, she was filled with it, especially as she looked at Jon with his arm in a sling, and Annie, who had been more quiet than usual. Her pretty face had always been pensive. But now it appeared haunted.

Sheila took a deep breath, pushing away the remnants of guilt she had been feeling. All of this madness had happened because of Sharon's twisted hatred for her. Four people dead: Allie, Harold, the FBI officer, and Sharon Milhouse herself. All that Sharon really wanted was one person's life: hers. She chilled at that thought. But all things considered, Sheila had never been happier than at this moment, surrounded by people she loved, breaking bread, swapping stories, and sharing gratitude.

"Tell us about the job," Beatrice said.

"I'll be starting at the end of January," Sheila said.

"Yay, Mom," came Donna's voice from the living room. "So proud of you!"

"Let's toast to Sheila's new job," Steve said.

"Here, here," Mike said, raising his glass.

Later in the kitchen, where most of the women gathered, while the men watched a football game, DeeAnn and Paige washed the dishes while Sheila sat at the table with Vera and Elizabeth. Annie was drying the dishes.

"Why are you so quiet?" Vera asked Annie.

Annie shrugged. "Not much to say, I suppose."

"You know, I'm sure being tied up like that was terrifying," DeeAnn said. "It's going to take some time."

Annie held up her wrists, pulled back her sleeves, and showed them the red circles of deep rope burn.

"Shouldn't you have a bandage on those?" Vera asked.

"I bandage them at night," Annie said. "I leave them on as long as I can take it, but they bother me."

"How are Mike and the boys dealing?" DeeAnn said.

"Mike's not happy with me," she said, reaching for another dish to dry.

"Same old thing?" Vera said. "He doesn't want you putting yourself at risk?"

Annie nodded. "That, and he walked into the B and B when Adam was holding me."

The room quieted.

"Oh, surely he understands what a mess you were. You just needed comfort," Vera said finally.

"I hope that's the resolution he comes to," Annie said, handing Vera a towel. "Right now, I don't think he's so certain."

Later, after everybody had left, Shelia sat quietly at the small kitchen table and reflected on the evening spent with her friends and family. And she thought about her mother and father and aunts and uncles and the holidays they had spent together when she was a girl. A tear sprang to her eye. This Christmas had been the most like those Christmases past. How had she lost those holidays of her youth? How had she become so focused on the outer trappings of it? It didn't matter one iota that she be able to gaze on her own tree with her own ornaments—what mattered was the people around her.

"You okay?" Steve asked, walking into the kitchen.

"I'm fine—better than fine, actually," Sheila said.

He sat down with her at the table. "You know, I've been thinking about Sharon all those years ago and wondering that if I'd handled things differently . . . if she would have . . . I don't know, been okay."

"We were all so young," Sheila said. "And remember that she had already been hospitalized before she'd gotten to college."

"I come back to that every time I think on it. There wasn't much I could do. I was in love with another woman. And I still am."

Sheila grinned. "You better be."

He reached out and rubbed his thumb along the ridge of her hand. "I guess there's no point in dredging up the past. But I'm sorry that she blamed you all these years. Blamed you enough to want to kill you."

"We don't need to worry about her anymore," Sheila said. "Let's hope she finally found some peace."

"What about you, Sheila? Have you found peace about this?"

She inhaled, then exhaled, and thought it over. "Not yet. I still need answers."

Chapter 66

Sheila had been to the police station and jail before, but never to visit an inmate. They were keeping Theresa in Cumberland Creek until her trial. No bail had been posted, but mostly for her own safety. Theresa was on suicide watch.

Sheila shivered as she took her place behind the glass. How did Annie do this kind of thing? Look at criminals through glass, stare them in the eye, ask them questions? Well, if Annie could do it, so could she.

She steadied herself and folded her trembling hands, placing them in her lap. She had had to beg and plead to see Theresa, and of course they would be watched every minute. There were guards posted in both rooms and a camera in each corner.

She just needed to know.

But as the guard escorted Theresa in, Sheila felt deflated. Theresa seemed different: hair unbrushed, hunched posture, and no makeup, of course.

"Hello, Theresa," Sheila finally said.

Theresa nodded, opened her mouth as if to speak, but didn't.

Silence ensued as the two women sized one another up.

"How are you?" Sheila finally said.

"I'm back on my meds," Theresa replied, after a moment. "Believe it or not, I'm glad to see you. I just . . . wanted to say . . ." Sheila sat forward. "My life sucks. I have four kids who'd rather live with their cheating bastard of a father than me. When I met Sam, um, I mean Sharon, it seemed he really understood."

"What happened?" Sheila asked. "Why did you kill her?"

Theresa shrugged. "I'm not a killer." She breathed deeply, as if she were willing away tears. "She switched my medicine. I thought I was losing my mind. It turns out that I was."

"She switched your medicine?"

"We met in a support group for schizophrenia. Mine has been very controllable with meds. But she swapped out my regular medicine. I was taking empty pills."

Sheila was flabbergasted by Sharon's deviousness.

"But I started to figure things out, even in my muddled state." It seemed as if each word was an effort for Theresa. She looked drained, as if someone could breathe on her and she'd fall right over.

"Please go on," Sheila said.

"I felt so stupid . . . when I realized . . . it was you, not me she was obsessed with. And when I was questioned by the FBI about the scrapbook, I realized what she had done. Sam . . . I mean Sharon, had used me to get to you." She managed a weak smile. "To get to your scrapbook to poison it."

"But why?"

"We develop obsessions," Theresa said, looking over at the guard, who watched them intently. "Steve broke her heart all those years ago and she thought it was your fault."

"Most people would get over it," Sheila said.

"You don't understand Sam. I mean Sharon," she said, and sniffed. "Extremely delusional."

"Yet she was smart enough to manage all of this," she said.

"Ha," Theresa said. "I keep asking myself—was she so smart or was I just stupid, seeing what I wanted to see?"

Sheila's heart sank. Was Theresa as much a victim as she was a killer? Annie often said that she felt many people would kill, given the right circumstances. Sheila didn't think she had a killer inside her—but if someone were to hurt her kids or come after them, she didn't know what she'd do.

"I look back and wonder how I didn't see that Sam was a woman, that the reason he wasn't interested in pursuing a physical relationship with me was because . . . well," she said, and shrugged.

"She'd taken a trip to Virginia the same time that the ship had first set sail. She met the ship the next day, at the second port, and met me on board.

"I was standing in your basement when I put it all together. I realized she'd been to your house before. She was stalking you. I figured it out when I noticed that she knew her way around your basement. Then something happened. Something switched in me. I don't know. I reached over and tried to take the ricin from her and we fought. Her shirt came off and I saw the straps around her chest. . . ." She took a deep breath. "I was trying to save you and your family, even before I knew he was a woman. But in that moment something snapped. I held her down—God, I don't know where I got the strength, something just came over me—and I force-fed her the poison."

Her eyes were ablaze now.

Sheila sat back as fear ripped through her. She and her family had come so close to being poisoned. Sharon had been to Cumberland Creek, knew her home, and probably had left the post-card in her box when she had visited right before she boarded the cruise, later than the other passengers.

The guard moved toward Theresa.

"I'm so sorry," Theresa said as she hunched over more, wilting as the guard moved toward her. "I wish . . ."

Theresa didn't finish her sentence. But it wasn't necessary. Sheila knew what was in her heart.

Chapter 67

Beatrice untangled herself from her blankets and quilts. Damn, something smelled good. Someone was making breakfast and she hoped it wasn't Jon, who was told not to use his right arm. He needed to take it easy. It was a miracle that a man in his seventies had survived that kind of trauma.

She bounded down the steps—well, as much as her bones could bound at eight-thirty in the morning—ready to give him a piece of her mind. But she was surprised to find Eric and Vera cooking.

Jon, who was sitting at the table, smiled up at her. "Good morning," he said.

"Hungry, Mom?" Vera said, holding up a plate of gingerbread pancakes. "This is one of Eric's mother's recipes. I thought we could try it."

Beatrice nodded as Elizabeth danced into the room. "Morning, Granny. Pancakes!"

"Good morning, sugar. They sure smell heavenly," Beatrice said, and smacked her lips together.

She poured herself a cup of coffee and saw the snow falling against the window. "Land sakes, look at the snow! There must be about six inches."

"And it's still coming down," Eric said, flipping a pancake.

"We were just talking about the past few weeks," Jon said, as Elizabeth skipped out of the room to watch TV. "Trying to make sense of it."

"Senseless," Beatrice said.

"I'm afraid Sheila is still feeling guilty," Vera said, setting down a plate of stacked pancakes. The table was already set, in a scattered way. Beatrice detected Lizzie's help.

"She probably will for a while," Beatrice surmised. "But none of it was her fault, of course."

"I hope she can stay focused on all the good things coming her way," Vera said, and sat down.

"Why did they let Sharon out in the first place?" Jon said. "I do not understand."

"They thought Sharon was okay. She'd served her term. And she might have been okay if she hadn't stopped taking her medicine after she left the Institute," Beatrice said.

Jon clicked his tongue and shook his head. "But what about the woman who shot me? Why was she free when she was so ill?"

Beatrice placed the pancakes on her plate and reached for the butter. Jon was doing the same. "She was ill too, and she and Sharon, dressed up as Sam, had met in a support group of some kind."

"Sharon really researched the scrapbooking community," Eric said, dropping a few fresh pancakes onto the stack. "It's a lot of effort to go to in order to kill someone. Such an orchestration."

"Yes, and a twisted one at that," Jon said.

"Lizzie, come eat," Vera called as Eric sat down at the table.

"You know, it was a wonderful Christmas dinner last night," Beatrice said. As usual, by her third or fourth drink of coffee, things were perking up.

"I agree," Eric said. "It was great to see the way everybody pulled together to give the Rogerses a decent Christmas since they couldn't get into their home."

"What's with them calling Cookie's house a safe house?" Vera said. "I thought that was a technical term for a place the cops always use to hide someone."

"I don't know," Beatrice said. "Maybe they're not using it in quite the same way. Maybe they are using 'safe' as a way of saying 'no ricin.'"

"Could be," Eric said. "Or it could be the property of the police since Cookie escaped from jail. I'm sure they seized it."

Beatrice's and Vera's eyes met, then lowered,

each to her own plate. They didn't like to talk about Cookie. Beatrice herself was fond of the young woman, but talking about her made it all seem too real. They would each come to terms with her disappearance in their own way.

"How does someone escape from jail these days? I thought it was supposed to be impossible," Jon asked.

"Well," Beatrice said. "Aren't you just full of questions this morning?"

Jon smiled. "Of course."

"The truth is," Vera said, "nobody knows how Cookie escaped. The security tapes from that day were a mess."

"I hear they've beefed up security since then," Beatrice said.

"They certainly botched the rescue attempt at the B and B," Eric said.

"I'm not so sure about that," Vera said, cutting into her stack of pancakes. "They had no idea there was a hostage situation inside, from my understanding. They were just there to question Theresa Graves. The FBI had pretty much fingered her as Sharon Milhouse's killer."

"In the meantime, Sharon had killed three people with her poison, while she was disguised as a man," Beatrice said.

"I'm not sure why she bothered dressing as a man," Vera said. "She used her name on the cruise registry."

"She had to—that's the name on her credit card," Eric said.

"It was just a disguise, and you know it was one that not everybody could pull off. But she was very masculine-looking, even without the disguise," Beatrice said. "A cruel one. Sharon fashioned herself into a perfect man for the sake of luring Theresa in and it worked. Theresa was so desperate. Sad."

"And in the end her desperation led to killing," Vera said.

"The mass of men lead lives of quiet desperation," Jon muttered.

"Quoting Thoreau now?" Beatrice said, eyebrows lifted.

"Why not?" he said, and shrugged.

Beatrice sat back and reveled in the people in her kitchen and the warm, spicy gingerbread pancake flavor that lingered on. She caught a glance exchanged between Eric and Vera. Was it love? Elizabeth was humming "Rudolf the Red Nose Reindeer" and eating the gingerbread pancakes in front of her.

Beatrice reached out and touched Jon's hand. "Merry Christmas, Jon."

Epilogue

"Really, Mike? When do you think I'd have time to have an affair with Adam Bryant?" Annie shot at him as she got ready to leave for the Saturday crop.

"I'm not saying you're having an affair. I'm just saying that it was a very tender moment between you and I felt like an outsider in your life," Mike said.

"Mike, I didn't know if I was going to live or die," she said calmly. "I didn't know if Jon was dead or alive. Or Elsie for that matter. I have no idea what I was feeling or thinking. But believe me, if I had seen you first, I would have been in your arms. Hell, if I had seen Steve first, he'd have been the one."

His eyes caught hers. Something was exchanged. A moment of truth. There was no need for talking at that moment. A few more beats of silence.

"I've noticed the way he looks at you, sometimes. Did you think I didn't notice?" Mike said, as if it hurt him to speak.

Annie felt like the breath was knocked out of her. She held her arms open and sort of shrugged. "I'm really not paying much attention to what Bryant does or how he looks at me. Mike, I love you. We are married. I'm not going anywhere."

Mike shifted his weight a bit. "You'd think I'd be used to other men looking at you."

"Hey, it goes both ways. I used to see other women checking you out all the time when we lived in Bethesda. Remember that Louise?" she teased him.

He smiled. "Yep."

She slid into the open space between his arm and shoulder, as he lifted his arm. He wrapped his arms around her. "Oh, Annie, I love you so much," he said with his voice cracking.

"I know that," she said, blinking back a tear. "And I love you, too."

"Hey, it's getting late. Don't you have a crop tonight?" he said, looking at the clock.

"I do, but I'm not going unless we are okay, Mike," she answered, looking into his deep brown eyes.

"Of course we are," he said. "Now, you better get going and rechristen the basement, now that you all are allowed back in there."

"Thanks, Mike," she said.

The boys were already in bed. She grabbed her roller-bag and headed for Sheila's. Thank goodness the Rogerses were back in their home. What would the croppers do without their basement every Saturday? Annie didn't want to think about it.

As she entered the room, she drew back a moment and took the scene in. Vera was hovering over DeeAnn, who was holding green lacey doilies. "You can paint these things any color you want," she told her. "I'm just loving the doilies."

"We saw them used every which way on the cruise. I saw a lovely border made with them. I've seen people using them for negative space. And oh, I loved the oversized one on pages where people used them as a background. Really creative," Sheila said.

Paige and Vera were already settled in and at work on their scrapbooks.

"Look who finally made it," Sheila said.

"What's that?" Annie said, noticing an old cardboard box on the floor.

"Those are Elsie's photos. We're doing a scrapbook for her. If you want to help, that would be great," Sheila said.

Annie nodded, thinking about all the times she'd helped put together scrapbooks for people who were killed. Too many. But she liked the idea of working on something together, something that had meaning, something that might provide some comfort to a traumatized woman.

Annie selected a few photos from Elsie's high school years, and next she chose a lovely lilac-colored paper. She started playing around with placement, thinking about embellishments.

"How is Jon?" Sheila asked.

"He's doing well," Vera said. "Mama is taking

real good care of him." She placed her scissors on the table and held up her page, grimacing. There was something about it she didn't like.

Annie got up, reached into the fridge for a beer, opened it, and took a swig.

"How are thing with Mike?" Vera asked.

"Good," Annie said. "I think I finally have him convinced I don't have the hots for Bryant."

"God, Annie, are you blind? We all have the hots for him!" DeeAnn laughed.

Annie didn't crack a smile, even as the others laughed and made leering noises.

"That is one hunk of a man. Here, darlin', have some chocolate peanut butter cookies. Good for you," said DeeAnn, and she slid the plate over to Annie as she sat back down at the table. "I'm so tired of baking right now I could scream."

"I bet you are," Vera said, not looking up from her work.

"Did the police ever find out who placed the postcard in your box?" DeeAnn asked Sheila.

"Yes," Sheila said. "Sharon came to town about the same time we were leaving. She was registered at the B and B. Nobody saw her do it, but Bryant says it's safe to assume."

"When do you leave for Minnesota?" Annie asked DeeAnn.

"Day after tomorrow. I'm not sure this is going to be a pleasant visit. But I'd like to see my mom—even if she doesn't know who I am,"

DeeAnn said. Her mom was riddled with Alzheimer's.

"It will do you good," Sheila said, sitting down at the table and opening her laptop. Then she looked up. "Well, here we are, cropping on a Saturday night, as if we don't have anything else to do."

Annie took another drink of beer.

Sheila's face said it all. She was glad to be home, off the cruise, away from dead bodies, and back in her own surroundings.

"I know I won't be sailing the high seas anytime soon," Paige said. "But it sure was nice spending time with Randy."

"I'd be perfectly fine to never step foot on another cruise," Vera said. "I did hear that Ahoy's chief of security has been fired. Imagine that. Firing a vampire."

The group laughed.

"Yes, I've gotten so many apologies from Grace Irons," Sheila said. "This is the first time they hired Ahoy Security. She was mortified. So was the cruise line. I know it's kind of funny, but it turns out that the chief has something called Renfield's syndrome, which is a kind of mental illness. He can get help for it."

"I imagine," said Annie, sitting down at her spot at the table. Her spot—she loved the familiarity. She picked up a postcard from Hannah, who had been in New York City a few days now.

Dear Annie,
    This place is . . . magic.
                  Hope you are well,
                  Hannah

Annie grinned.

"How is she?" Vera said, looking over her shoulder.

"She's smitten, I'd say," Annie said. "I have to wonder if she will come back and marry like she's supposed to."

"Time will tell," DeeAnn said.

Just then, Annie heard the sliding glass door open. Who could it be? All of the croppers were here: Vera, Paige, DeeAnn, Sheila, and herself. Sometimes Beatrice stopped by, but she was certainly home with Jon as he was recuperating.

Annie started to look over her shoulder, but Vera glanced up first and her mouth dropped open. Paige dropped her scissors. DeeAnn's fork hit her plate with a clank. When Annie finally turned around, she glimpsed why her friends had been rendered senseless.

Their old friend Cookie Crandall stood there.

"Any room for me at the table?"

Glossary of Basic Scrapbooking Terms

Acid-free: Acid is a chemical found in paper that will disintegrate it over time. Acid will ruin photos. It's very important to use papers, pens, and other supplies labeled "acid-free," or eventually the acid may ruin cherished photos and layouts.

Adhesive: Any kind of glue or tape can be considered an adhesive. In scrapbooking, there are several kinds of adhesives: tape runners, glue sticks, and glue dots.

Brad: This is similar to a typical split pin, but it is found in many different sizes, shapes, and colors. It is commonly used for embellishment.

Challenge: Within the scrapbooking community, challenges are issued in groups as a way to instill motivation.

Crop: Technically, to crop means to cut down a photo. However, a crop is also a gathering of scrapbookers who get together to create scrapbooks. A crop can be anything from a group of friends getting together to a more official gathering where scrapbook materials are for sale, games are played, and challenges are issued, and so on. Online crops are a good alternative for people who don't have a local scrapbook community.

Die-cut: This is a shape or letter cut from paper or card stock, usually by machine or by using a template.

Embellishment: An embellishment is an item, other than words or photos, that enhances a scrapbook page. Typical embellishments are ribbons, fabric, and stickers.

Eyelet: These small metal circles, similar to the metal rings found on shoes for threading laces, are used in the scrapbook context as a decoration and can hold elements on a page.

Journaling: This is the term for writing on scrapbook pages. It includes everything from titles to full pages of thoughts, feelings, and memories about the photos displayed.

Matting: Photos in scrapbooks are framed with a mat. Scrapbookers mat with coordinating papers on layouts, often using colors found in the photos.

Page protector: These are clear, acid-free covers that are used to protect finished pages.

Permanent: Adhesives that will stay are deemed permanent.

Photo corners: A photo is held to a page by slipping its corners into photo corners. They usually stick on one side.

Post-bound album: This term refers to an album that uses metal posts to hold the binding together. These albums can be extended with more posts to make them thicker. Usually page protectors are already included on the album pages.

Punch: This is a tool used to perforate paper or card stock with decorative shapes.

Punchies: The paper shapes that result from using a paper punch tool are known as punchies. These can be used on a page for a decorative effect.

Repositionable adhesive: Magically, these adhesives do not create a permanent bond until dry, so you can move an element dabbed with the adhesive around on the page until you find just the perfect spot.

Scraplift: When a scrapbooker copies someone's page layout or design, she has scraplifted.

Scrapper's block: This is a creativity block.

Strap-hinge album: An album can utilize straps to allow pages to lie completely flat when the album opens. To add pages to this album, the straps are unhinged.

Template: A template is a guide for cutting shapes, and for drawing or writing on a page. They are usually made of plastic or cardboard.

Trimmer: A trimmer is a tool used for straight-cutting photos.

Vellum: Vellum is a thick, semitransparent paper with a smooth finish.

Scrapbooking Your Holidays

Other than the typical holiday scrapbooking, with simple photos of the day and gifts exchanged, here's a few other ways to create your holiday scrapbooks.

1. Include your Christmas cards.
2. Don't forget to record your own personal holiday traditions. We leave a plate of cookies out for Santa every year and carrots for the reindeer. What do you do?
3. Include your preparations—picking out the tree, decorating, baking, and so on.
4. If you are a list person, save your holiday to-do list to use as part of your layout. Also, save your children's wish list for Santa.
5. Include your recipes for special holiday food.

Scrapbook Essentials for the Beginner

When you first start to scrapbook, the amount of products and choices available can be overwhelming. It's best to keep it simple until you develop your own style and see exactly what you need. Basically, this hobby can be as complicated or as simple as you want. Here is all you really need:

1. photos
2. archival scrapbooks and acid-free paper
3. adhesive
4. scissors
5. sheet protectors

Advice on Cropping

Basically, two kinds of crops exist. An "official" crop is when a scrapbook seller is involved. The participants sample and purchase products, along with participating in contests and giveaways. The second kind of crop is an informal gathering of friends on at least a semiregular basis to share, scrapbook, eat, and gossip, just like the Cumberland Creek croppers.

1. In both cases, food and drinks are usually served. Finger food is most appropriate. The usual drinks are nonalcoholic, but sometimes wine is served. There should be plenty of space for snacking around the scrapbooking area. If something spills, you don't want your cherished photos to get ruined.
2. If you have an official crop, it's imperative that your scrapbook seller doesn't come on too strong. Scrapbook materials sell themselves. Scrapbookers know what they want and need.
3. Be prepared to share. If you have a die-cut machine, for example, bring it along, show others how to use it, and so on. Crops are about generosity of spirit. It can be about something as small as paper that you purchased and decided not to use. Someone will find a use for it.
4. Make sure there's a lot of surface space, such as long tables where scrapbookers can spread out. (Some even use the floor.)
5. Be open to both giving scrapbooking advice and receiving it. You can always ignore advice if it's bad.
6. Get organized before you crop. You don't need fancy boxes and organizing systems. Place the photos you want to crop with in an envelope, and you are ready to go.
7. Go with realistic expectations. You probably

won't get a whole scrapbook done during the crop. Focus on several pages.

8. Always ask about what you can bring, such as food, drinks, cups, plates, and so on.
9. If you're the host, have plenty of garbage bags around. Ideally, have one small bag for each person. That way scrapbookers can throw away unusable scraps as they go along, which makes cleanup much easier.
10. If you're the host, make certain there is plenty of good lighting, as well as an adequate number of electricity outlets.

Frugal Scrapbooking Tips

1. Spend your money where it counts. The scrapbook itself is the carrier of all your memories and creativity. Splurge here.
2. You can find perfectly fine scrapbooking paper in discount stores, along with stickers, pens, and sometimes glue. If it's labeled "archival," it's safe.
3. You can cut your own paper and make matting, borders, journal boxes, and so on. You don't need fancy templates, though they make it easier.
4. Check on some online auction sites, like eBay, for scrapbooking materials and tools.
5. Reuse and recycle as much as you can. Keep a box of paper scraps, for example, that you

might be able to use for a border, mat, or journal box. Commit to not buying anything else until what you've already purchased has been used.

6. Wait for special coupons. Some national crafts stores run excellent coupons—sometimes 40 percent off. Wait for these coupons, and then go and buy something on your wish list that you could not otherwise afford.

Mollie Cox Bryan, author of the Cumberland Creek mystery series, is also the regional bestselling author of *Mrs. Rowe's Little Book of Southern Pies* and *Mrs. Rowe's Restaurant Cookbook: A Lifetime of Recipes from the Shenandoah Valley*. An award-winning journalist and poet, she currently blogs, cooks, and scrapbooks in the Shenandoah Valley of Virginia with her husband and two daughters. Her first Cumberland Creek mystery *Scrapbook of Secrets* was nominated for an Agatha Award for best first novel. Please visit her at molliecoxbryan.com.

Center Point Large Print
600 Brooks Road / PO Box 1
Thorndike, ME 04986-0001 USA

(207) 568-3717

US & Canada:
1 800 929-9108
www.centerpointlargeprint.com